PENGUIN BOOKS

# The Drowning Lesson

While working as a GP, Jane Shemilt completed a post-graduate diploma in creative writing at Bristol University and went on to study for the MA in creative writing at Bath Spa, gaining both with distinction. She was shortlisted for the Janklow and Nesbit award and the Lucy Cavendish fiction prize for *Daughter*, her first novel. *Daughter* was a *Sunday Times* bestseller and was selected for the autumn 2014 Richard and Judy Book Club as well as winning the public vote for Best Read. It was 2014's bestselling fiction debut.

She and her husband, a Professor of Neurosurgery, have five children and live in Bristol.

# The Drowning Lesson

## JANE SHEMILT

PENGUIN BOOKS

PENGUIN BOOKS

UK | USA | Canada | Ireland | Australia
India | New Zealand | South Africa

Penguin Books is part of the Penguin Random House group of companies
whose addresses can be found at global.penguinrandomhouse.com.

First published in Great Britain in Penguin Books 2015

001

Set in 13/15.25 pt Garamond MT Std
Typeset by Jouve (UK), Milton Keynes
Printed in Great Britain by Clays Ltd, St Ives plc

A CIP catalogue record for this book is available from the British Library

ISBN: 978–1–405–91531–1

www.greenpenguin.co.uk

Penguin Random House is committed to a
sustainable future for our business, our readers
and our planet. This book is made from Forest
Stewardship Council® certified paper.

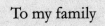

To my family

# Chapter One

The hot evening closes around the track, the rasp of cicadas is dense. My feet crunch on deep grit. Walking seems as easy as breathing; my thoughts loosen and drift in the warm air.

Adam will be sipping beer, happy; that new word . . . Zoë, maybe under the trees with a lizard in her hands. Alice will be near Teko, reading, dark hair sweeping the page, calmer than this morning. The scent of supper diffuses into the garden; Elisabeth puts flowers in a glass.

A crested bulbul startles up from the track, his staccato call tearing the peace: *be quick, be quick, Doctor, be quick.* The gold light darkens between the trees; a desert flower flares red in the shadows, and then it's dusk.

Supper time. Bath time. Sam might be crying.

Another bird answers the first and another, then all the trees are full of broken sounds. The darkening air feels thick as cake in my mouth.

In front of my feet a thin snake slithers lightning fast across the track and disappears into a gully. I want a drink with gin in it. I want Adam to be impressed I made it home on foot – sorry he forgot to check the car, sorry he didn't charge his mobile.

The gate is shrouded in shadow by the time I reach it, though the wood is still hot under my hand. It swings back with the familiar two-tone whine. The frogs have started their night-time belching in the pond behind the house. When I kick off my slimy flip-flops, the dust is soft under my feet. Relief at being home blooms like a pain under my ribcage and I round the curving sweep of the drive, impatient to see the first lights pricking across the scrubby lawn.

It takes seconds to register that all the lights in the house are blazing, that torch beams are moving jerkily across the lawn. Adam is shouting, his voice a low-pitched bellow like an animal in pain. He's over by the trees. When I start running, his face turns towards me, glimmering white through the dusk. Zoë, inside, stands against the wall, crying quietly. It's not her then. Alice squats in the corner; she sees me and stands with fluid grace. It's not her either.

And then I know.

The shadows in our bedroom flicker differently: it takes me a second to see that the curtains are torn, and moving a little in the slight wind. A glittering pile of glass lies in front of the window on the carpet, a few jagged shards still lodged in the frame.

The cot is empty.

# Chapter Two

*London, March 2013*

It was a bad time to start a conversation. Midnight. Rain crackling at the windows, an empty wine bottle on the table between us. Adam's slim face was flushed, his dark hair sticking up where he'd run his hands through it so many times. I wanted to smooth it down and put my lips against the lines between his eyebrows, but there was a secret gleam about him that kept me away.

The kitchen was messy: Sofia had gone to see a Polish film with her friends, and the children's shoes and bags were strewn about the floor. Our glasses and the food cartons needed clearing away. Zoë's drawings lay in sliding heaps on the sideboard, Alice's maths neatly piled, both waiting for my approval.

Tomorrow's list started at eight a.m., with two hysterectomies. I pushed back my chair and got up. Adam's expression was inward, as though he was working out a difficult sum in his head. I began to clear the table, stacking bowls on the crowded draining-board.

My father had an antique weighing machine: it sat on the desk in his study but it disappeared after he died. It was made of polished wood and brass, with embossed metal weights; he'd let me use it as a child, to weigh his letters and parcels. A thin sheet of paper could make all the difference. My relationship with Adam was evenly weighted with work and success, but the balance could tip at any moment. I clattered the cutlery into the sink. I loved him. I loved almost everything about him: the smile that deepened the creases around his eyes, the way he swung up the children at the end of the day, the warmth of his body in bed next to mine; but if he was winning, it meant I was losing. I wanted him to do well, just as long as he didn't do better than me.

'Tell me.' I reached for his plate. This needn't take long. It might be nothing, a clever diagnosis, perhaps, or the winning shot in his lunchtime game of squash.

'A research opportunity has come up.' He cleared his throat, an unnecessary sound that grated. His voice was monotonous, but as his eyes tracked mine, the dilated pupils gave him away: this was no routine project. I dumped the plate in the sink on top of the knives and forks and sat down to face him, hands on the table, braced.

'Let me guess. The Wellcome Trust agreed funding for your cancer stem cell project?' Pride and jealousy curdled in the pit of my stomach.

He shook his head; his eyes skated sideways. 'Remember when you did that research post in San Francisco twelve years ago?'

I nodded, though it seemed longer ago than that, a strange and distant time of missing Adam, of walking alone up and down the foggy hills to the hospital, and of the faint strains of jazz reaching through the open windows in the lab. I'd spent my days and nights staining and studying slides, then analysing results; hours writing up my findings.

'. . . just married but it was your big opportunity and I let you go,' Adam was continuing.

The memory of the shining midnight lab, the racks of slides and empty coffee cups faded. Adam was staring at me, tapping his fingers.

I stared back at him. 'What's this really about, Adam?'

His eyes flickered downwards. 'I've been offered a research post for a year in Botswana.'

In the silence that followed, the dishwasher clicked: the end of the cycle. We often pretended not to notice it needed emptying, but this was a whole new game. It was as though he'd punched me in the gut, more a fight than a game.

'Offered? You applied some time ago, then.'

Around us the children's paintings were stuck on the cupboard doors; Zoë's clay animals cluttered every sill. A squash ball lay among the oranges in the fruit bowl. Alice's violin was in the corner ready for tomorrow, swimming-pool times were pinned to the fridge with a heart-shaped magnet. My on-call rota was Sellotaped to the wall above the phone. Adam's news could change everything but he had kept it completely secret until now.

'The offer came out of the blue, Em. I'd have discussed it first if I'd applied. Of course.'

A muscle in his cheek flickered. The movement was minute – if I hadn't been watching so closely I would have missed it.

'That can't possibly be the whole story, these things take discussion and planning. Why didn't you tell me before?'

'It's difficult to talk to you sometimes . . . You get so wound up by my success.'

'So you kept it secret?'

'I couldn't find the words.'

'Tell me now.'

'Chris Assazar emailed me from Johannesburg.' Adam leant forward. 'He's read my paper on serum markers for lymphomas and he thinks an oncologist could do something useful out there. He'd supply funding.'

'Useful . . . Meaning what, exactly?'

'He runs a research center for HIV in southern Africa. Botswana has the fastest growing infected population in the continent. We know AIDS patients are at risk of lymphomas . . .' He was beginning to sound portentous, as he probably did when lecturing the medical students. He caught my glance and his voice quickened: 'So if we can tell from serum markers who is at particularly at risk, we can give anti-lymphoma treatment early and extend normal life by months, years, maybe.'

'What about our normal lives?'

Our lives weren't normal, but one of us was around, at least for part of the time, and the au pair filled in the rest. We took turns to be on call. Last weekend I'd done four Caesareans while Adam held the fort at home. I often did my research in the evenings while he read stories to the children. I took them to school in the mornings. With Adam in Botswana, I would be responsible for everything; there would be no time for research as well as clinical work. He would be free to work as hard as he wanted. He'd publish new work. I'd achieve nothing.

He'd win. He'd always denied it was like that, but I didn't believe him. My eyes burnt with tiredness and in that moment I was back at school, pulling through the pool, watching rivals, eyes stinging with chlorine, on fire to touch first. How could anyone not want to win?

Adam's chair grated against the slate floor as he

stood up. Next to him was the silver-framed photograph of my father on the windowsill. White-haired, high cheekbones, deep-set eyes behind half-moon glasses. The picture didn't show his hands, which had been tough-skinned, broad as spades. Warm. Because he was an obstetrician, people said they were surgeon's hands, skilled at saving life. It hadn't seemed like that to me in the quarry. *You can sink or you can swim*, he'd said. I was five years old.

*The quarry is silent. Secret.*

*The lake is a deep scoop of shadowed green between cliffs. We are together in his boat.*

*It's a hot day but I'm cold. I'm wearing a swimming costume. I don't know why, I can't swim. We usually come to fish but today he hasn't brought the rods.*

*'You can sink or you can swim.'*

*I don't know what he means but I feel frightened.*

*'It's up to you,' he says. He bends to me; his hands fit round my waist. He picks me up, holds me over the edge of the boat and then, very carefully, drops me in.*

*I hit stones at the bottom, mud soft as flesh, like Mum's grave. I open my mouth to scream and gag on water.*

*Thin yellow light comes down though the green above me. Bubbles stream upwards.*

*A voice shouts my name.*

*I lunge to the surface, reeds scraping my legs as I rise.*

*

Adam began to pace a few steps, turning back and forth as he gesticulated. His words fitted smoothly together, as though he'd been practising what to say out loud in the car coming home. '. . . good for both of them. It wouldn't matter if Zoë skipped Reception – in Scandinavia, five-year-old kids wouldn't even be at school; Alice is so far ahead she could take the rest of year five off and it would make no difference at all.' He sat down again and opened his hands as if offering me a gift. 'You could take a sabbatical, do any research you liked.'

So he wanted us in Botswana with him. I stared across the table but didn't see him. I was back in the early-morning kitchen ten years ago, downing coffee and writing papers while Adam and baby Alice slept. It was the same when Zoë was born. Since I'd been made consultant, life had been a constant round of clinical work and research. I hardly took a day off – how could I go away for a year? Adam had published more than me but I was younger. I'd catch up. None of it was easy, time was still scavenged. Family flowed into every gap there was, buoying me up, weighing me down.

'Please, Em?'

Across the table Adam was leaning forward, waiting for me to agree. Two years ago he'd wanted a third baby. He'd begged then, but I was new to my post and responsible for a team. The timing wasn't right. We had Alice and Zoë; everything balanced. Just. I'd said no. I'd say no to this. Adam's research in Botswana would take longer than a pregnancy. I'd sooner have a baby than spend a year abroad: babies slotted in. It was Adam's turn to give something up.

'When is all this supposed to happen?' I asked.

I had to marshal my thoughts but I needed sleep. If this had been a normal evening, like any other, the kitchen would be peaceful by now. The main light would be turned off and the room lit by the glow from side lamps. Adam would be reading a paper with his feet up, sipping tea, while I glanced through the girls' work. The only sounds would be the clock ticking and the pages turning, maybe Adam's favourite Mozart quartet playing quietly as the day knitted together.

'It will take a little while to set up, confirm funding, and organize the team.'

His voice was quieter. He thought he'd won.

'Megan said she'd help. Her parents used to work in a mission centre out there. It's where she grew up. It'll take nine months to organize the research, starting from now. Ten tops. We could be there around Christmas time.' He was smiling now. 'It would be a chance to help people, get some real meaning in our lives.'

But we helped people already. Our lives were full

of meaning. I pushed myself up and, ignoring the dishwasher, ran the tap over the pile of cutlery and plates in the sink, splashing water on my clothes. Megan, his loyal secretary. She'd do anything she could to help him achieve what he wanted. She didn't have children, though: she might not realize the effect Adam's plan would have on ours. They were doing well, but what would happen if we pulled them away from their routines? They deserved the choices I'd had. That meant keeping pace, working hard.

Adam's arms slid round me from behind. 'It would be an adventure,' he said.

I used to love that word. It meant bicycling across Europe with tents or hitching through America, rucksacks on our backs. I scraped a smear of pesto off a dish with a knife; I didn't need that kind of adventure now. Everything I wanted was here, in London. Adam's arms were pressing into the skin of my pelvis. Despite the tiredness, I felt desire heat my face.

'What d'you think?' His lips were on my neck.

I turned to face him. His mouth was slightly open and I could smell the wine on his breath. My head was swimming with alcohol. He'd said nine months, starting from now: that gave me time. I'd work something out; I knew about survival. I'd survive this.

'Let's not deal with it now.' I kissed him. 'We're too tired. There'll be time to go over it tomorrow or at the weekend. Come to bed.'

I took his hand; I could look through the paintings and homework tomorrow. As we turned to go, I heard light footsteps scurrying up the stairs ahead us, then a door closing quietly. Sofia must have crept in unnoticed. She was on the top landing in the room next to Alice. Alice had been so tired recently – I hoped Sofia hadn't woken her up.

We closed our bedroom door and leant against it in the dark, out of breath and clinging to each other, wine and exhaustion loosening the moment. Adam started pulling off my jersey. I unbuckled his belt. We were laughing.

He pushed me back onto the bed, sliding his hands under my skirt. We had to stop. I needed to put in my cap. He'd forgotten I wasn't taking the pill any more.

I unbuttoned his shirt with trembling fingers; my heart was beating very fast, the thoughts coming faster. To an obstetrician like me, nine months meant heart formation, brain enlargement, facial elements coming together, the laying down of bones and fingernails. I smiled and reached up to him. He'd kept his own plans secret until tonight; that gave me the right to have a secret plan too, one that could trump his, if only I could think more clearly. I shouldn't have drunk so much wine.

He pushed inside me and began to move. His mouth lowered to mine. It was becoming too late, I began to let go. Nothing would happen, it had taken months to conceive Alice and over a year for Zoë. I was older now, less fertile. Besides, I'd forgotten the cap several times before now and my period had always arrived exactly on time. In a few moments my body was moving with his and my last conscious thoughts dissolved.

# Chapter Three

*London, April 2013*

'Why do you have to drive so fast?' In the rear-view mirror Alice's black fringe, squashed flat by the beret, made her skin very pale. Her small face looked scared.

'I have to get you to school, drop off Zoë, see Mrs Philips, do a ward round and start my operations . . .' She didn't need this litany but it had been in my head since five a.m. Zoë, tucked in beside her, was deeply asleep, her face pushed sideways by her sister's elbow, a moustache of milk and crumbs around her mouth. A strand of blonde hair stuck to her lips.

I saw in the mirror that she wasn't wearing a seat-belt. I'd forgotten. The cars were parked bumper to bumper both sides of the road. I'd have to stop in a driveway, more time lost.

'It's not allowed to drop me off so early.'

'Of course it is, Ally.'

'There's nowhere for me to go.'

'You can read in the classroom, talk to the others. . .'

I twisted round to smile at her and looked back at

the road just in time to take in the red lights up ahead. I jammed on the brakes, skidding to a halt. A young woman with rain-flattened hair glared at me as she shepherded her bundled child over the road. Behind me, Zoë started to cry loudly. She had been jerked forward and was crumpled in the trough between the seats. Sweating with guilt, I got out of the car, and yanked the door open. She was tightly wedged, her face streaked with tears of shock. I pulled her out and stood her upright on the pavement. No damage. I gave her a short, hard hug and put her back into the seat, this time fastening her belt. Behind us a line of traffic was forming. There were angry faces and horns blaring. I got into the car again, trembling. I rarely made careless mistakes but this morning I'd been in a hurry and distracted by the day ahead, forgot to check if I'd fastened the seat-belt. Was I becoming the kind of mother who put her career before her children's safety?

'I feel sick.' Alice's voice was unsteady.

At school, she got out of the car and walked slowly across the empty playground without saying good-bye; she knew it was my fault. She disappeared down the steps leading to the cloakroom, her narrow back bent by the weight of the rucksack, shoulders hunched against the drizzle.

Despite what had happened, Zoë had fallen asleep again. I carried her to Reception, trying not to dislodge the thumb from her mouth. We were greeted by Susi, the teacher's assistant, who smiled as she took her. Too late, I noticed Zoë's hem was coming down, her cuff was stained with felt tip and she was wearing unmatched socks. Susi carried her carefully from the door. I imagined how gently she would lay her on the deep cushions in the rest room. I had seen them when I'd looked round the school before the children had started there; that detail had been decisive. Now I was worried: why had Alice's teacher asked to see me?

Mrs Philips was waiting for me in the empty year-five classroom. She must have been cleaning the board – chalk dust hung in the air. She watched me, her head held sideways, a long orange earring touching her shoulder. Her fingers, tipped with matching orange, rested on a small picture of Alice that was fastened to a closely typed sheet; the nails were sharp and shining like the talons of a minor bird of prey.

'I got your email,' I began.

'Thank you for coming in. I've sent Alice to breakfast with the boarders. I wanted to share my concerns in private, Mrs Jordan.' Her voice was burdened with sincerity. She leant forward. 'I think you should know that Alice has been taking things, small things.' The earring swung and trembled.

I had a vision of a shining pile of mobiles, watches and coins. 'What kind of small things?'

'Pencils, rubbers, scrunchies, a pair of socks.'

'Is that all?' I wanted to laugh. 'She was probably only borrowing this stuff temporarily and then forgot. At home we tend to share things, so –'

'The items were found in her desk, in a little box, labelled with her name.' She smiled gently.

'Does she know you know?'

'I removed them and told Alice I would have a discussion with you. No one else is aware of the situation.'

I glanced out of the window; I disliked this woman though I wasn't sure why. Small knots of children of about Alice's age were beginning to walk across the playground in twos and threes, holding hands, chatting. They looked happy, but perhaps they secretly minded about losing their pencils or scrunchies. They might be plotting revenge. I felt a pang of worry for Alice.

'I'll talk to her,' I said. She usually told me about school, though not so much lately. I looked at my lap where my hands twisted together. Surgeon's hands, like his, Dad had said. Clever hands that could dissect to the problem and cut it out. I ought to have known if Alice had a problem: it should have been something she'd confided to me in whispers at the end of the day when I tucked her in. But I often wasn't there then. Adam was. Even if I asked her what was wrong, would she tell me? She might have decided on the evidence that I didn't care.

'I think Alice is self-validating,' Mrs Philips was continuing. 'Ten-year-old children who steal may be looking for ways to reward themselves. I wondered if she was getting sufficient positive feedback from . . . all her caregivers.'

I felt my face heat. The clock behind her head showed eight. I would be late if I stayed to argue. I stood to go. 'She gets plenty of feedback at home. We praise her all the time. Perhaps you could make sure that happens at school, too, instead of accusing her of theft.'

She didn't reply but I could feel her eyes watching me as I walked to the door. Iridescent lines danced at the corner of my vision: a migraine was approaching. I delved in my bag for paracetamol as I crossed the playground, fine rain driving against my hot cheeks. My heels tapped the tarmac, jarring my head with each step. Bloody woman. I shouldn't have lost my temper but I was worried for Alice. As I swallowed the bitter tablets I wondered whether any of the sweet-faced children running past me in the opposite direction had retribution in mind.

The operating theatre was brightly lit, warm and calm. Classical music flowed from speakers in the ceiling. It was easy to empty my mind of everything except what I had to do. The patient lay in front of me, unconscious, intubated, eyes taped shut. Cancer had invaded the bladder from the uterus. The task distilled and became, simply, careful dissection and painstaking repair. The anaesthetist nodded. It was safe to begin. The theatre sister quietly handed me the knife and I started to cut. The music and murmurs of my team faded into the background as I worked, blinking away the sweat as it stung my eyes.

Two hours later the skin was neatly sutured, bladder function preserved.

Back in my room, I took more paracetamol, this time with a palmful of metallic tap water from the basin. I sat at my desk massaging my temples; on the screensaver in front of me Alice and Zoë were laughing on a sunny beach. Alice's face in the mirror this morning had been bleak. Perhaps what Mrs Philips had implied was true: perhaps there wasn't enough positive feedback at home – perhaps there wasn't any. We didn't praise her all the time; in spite of what I'd said, I couldn't remember the last time we had. The opportunity never seemed to present itself, or maybe it was simply lack of time. It might be worse than that.

I got up from my desk and stared out of the window. In front of me was a panorama of north London: sky, houses, roads, the grassy slopes of Hampstead Heath. The hidden ponds behind the trees where the water was green and deep. Had I become like my father in some way that was hidden from me? Did she feel she had to win to make me happy?

If I worked through lunch I could finish my review paper on intrauterine growth retardation for the *Journal of Reproductive Medicine*. I'd get home earlier for once – I could catch Alice and we would talk.

In the early-afternoon gynaecology clinic I was called back to theatre to help with an obstructed labour. The monitor showed the baby's heart rate was dipping between contractions. As I tugged on the McIndoe's forceps, the small bloodstained face appeared at the bulging introitus, the tiny nose squashed flat. A deep episiotomy, one last tug and the delivery was done. The tiny boy went straight to the waiting paediatricians to be checked, then, wailing, was handed to the exhausted mother. The father bent over them, too overcome to speak. Nodding congratulations, I stripped off my gloves and left, leaving the placental delivery and vaginal stitching to my registrar. Suffused with anxiety about my own child, I had nothing to say to these parents – they wouldn't thank me if I was honest, if I warned them that labour was trivial measured against the worries that lay ahead.

As I walked back to the clinic along the corridor, several colleagues hurried by, all of them intent on the next ward round or clinic. I felt in my white coat for my mobile: I wanted to talk to Adam. When we were first qualified and up all night with emergency admissions, we would meet in the hospital canteen at two a.m. As we leant wearily against each other, with our cups of watery hot chocolate on the Formica table in front of us; we would try to make sense of the demands and the suffering. We never talked about those things now. I was put through to Megan's answering machine and cut the call without leaving a message.

The last two patients of the day had cancelled so I left early. Alice wouldn't be back yet and I had time for a swim in the leisure centre. The poolside seats were full of parents at this time of day, chatting as their children changed after swimming lessons.

My father had been sitting three rows back at my school's gala day, a Wednesday – I remember that. He never came to galas, he always worked Wednesday afternoons, but it was my tenth birthday and he'd swapped things around. His shoulders had been hunched, his mouth turned down. He looked unhappy; he'd looked unhappy for five years.

*Can you die of a broken heart? My teacher says you can. My toes curl around the lip of the pool. My heart is banging so hard I can't think.*

*The whistle goes into my spine, like hot electricity.*

*My legs are beating as I hit the water, my arms already slicing. At the first turn, I'm in third place. By the time I turn again I'm lying second. On the last length I don't turn my head to breathe, not once. I draw level halfway down then pull ahead. Bursting for breath, I touch first.*

*The roar from my school echoes round the pool. I pull myself out and turn to check on Dad. He's smiling. Really smiling. I haven't seen him smile since Mum died.*

*Now I know exactly what to do.*

In the evening, Alice didn't want her supper. She was quieter than usual.

'Is anything wrong, sweetheart?'

'Not hungry.' She shrugged, pushing mashed potato round the plate.

'You know I saw your teacher today . . .'

Zoe looked up, interested.

Alice pushed her plate away. 'I've had enough, thanks,' she said. 'I need to practise.'

I followed her upstairs but by the time I reached her room she had her violin in her hands. She looked up, her face a polite, questioning blank.

'Ally, you probably want to know what Mrs Philips said . . .'

Her fingers tightened around the bow but she didn't reply.

'She told me you might have some things that belonged to the other girls. I knew if you'd taken them, there'd be a reason –'

'They wanted me to look after their stuff.' She pulled the bow over the strings, sounding a small discordant note. 'I said I'd keep it safe for them.'

'All the same –'

'I gave it back today. They can look after their own things.' She turned over a page of music, frowning. 'I've got to practise, Mum, okay?'

I could come back when she'd finished. She might be ready to talk later but the violin scales went up and down for half an hour, then her Mozart piece started; it stumbled a little with a couple of long pauses. I waited until I was sure she had finished, but when I went up again the room was dark and she was already in bed. Her eyes were closed and her breathing was regular. I kissed her and she didn't stir. Everything seemed normal: her shoes were neatly side by side, her clothes carefully folded, but the ceramic Russian dolls on the mantelpiece caught my eye. They were lying down for once, spaced out evenly in size order, though usually they were stacked one inside the other. I'd brought them back from Moscow years ago after an obstetrics congress. I picked one up. The china was sharp beneath my fingers – the doll was cracked. Checking each in turn, I saw they were all broken, the smallest in several pieces, its bright fragments scattered on the carpet. The curtains were moving in the breeze: the window had been left open. Perhaps the dolls had simply blown over. I slid the pane down quietly.

We would chat tomorrow on the way to school; she could tell me what had happened then. It was often the only time we were together with nothing else in the way. I closed the door and went downstairs. The morning's migraine had started up again and was playing itself out in a drumroll of pain. I needed quiet and dark.

Sofia was washing up in the kitchen, ponytail swinging as she jigged from foot to foot in time to loud pop music. She was responsible for dusting the children's rooms. I switched the radio off and she turned, her dark eyes round with surprise.

'Sofia, do you know how Alice's Russian dolls got broken?'

Her face reddened. There was a pause. She met my gaze for a second, then looked down, shaking her head.

The blush and her silence were telling: she must have broken them but wasn't going to own up. The dolls were special to Alice – she used to play with them all the time, making little family groups, the larger dolls arranged in a ring around the smaller ones, with the baby in the middle.

'Well, please take Zoë up to bed now. Perhaps you could mend them tomorrow.' Despite her carelessness, I needed Sofia. 'There's ceramic glue in the right-hand cupboard in the utility room.'

She shrugged, pulling off rubber gloves, her face wiped of expression.

I bent to kiss Zoë. 'Night, sweetheart. I'll be up later.'

Zoë held up her stuffed dog for a kiss, then trailed after Sofia.

24

Adam was writing at the large desk in his study. His face looked empty. When I'd told him we wouldn't be coming to Africa he'd been disbelieving, then angry. Now, three weeks on, it had finally sunk in.

'How's it all going?' Laminated maps were stacked in tidy piles on the surface in front of him, and the invoices lay in ordered rows. My own desk was deep in layers of paper. He was annotating a list in neat red capitals: blood bottles, syringes and centrifuging kit, mosquito net, trekking boots.

'Anything I can do?' Close up, I could see the eczema flaring in a red line along his collar.

'It's coming together.' Then he put his pen down and stared up at me. 'Though I still wish you were all coming. Em, are you completely sure?'

'We've been through this a hundred times. You know I can't leave.' I felt giddy and sat down quickly on the sofa, wishing I'd eaten lunch. 'Let's not tell the girls you're going till nearer the time – Alice might worry. I saw her teacher this morning.'

I described the meeting with Mrs Philips. As Adam listened, his fingers were constantly moving, stacking papers edge to edge, and placing pens in parallel rows.

'I don't think she needs more discussion about stealing,' he said, when he'd heard the story. 'We ought to simply –'

'Do nothing? Let things completely unravel? She'll

get isolated. Kids don't like it if their stuff gets nicked, even if she has given it back.' I glared at his hands arranging his phone and calculator side by side, like little black soldiers. 'Can you stop fiddling? It drives me insane. We ought to simply what?'

'Love her, I guess,' he said. His fingernails raked under the edge of his cuffs. 'Make home a safe place for her to be.'

'For God's sake, stop scratching.' I felt winded with hurt. 'How can you imply I don't love her? She knows she's my top priority –'

'Which particular top priority, Em?' Adam stood up, patting his pockets for an inhaler. 'There are so many: operations, clinics, research . . .'

'That's a fucking hypocritical thing to say. It's exactly the same for you. And now you're completely preoccupied with this Botswana project.' My cheeks were burning with fury. 'When did you last really talk to Alice?'

'This very evening. I went up when she was prac-tising her violin.' He inhaled a couple of puffs of Ventolin, then leant back against the desk, frowning. 'I noticed all her Russian dolls were broken. She did it on purpose.'

'She didn't do it, Adam. Sofia did. It was an acci-dent, I'm sure, but Sofia looked so guilty when I asked her, it must be her fault. Alice might be taking the blame to protect her.'

Adam looked doubtful. 'My guess is that it's less complicated. Alice is bidding for attention. Negative attention is better than none. Maybe she needs more of our time . . . Perhaps she doesn't realize how much we love her.' He paused, scratching his neck.

'Of course she does.'

'How?' He sounded genuinely curious.

'I tell her all the time.' That wasn't true, though. I never told her. I took it for granted she knew. 'I show her as well.'

Did I? When? Amid the hurry to school in the morning so I could get to work on time, or in the evening's rush to catch up with paperwork? She couldn't read my mind. She might not realize she was loved. Adam could be right.

I turned my back on him and stared out at the streetlights. In the silence, the rain started again, hitting the study window like handfuls of tiny stones. Six thousand miles away the sun would be shining on an emerald landscape. It would be hot. Adam had emailed some pictures the other day, in an attempt to change my mind. One showed a large flat-topped tree by a lake. The water had been shimmering in the sun, and under the tree the grass had looked thick and soft. I closed my eyes and let myself imagine sitting in the shade with Alice. There would be the sharp scent of young grass and the peaceful calling of birds across the water. Alice would have bare feet.

We both would. There wouldn't be a briefcase in sight.

Adam came up beside me, staring at the drops sliding down the dark glass. 'I booked Provence today. Same villa, same fortnight. You're not getting out of that one.'

Sunshine and peace for two weeks. I took his hand and brought it to my mouth, turning it over to kiss his wrist. The rash felt hot and bumpy under my lips.

# Chapter Four

*London, May 2013*

I slid the cold probe over my pelvic skin while looking at the screen by my head. I was lying on the carpeted floor of my office, doors locked and blind pulled down; this was just a quick check. Missing periods happened with stress, with exhaustion, with not eating enough. I'd been so busy recently that any of these could apply.

At first I thought it was a mistake, that the dense curved shape in the uterus was a scrambled image of some kind. I ran the probe backwards and forwards, pressing deeper each time. It wasn't a mistake. There was a tiny beating heart in the darkness, small blocks of vertebrae, the thick umbilical cord. No wonder I'd been emotional recently – even now, tears were sliding down my cheeks. This was a baby, ours. A few moments later concern cut into the unfolding sense of gladness. I had let this happen. Six weeks ago there had been a moment when I could have drawn back but I'd chosen not to. What would Adam say? I closed my eyes. He'd be pleased. Of course he would.

He'd been desperate for another child. There would be a second of disbelief, he might struggle to take me seriously, but then his face would break into a smile. He'd remember this was exactly what he'd longed for.

A door closed softly. Sarah had arrived in the adjoining office. Muted steps sounded across the floor, followed by a brief clanging tune as she started the computer. The ridged carpet was uncomfortable now; I'd have to get up soon and carry on as if unchanged. But, then, I hadn't changed. I still wanted everything; everything exactly as it was. Family, work, achievement. I wiped the tears away. I'd be going back to work once this baby was born; I couldn't afford to be emotional, now or later.

*'Emmie?'*

*I stuff my jersey into my mouth but he hears anyway. He comes into my room.*

*'Stop that now.' He sits down on the bed. 'She wouldn't want you to cry.'*

*Mum wouldn't mind: whenever I cry she holds me . . . held me.*

*'The funeral's in two hours. I need you to help me. Look at me when I'm talking.'*

*His face is puffy. His eyes are red and small. My chest hurt. So he's been crying too.*

*'Emotions pull you under. Be strong,' he says, and wipes his*

*scratchy thumb over my cheek. 'The only thing that lasts is you.
It's called survival.'*

*A week later, he takes me to the quarry for the first time.*

I had to hurry. I examined the measurements on the
screen. Crown–rump length: 1.46cm. Heart rate: 164.
Limb buds: present. On course at six weeks. I wiped
the sticky trail of blue gel off my skin, got to my feet
and printed off the scan, slipping it into my
briefcase.

The room felt smaller than usual; stale, as if the
cleaners hadn't been in that week. I wanted to open
the window but the heavy glass pane had no hinges.
Light poured into the room but not air. If I wanted
fresh air I had to go down in the lift, along corridors
and make my way through the ambulances into the
crowded car park and stand on the tarmac by the
rubbish bins where the smokers gathered. Somewhere there was a huge sky, a sweep of sun-lit grass,
flat-topped trees. Peace.

My mobile sounded. Adam. Six weeks ago, I'd let
Fate decide, thinking if a pregnancy happened it might
help in some way. I hadn't worked out exactly how,
which was unusual for me, but Adam's plan had
thrown me. I'd been tired, a little drunk. Now I had to
focus. I put my phone down unanswered, and after a
few seconds the ringing stopped. If I told him I was
pregnant he'd leave for Africa sooner than planned to

be back in time for the birth. My fingers drummed on the sill. He mustn't leave at all. Alice needed him. I needed him. Already I was more tired than usual. In fourteen weeks, the pregnancy would be five months along. I'd tell him then; leaving at that point wouldn't be worth his while. Africa would be cancelled. Life would continue as normal. He'd be delighted about the baby so he'd forgive me. He'd have two weeks off at the birth as he'd done with the girls; I'd go back after six. Now, as well as after the baby was born, we'd continue as normal, together.

All morning I carried the secret as tightly and silently as I was carrying the tiny nub of life inside me. It was my half-day but I decided to stay on to start collecting the research papers for an umbilical-cord clamping project that interested me.

My secretary had to knock twice. 'Your husband's on the phone.'

'Darling?'

His hesitant, about-to-ask-a-favour voice: he knew it was my afternoon off. As I waited, I wanted to blurt out the news but I couldn't. My skin tingled with guilt.

'I've left some scans I need at home. I'm in a meeting I can't get out of, and then it's the neuro-oncology clinic when I need them for the first patient.' I heard him turn away from the phone and sneeze. Asthma again. Stress.

'And?'

'They're on the table in the dining room, or maybe the floor by my desk in the study. Megan said she'd go over now if someone could let her in, but it's Sofia's day off.'

'Can't you give her a key?'

'I almost did, but then I thought if you were around to offer her a cup of coffee, it would make it seem less of a favour. Have you got time?'

I stood to pack the papers away. 'You owe me one.'

'You're an angel. I'll fetch the girls today.' He rang off.

I'd met Megan once in the hospital car park. Middle-aged, hair pulled back tightly, she'd seemed tired, slightly remote. She'd always refused invitations to our Christmas party; I was never quite sure what I had done wrong.

The woman waiting on our doorstep took me by surprise: younger than I'd remembered, auburn hair curling to her shoulders, her smooth face lit up when she saw me. She stepped forward. 'Thank you so much for coming back specially.'

'It's kind of you to rescue Adam. Coffee?'

She hesitated, glancing at the neat watch on her wrist.

'I'm sure he can spare you for another ten minutes. The neuro-oncology clinic starts at two, doesn't it?'

'You're right. I'd love a quick cup.'

She followed me to the kitchen. 'I should have sent a reminder last night, but he's normally so careful.'

'Adam is beyond careful.' I glanced at her as I flicked the kettle on and pulled out two gold-rimmed mugs, the last of a wedding-present set. 'Does he line his pens up on his desk at work as well?'

She raised her head from unbuttoning her coat. 'Yes!' Then she blushed: she was wondering if she'd been disloyal.

'Don't worry.' I took her coat. 'I won't tell.'

The colour of her dark gold shirt matched her hair exactly. As I put the mug in front of her, I caught the echo of expensive scent. Was this for Adam's benefit? I wondered if he knew. I appraised her again: lovely skin and clear brown eyes, a dimple on her left cheek. Wholesome, self-contained. Not his type, though that was unfair: Adam didn't have a type. As far as I knew he had never glanced at another woman. I saw Megan taking in the polished Aga, the gleaming granite surfaces, the neatly stacked china in the dresser. The mess of the night before had been tidied away. The slate floor was spotless. Sofia was good at making a room look tidy.

'Lovely house.' Megan's voice was warm.

For a moment I was tempted to pretend I did it all but the truth was easier. Megan had a busy life, she'd understand about priorities. 'I have help. The kids leave a mess but I never have time to deal with it in the mornings.'

'Alice and Zoë?' She was studying the large black and white photo of us on the wall taken a couple of years ago. We looked slightly unreal. My hair had been carefully tousled – I could have been in my twenties, not late thirties. The camera had caught Adam as he was laughing. The children were between us, beaming adorably. Megan's eyes tracked rapidly back and forth between the images. 'Beautiful children.' Her tone was serious.

'I'm straight out of the door with them in the mornings so . . . well, you know how it is . . .' But Megan didn't have children. Wasn't there some issue with her husband's health? Adam must have told me and I'd forgotten.

'My husband's always at home,' she said and I caught a flicker of emotion in her tone. Defensive, embarrassed.

'Lucky you. Adam's never here to help. Sometimes I think it's easier without him.'

'Easier?' She sipped her coffee.

'If he's not here to help with the kids, at least it means one person less to cook for . . . kind of cancels out, with the added advantage of no sex when you're tired.' I caught myself. What was I saying? I hardly knew her: my guard must be down. I wasn't used to friendship from women. I didn't know many.

She leant forward. 'You'll have help in Botswana, I know. I grew up out there.'

So Adam hadn't told her that I wasn't going with him. Was he still hoping I'd change my mind?

'I've still got some contacts,' she said eagerly. 'Adam told me he'd be very grateful for anything I could arrange.'

My thoughts flickered between possibilities: was this an innocent offer, or did she know I'd decided not to go and was seeing if she could persuade me? Was this something she was doing for Adam? Maybe why she was here?

'Actually, Megan, I won't be going,' I said crisply. 'Adam knows I couldn't possibly uproot the children or take a year away from my job.'

'Ah. He hadn't told me. I'm sorry.'

It might have been those simple words, her smile or even her hand, which was lying loosely open on the table, but in the little silence that followed, something inside me seemed to unlock. 'I can't take time out simply because it suits Adam. It's been tough to get to this point. I've had to sacrifice time with the children . . .' Though last night I'd left the hospital early to catch Alice before bedtime. I sat on her bed as she read; she glanced up and smiled. 'I thought about you today, Ally,' I said. 'I had a patient who needed help for her little girl to be born. She had black hair, like you. When you arrived you were so tiny, Dad put you on my tummy.'

Alice pretended to vomit. 'Yuk. Disgusting.'

I watched her eyes return to her book. 'Darling, you do know how precious you are . . .'

But she put her hands over her ears, and burrowed into the pillow. I stroked her back. Normal behaviour, but I sensed we needed days together, weeks probably, time I didn't have. I was organizing the summer conference in obstetrics this year. I'd just have to find extra moments like this where I could.

'I was made consultant three years ago and I've got research planned.' My voice sounded brittle in the peaceful kitchen. 'My father made me promise –' I broke off. In a moment I would be telling her I was pregnant.

'You must feel that everything you've achieved is threatened. I know exactly what that's like.'

Did she? With her round eyes and buttery skin, she seemed sealed in an invisible envelope of calm. It was unlikely she fought the kind of battles I did every day. In the mirror earlier, my face seemed made of angles and shadows. I'd been surprised by the thin lines round my mouth and the strain in my eyes.

'Andrew worked in the path lab at the hospital while I was studying law, but he kept dropping test tubes and lost his job so . . .' She gave a little shrug. No wonder they didn't come to parties. I was wrong to think she was unscathed; she'd faced far worse battles than me.

She looked up, smiling. 'He's at home all the time now, so that's good. He helps with the animals.'

'Animals?' Did she have a smallholding of some kind? I couldn't imagine her with muddy boots and buckets of feed.

She must have seen the surprise on my face because she laughed. 'Knitted ones for the hospice children. Andrew chooses the wool. Let me give you a couple for the girls.'

'Thanks. They'd love that.'

She was making light of her sacrifice, but what she had given up was so far beyond what I would be willing to that it didn't touch how I felt about Adam and Africa.

'You could carry on working out there. If you change your mind, just let me know. I'm sure I could find someone . . .' She looked down: the cat had come in and was winding around her legs. She scooped him up and sat down with him on her lap. He was a stray that Zoë had begged to keep, and was usually intolerant of strangers.

'Careful. He can be nasty with people he doesn't know.'

'Cats love me.' Richard began to purr loudly. 'I could look after him if you go.'

I didn't reply and she continued, 'The children would love it in Botswana. Especially Alice. She could get away from that wretched school.'

I felt my mouth tighten. *Especially Alice? That wretched school?* How much had Adam told her about our family? There was a hovering sense of unease, of boundaries being crossed.

'That clinic will be starting soon.' I lifted Richard from her arms as I spoke and put him on the floor.

She got to her feet, catching a mug with her elbow. It fell with a crash, the china splintering into tiny fragments on the slate.

'I'm sorry . . .' Megan tried to gather the broken china in her fingers.

'It's not important. I'll sweep it up in a minute.'

She reached for her coat, pulling it round her tightly. She'd been caught off guard. I should have been less abrupt; it wasn't her fault that she knew about Alice's problems. If Adam shared family worries with her, I'd just done the same. There was something generous about her that invited confidences. As I led the way to the front door, I picked up the scans from the dining-room floor and slipped them into their envelope. 'Thanks for coming.' I handed the packet to her. 'Don't worry about the mug. It really doesn't matter.'

She gave an awkward little wave as she walked down the steps to the street.

I began to sweep up the pieces of china scattered on the floor. The girls came down here with bare feet in the mornings. I leant further to reach the fragments that were under the stool and a shard lodged in my palm, diamond sharp. I pulled it out; a drop of blood welled and I put the tiny wound to my mouth. We didn't need china to remember our wedding. I tipped the shattered remains into the bin and went upstairs to my study.

I didn't sit down straight away, I felt restless and stood at the window for a while. Richard was outside again, crouching by the apple tree at the edge of the lawn. The garden was immaculate. Adam's territory: the neat beds and edged grass were as ordered as his desk. I'd wanted a wild-flower patch, but when I looked it up online, it seemed complicated and I knew I wouldn't have time. The cat was crouched low, staring into the twiggy depths of a laurel bush, paws folded under his sleek body, tail twitching. Above him, the dark branches of the apple tree were thick with white and pink blossom. How had I not noticed before? The buds must have swollen, then opened unseen. In the gardens that lay alongside ours, there was blossom everywhere, tender flashes of brightness close-hemmed by walls and fences. I'd missed it all. Putting my hand low on my abdomen I closed my eyes, feeling the warmth of my palm seep through my clothes to my skin. Inside me the tiny heart was the size of a poppy seed; it would be beating twice as fast as mine. At this stage her skin would be as translucent as a petal.

The back door slammed below me: Sofia back from her English class. I pulled out my papers, accidentally smearing the top one with blood. I wedged a tissue into my palm and settled down to read.

# Chapter Five

*Botswana, March 2014*

No, wait. The cot isn't empty.

There are a few blond hairs in the dip where his head has rested; a shiny circle of dried mucus from his mouth.

'For Christ's sake, Em, don't fucking touch it,' Adam shouts.

There are bloody footsteps on the rug and on the crumpled mosquito net, but it's my blood: the sole of my foot has been cut by a piece of broken glass. His white blanket is missing.

'We need to move out of here.' Adam bundles me from the room. 'The police will want to take it apart.'

So it's a crime scene now. A criminal has my son. I twist out of Adam's grasp and put my hands to my cheeks, clawing the skin. 'What did you see? When you got home, what did you see?' I'm shouting at him as we walk down the corridor. Alice backs against the wall in the sitting room. Zoë stands close to her, sucking her thumb, watching us.

'No one ... everyone ...' Adam is wheezing

badly – he can hardly talk. The girls glance at him, scared. 'I phoned the police. They're coming.'

'What did you see, Alice?' Ashen, she stares at me. Sliding my arm round her, I feel her body shake as though in the grip of a fever. 'Ally, did you hear anything?'

She twists away.

'I'm going back outside with Kabo,' Adam gasps. 'Don't move. Stay with the girls.'

Sitting on the floor, I pull them to me. Zoë climbs onto my lap. I hold Alice's arm, which is as cool and stiff as a doll's. Adam disappears from the room.

'What happened, Zo-Zo?' I put my face against hers but she begins to cry again, deep shuddering sobs. I hold her tightly. There is a roaring noise in my head. Someone touches my arm: Elisabeth, with a glass of water. I tip it into my mouth, swallowing quickly.

'What did you see, Elisabeth?' The children cringe at my harsh voice.

'Nothing.' Elisabeth looks frightened. 'I was in the garden with the girls.'

'Josiah? Teko?'

'Josiah is sleeping. Teko found that the baby has gone.'

'Where is she now?'

Elisabeth points through the back window. I stand to see: Teko is faintly visible, her white shirt glimmering as her torch sweeps over the reeds by the pond. The noise in my head gets louder.

'I can't sit around doing nothing when everyone is looking.'

'Chief Momotsi lives in the village,' Elisabeth says. The name is familiar, my patients have mentioned him: an important man, a leader. 'He will help you.' She nods.

'I'm going right now.' I move from the children and fumble for Adam's keys on the row of hooks, grab the remaining torch on the shelf above and call the girls to me again.

Adam meets us at the door, bent over and gasping for breath; he puts a hand on my arm. 'Wait. The police . . .'

I shake him off. 'For Christ's sake, get a fucking inhaler, top drawer of the chest in our bedroom. The police could be hours. I'm going to the chief in Kubung, I'll keep the girls with me.

'Emma –'

'And ask Teko why the fuck she wasn't with Sam this afternoon,' I shout back, running down the steps to the open-sided jeep. 'She should have protected him.'

The girls flutter after me, little moths in the darkness. They climb up quickly, over the top of the door, and fall into the front seat when the engine starts. Alice puts her arm round Zoë. They sit jammed together.

Adam appears, waving and running towards us. As I swerve to avoid him, the jeep glances off the jacaranda tree, and a bird flies shrieking from the branches. White discs around orange eyes, a Verraux owl. It swoops off into the darkness. How strange: he's been waiting for weeks to see one.

As we turn onto the track, the headlights dance with insects; beetles clip the windscreen and crack open. My breasts, bursting with milk, are jarred as the car jolts over potholes. Sam will be starving, tears soaking his face. My abdomen cramps viciously.

Alice searches her side of the road; I search mine. After a few minutes she yells at me to stop, pointing into the ditch. I brake, scramble down, fumbling, and almost dropping the torch. The curved shape resolves itself in the light as Josiah's dog. The yellow fur is pale in the torchlight. Half the head is missing; the back is covered with a moving blanket of maggots.

# Chapter Six

*London, May 2013*

The neuro-oncology clinic dragged on till late. It was nine by the time Adam returned bringing roses, their tight buds already wilted. He set a bottle of wine on the table, and pulled a stack of cardboard boxes from a carrier bag, the foil lids seeping orange grease.

I was curled on the kitchen window-seat with my laptop, the window a crack open to catch the faint scent of apple blossom. I'd forgotten about food. He poured the wine carefully, then handed me a glass. 'Megan said you were very kind.'

I shook my head. I hadn't been kind. She'd been unhappy as she'd left. I put the glass on the window-sill, watching the red meniscus rock against the curved sides. I'd contact her, reassure her that it didn't matter about the mug. I'd offer to buy her lunch.

Adam put the roses in the jug and began to ladle out piles of bright yellow rice and orange chunks of chicken; the spicy scent of tikka masala rose in the air. My stomach turned. 'I only want half that, Adam.'

His spoon hovered over the steaming containers. Usually I was starving.

'I ate with the girls earlier.' Untrue, but I'd been with them in the kitchen taking a call from the hospital as they'd had their supper with Sofia. She made Polish dumplings, herb-flecked and glistening, compensation, I guessed, for breaking the dolls. Alice looked pale though she chatted to Sofia.

'Naan?' Adam handed me the warm slab, and I sat at the table, biting into its doughy blandness. 'Interesting day.' Adam sat opposite me with a little sigh of relief. 'I had a phone call from Botswana, a man called Kabo. He's studying for his doctorate in Jonathan's lab. He'll be the one I work with. He sounded very friendly. He wanted to run the protocol by me. He said how sorry he was not to be meeting the family . . .' Adam glanced at me, then he talked on: funding had come through, there were recruitment problems, the testing centre had yet to be decided . . .

I stopped listening. A sense of guilt was at my throat. Adam didn't know his plans would be wasted. How would he feel when he discovered I was pregnant and that there wouldn't be time to go to Africa? He caught my eye and gave a quick grin. We tapped our glasses together. I replaced mine untouched but he didn't notice. Should I show him today's scan now, while he was smiling at me? Warn him he ought to go quickly before it was too late?

I put my fork down and looked out of the window into the darkness, forcing myself to remember the time I'd taken off for the children, how I still organized the family, the greater freedom he'd always had. I kept up through the previous two pregnancies, but Adam was there, in the background. Alice's pale face threaded through these thoughts; she needed both of us. I had to remember that and once this baby was born, his disappointment would quickly fade.

'You're quiet tonight, Em. Anything wrong?'

I must pull myself together. 'Thinking about Alice.'

It was true: I was always thinking about Alice. Beneath a constant hum of anxiety, the questions whispered relentlessly: should we push for answers about the pilfering or say nothing more? Give her space and time, or try to get closer? Decisions at work were simple. There were set procedures to follow: when to expedite delivery, what to do if a patient bled at hysterectomy, how to treat an advanced ovarian tumour. If only there was a protocol for bringing up children, something I could stick on the back of a cupboard door and refer to in emergencies. Tonight, as we began to talk about Alice again, our words followed each other round and round in tired circles, going nowhere.

We went up to see her. She had fallen asleep over a

book, her dark hair fanning out on the pillow. I kissed her, then Adam did. She half woke, murmured and turned her head into the pillow. The china dolls were upright now, all neatly mended. I slipped them carefully back, one inside another. The hairbrush, comb and little deodorant bottle were evenly spaced on her dressing-table. Even the hairclips were in colour-coded rows. We stared at them for a moment. Adam gave a guilty little shrug; his genes.

Zoë was asleep, her thumb in her mouth, surrounded by toy animals. Her clothes were scattered all over the floor. I picked them up. When we kissed her she didn't stir.

Later, as we undressed, I thought back to the scan hidden in my briefcase. My pregnancy still felt unreal. Disbelief was woven through with strands of guilt and excitement. I turned to Adam, sliding onto his body. We made up the rules as we went along and tonight I had the power, though he had no way of knowing how much. At the end our soaked bodies slipped apart.

We lay holding hands. His head turned towards mine as I gazed at the tiny pinpoints of stars through the sash windows. I'd never hung curtains: I loved the fragment of night sky we could see from our bed. Though it was orange-stained and cut by high buildings, I could still imagine the space beyond the stars.

I used to look for my mother in the sky. If she was here, I could have shared my news. She would have been happy – at least I thought she would. I was only five when she died, I remember the cake she made for my birthday and her smile, lit by the candles. She had dark hair, like Alice. Freckles like Zoë. A brain tumour. It had taken six weeks, he told me afterwards, but the smell of the hospital, her thin blue-veined hand on the sheet, the taste of neighbours' food, coloured the years of my childhood. I looked at the stars on the anniversary of her death and on my birthday. I'd been looking for her the night before I turned ten.

*The grass is stiff under my feet. Moonlight is on the trees.*

*Wind presses my nightie. My face is cold.*

*Are you there? Hiding between the stars somehow, or behind the moon? Can you see me?*

*A door opening. Footsteps on the gravel. Whisky breath. 'Emmie? What are you doing, child? It's gone eleven.'*

*He lifts me up, though I'm too heavy. 'Don't cry. You didn't think I'd forgotten it's your birthday tomorrow, did you? Look, I'll come to your gala.'*

*His face against my cheek is wet. His tears or mine?*

*Later I sneak down to check: he's in the kitchen, head lolling, a half-bottle of whisky on the table. A parcel wrapped beside it.*

*I tiptoe back to bed, my heart banging. Will he die too? Die of sadness? Die of drinking?*

\*

'How will you manage when I'm gone?' Adam's sleepy voice was easy to decode in the dark. I could tell he thought we would manage fine without him.

'I might get an extra pair of hands,' I said, turning away and pulling the duvet close around me. 'Maybe a tutor to help with the girls' homework, when I'm on call.'

When he saw me vomiting the next morning, I blamed the curry.

That evening, Sofia handed me a package that had come in the midday post. The card was simple:

*Dear Emma,*

*Thank you for the coffee. I'm sorry I broke the cup. Yours, Megan*

Inside the layers of wrapping was a painted china mug with a delicately curved handle and an exquisite pattern of pale pink flowers; it shone on the shelf in the row of dull white china.

During the day, a case was cancelled. I waited for the next patient in the staff room, nausea hovering; the smell of cheap biscuits and milky tea seemed to leak from the broken upholstery. Two theatre nurses sat close together opposite me. One was middle aged; her grey hair emerged in wisps from her theatre cap, the sleeves of the regulation greens stretched tightly over plump upper arms. Her friend was younger, neater, her dark hair tucked away, a glinting cross on a chain round her neck. They laughed and whispered together, eyes darting round, hands dipping into the same crisps packet. When the older woman's gaze met mine, I looked away, ashamed, as if caught out coveting something that wasn't mine.

My colleagues were mostly men: we had jovial working friendships that didn't go deep. Joan Ridley-Scott, the only other woman on the team, was always preoccupied. She twinkled at me over the top of her half-moon glasses as she passed me in the corridor, her grey hair pinned in an untidy knot. She was kindly but remote. Dropping the children off early and collecting them late, I never met other mothers at the school gate. In any case, friendships seemed to demand complicated input, obligations accumulated; time was needed for groundwork. Today, though, I envied the easy closeness of the nurses. Like sisters, though I'd never had one. Adam and I were only children of dead parents. Sometimes it felt as though there was an echoing space around our family where a larger family should have been. Was that what I was missing? I wondered, as I sneaked another glance at them. A sister?

I got up and threw my cup into the bin. As I went through to the scrub room, I pulled out my phone and texted Megan, thanking her for the mug and suggesting we meet for lunch next week in a café near the hospital. I scoured my hands with the little brush, turning them this way and that under the stream of hot water. The palm muscles were stronger and larger than most women's. My hands had to battle with implements against the clock, gripping, cutting and sewing. Megan's hands came into my mind as they had been on the kitchen table, smooth-skinned, tranquil, acquiescent, like she seemed to be, as if they were waiting calmly, with all the time in the world.

The noise of women eating, talking and laughing hit my face, like a wave. I hesitated inside the café door. I should be at my desk; this wasn't my world. As I began to text an excuse, I caught sight of Megan in a far corner. She hadn't seen me. She was wearing a flowery blue jacket, her hands clasped on the table, her head tilted as she waited. I put my phone away.

'This is lovely,' Megan said, as I slid into the seat opposite her. 'Andrew and I never go out to eat. Not that I mind, of course, but I'd forgotten . . .' She was staring at the pink roses in a vase on the table, as though contrasting this with mealtimes at home, the unremitting chore of getting food to table every evening so that it had long ago stopped being a moment to celebrate or even relax. I wondered if she had to feed Andrew sometimes.

'We don't go out either,' I said. 'Only on holidays.'

We talked about holidays as we waited for food. She showed me pictures on her phone from three years ago: Megan on a beach with a tall man leaning on a stick, dark hair blowing in his eyes. She leant to look at mine. They were mostly of the children on beaches in France. Scrolling, I paused at a close-up of Alice on a boat: her eyes, reflecting water, were dancing with light, her mouth open in a wide grin, ice cream smeared on her cheek. An ill-defined sense of loss hovered. I put my phone away, looking round, as though somewhere among the crowded tables and chairs I would spot what had vanished, though I wasn't even sure what it was.

As she talked, Megan touched the roses unconsciously, as if tidying the petals. She was telling a story about Andrew. The background noise had faded, and the sun poured through the open window next to me; the cutlery on our table glittered like treasure. It was peaceful, as if I had stepped outside my normal world and found another one.

Over coffee her phone sounded. Gesturing an apology, she left the table almost immediately. Andrew had fallen and couldn't get up. She hurried out, her face tight with worry.

There was a bumpy brown package by my plate. She must have taken it out of her bag along with the phone. Inside there were two small knitted lions, complete with woolly manes and labels tied around their necks with red ribbon: 'For Alice' and 'For Zoë'. Texting me later, she told me Andrew had panicked; he was fine now. We arranged to try again a fortnight later.

# Chapter Seven

*Provence, August 2013*

When Alice had finished her croissant, she tipped her chair back and shut her eyes. I registered a fluttering sensation deep inside my pelvis, the kind a butterfly might make if trapped in a palm. The courtyard was quiet, apart from the warm thrum of bees in the thyme. We were surrounded by the dusty scent of hot stone.

'I never want to go home,' Alice whispered, as if she was speaking to herself, or even praying.

I caught Adam's eye above her head. We had two days left. What would it be like if we could stay on? These easy days would continue: swimming, playing and resting, my work fitting into the tranquil routine. There would be time to talk and cook and read. Adam was silent, perhaps thinking the same.

A bee landed on my plate, crawling over a smear of apricot jam. Another joined it. I pushed my chair back as I got up, the metal scraping on old stone. It took a few moments for my eyes to adjust to the cave-like darkness of the kitchen. We would, of course, go home; we would pick up the threads of our London life. The girls would resume school. Adam would go back to work and so would I. Normal life would take over again.

*What about our normal lives?* The question I'd asked Adam when he'd told me about Botswana seemed to echo around the silent kitchen, with its high shelves full of blue and red china and the thick, uneven walls. What had I meant exactly? Normal life was the daily drive to school fighting traffic, then ward rounds, clinics, a sandwich in front of the computer in my office, operating till late, meetings in the lab, then home, snapping at the children and Adam. Ready meals slapped on the table. Evenings answering emails. In a few days that rush would start again, until the next holiday a year from now apart from a brief break at Christmas. I picked up my laptop from the dresser and walked out through the front garden to the table under the olive tree at the far end of the pool.

The children followed in a few minutes. Alice dived into the pool, neat as a swallow. Zoë leapt into the air and landed with a noisy splash. Adam slid in after them. I took a photo on my phone; in some future traffic jam with November rain slanting against the windscreen, I would glance at the picture and retrieve the blue of the water, the scent of lavender in the fields around the villa, the sharp taste of the soft yellow apricots that fell onto the grass from the tree by the wall.

Adam's shoulders gleamed as he pulled through the water. Zoë clung onto him, shouting encouragement, while Alice kept pace, her arms flashing through the water. I watched her face, as she turned her head for breath with each stroke: it was lit with a fierce joy, and for the first time, I wondered if I could be making an enormous mistake.

Megan had painted pictures of Botswana, adding brushstrokes each time we met. I could see the silent plains clearly now, the friendly people, the engulfing sun. I leant back and stared up through the thin green leaves to cloudless blue. In the last two weeks I'd worked far better here than at home, better in the flimsy shade of this olive tree than in my stuffy office. Was it the clarity of light? The heat? Even though my cotton dress stuck to my back, my hands flew over the keys. I was as focused as if I had a scalpel in my hand. Yesterday I'd updated notes for my performance appraisal and written a case report on uterine cancer. It had been overdue, but until we'd left for France I'd been preoccupied by the summer conference. This had been my first chance to catch up and now I was writing as fast as I could think.

'Come in, Mummy!'

Alice's wet fingers were cool on the hot skin of my swollen feet, one of the few signs of my pregnancy so far. As she reached from the pool to touch me, her other hand was on Adam's head while he rested, wheezing slightly, between lengths. I was caught by the light in her tilted face. When had I seen her look as happy as this? Last year? Three years ago? When she was a toddler?

I watched the net of gold light expand and contract in the rocking water. Anchoring the family in London had made perfect sense, but as I closed my eyes I saw Alice's sunlit face change: in the darkness behind my eyelids it became pale and tense, her eyes closed.

It would be hot in Africa, like here. The light would be as clear. There would be time to connect with Alice, and Adam would get to do his project. Zoë would be in her element. The baby would start life in the sun. If I worked as well as I was working here in France, I could keep pace with Adam. I'd get my research done, combine a sabbatical with maternity leave and come back with several papers to my name. The scales would still balance.

I had started to show a small curve in the last four weeks but clothes had disguised it. I'd complained loudly about getting fat and Adam had been completely misled. He said he'd always wanted a plump wife and that perhaps I'd slow down now I had so much weight to carry around.

I peeled off my kaftan and stood in the sunshine in

my bikini; my skin felt bathed in warmth and light. I wondered if the baby could sense the brightness. Adam glanced over, away, then back again, a smile spreading over his face as I dived in.

He was waiting for me in the shallow end when I came up for air and imprisoned me against the wall. His mouth was warm in the cool water. 'You kept that pretty secret, didn't you?'

Against his tanned skin, his brown-green eyes were very clear. I watched them as I wondered how to answer. There seemed little point in telling him it had been a deliberate ploy.

'It was a mistake. I was so . . . surprised when it happened, I didn't know what I wanted,' I told him, my heart beating hard. Would he believe me? 'It took time to work things out. But I have now.' That was the truth, after all.

'Meaning?' He cupped my chin with a wet hand.

I held on to his shoulders, letting my body float up behind me in the water. It was a relief to feel weight-less. 'We'll go to Africa together, all five of us.'

His eyes narrowed, as if he sensed my evasion. Was he about to challenge me? Ask for more details? Then his face relaxed. I watched him decide to lay doubts aside. After all, he wouldn't want to spoil the moment either: he was being given everything he'd wanted. His hug was so tight I could hardly breathe.

Alice was swimming towards us, grinning widely.

I didn't want to spoil her happiness – she might feel threatened by so much change. 'Let's tell them we're going to Africa, but not yet about the baby,' I whispered into the wet curve of his ear. 'One thing at a time?'

He nodded and, turning, swept Alice into the hug.

I was in the courtyard, snapping off stems of basil before lunch, when Megan phoned. I could hear the smile in her voice. 'I got your text. So you're all going. Wonderful.'

'Isn't it?' I held the shiny leaves to my face. The green peppery scent was so strong that my eyes stung.

'What made you change your mind?'

'Alice mainly, the sunshine and . . .' I hesitated. The secret had been so closely held.

'You needn't say. I know.' Her voice was amused.

'How?' I walked into the kitchen and laid the herbs on the chopping board.

'Emma, we've had, what, six lunches now?' She sounded affectionate but exasperated. 'How could I not have noticed? Your looser clothes maybe? The shape of your face?'

I looked into the little mirror by the fridge; even in the gloom of the kitchen I could see my rounded cheeks, my eyes glowing like a cat's. My hair was thicker. I had been too busy to notice, and so had Adam. He left the tomatoes he was slicing and put his arms around me, his face beside mine in the reflection. 'Hello, pregnant wife,' he whispered, kissing my shoulder. 'We're starving to death here.'

I said goodbye to Megan.

That evening, I lay on Alice's bed. Tired out from swimming and the excitement about Africa, she tucked in close, her back towards me as she looked at the olive trees in the moonlight beyond the open shutters. Her warm toes curled and uncurled against my leg. The faint scent of lavender and thyme came to us from the garden. Zoë pushed into my other side. I read 'Hansel and Gretel' from *Grimms' Fairy Tales*, which Zoë brought on every holiday. She dreaded and loved the telling. Halfway through, she cuddled closer, glancing outside. 'Are there witches in France?' She pulled her thumb from her mouth. 'Do they eat people?'

'It's just a story, Zoë.' Alice's voice was sleepy. 'There's no such thing.'

'Okay,' Zoë said obediently, slipping her thumb back in. A few moments later she had fallen asleep.

I lay with my arms around my daughters, watching the moon rise in the darkening sky. I could think of no reason at all why life in Africa wouldn't be this perfect.

# Chapter Eight

*London, September 2013*

Three a.m., emergency Caesarean. The skin edges sprang apart under my scalpel; small packets of red-rimmed fat bulged into view. A wet meat smell seeped upwards into the room.

Foetal distress. Obstructed labour. Undiagnosed breech, inexperienced registrar. The decision to operate had been easy. The operation was easy. Dissect to the fascia, separate the rectus abdominis muscles, slit the uterine wall, suck out the meconium-stained amniotic fluid and reach inside, my own swollen belly making the movements awkward. A few tense seconds spent pulling the wedged shoulders free with a see-saw motion, and then the small, greasy body was out. A stuttering wail, string-white arms widely outstretched: a blood-wet, healthy girl. I handed her to the waiting paediatrician. My back ached. Bending was difficult now I was twenty-four weeks pregnant. I couldn't stop now, though I could have handed the sewing-up to the registrar at my elbow. Giving up wasn't an option.

\*

*'When the going gets tough the tough get going.'*

*He smiles as he says it. We're in the car, on the way to the pool. Six a.m. and raining. I smile back. It's easy now. When I win, he smiles. I can tell he's happy. He eats more. He's reading books again. He's stopped drinking.*

*Practice makes perfect; that's another thing he says. He tells me I must never, ever give up.*

*Every morning is the same. He reads the paper and does his work by the side of the pool. I train. He thinks he's doing this for me. How can I tell him it's the other way round?*

*I have a coach, and we concentrate on different things. Today it's my hands: how to tilt them in as they go into the water and how to cup the fingers. I swim length after length after length just focusing on my hands.*

*Never, ever give up.*

I concentrated on the open wound, the placenta and the bleeding. The midwife's chatter faded as I worked, the mask damp against my face.

Twenty minutes later I was done. Fifteen more, I was driving slowly across Hampstead Heath in the slate grey of early dawn. Leaves lay in dark piles around the trees and in blown heaps along the gutter. A young fox trotted over the road, almost under the car wheels, head high – I had to brake quickly. He must have seen the car but hadn't taken in the danger: it was too big, too near, too alien. The white-tipped brush disappeared into the bushes. The wildlife on the Heath was hidden by day and, drawing into the kerb, I slid the window open to absorb more. The cool air was sharpened with the scent of wet grass and rotting wood; a few moments later, birdsong unspooled from the surrounding trees. My hands relaxed; the sudden tears were cold on my cheeks.

A police car drove by slowly; a man's weary face glanced, not unkindly, through my window. I started the ignition again and pushed my head hard back into the seat to stretch my aching neck muscles, turning my head from side to side, while I replayed the operation I'd just done, checking for mistakes. There had been none. It had all gone smoothly, though I'd forgotten the patient's name; had I ever known it? Did it matter? I was her obstetrician, not her friend. She didn't need my friendship, just my skill. I turned the car into our street, then let it glide down the hill to our house. The operation had been swift: the child's brain had remained oxygenated; she would be normally intelligent. The mother's wounds would heal. That was enough. I got out of the car, glancing around at the empty street, with its row of curtained houses. If there was something more I should be doing or being, it was hidden from me.

Adam was lying on his side in the bedroom. I pulled up the blind to let in the light, opened the window, then sat on the bed to watch him. Sleeping, he looked younger, more as he had when I'd first met him, though he was already older than the rest of us. Changing career from the City, he had been more mature, schooled in organization. His notes had always been filed, cross-referenced, indexed; everything to hand. Mine had been in untidy stacks around the room, notes spilling across the desk, on the radiator and spread all over the floor. I was untidy by nature; his orderliness had seduced me.

I bent forward to touch my lips lightly to his hair, feeling the strands of wiry grey distinct from the black softness. Then I pulled off my clothes, throwing them towards the chair where Adam had left his carefully folded trousers. Some landed on the floor, the rest on top of his. He'd notice and mind. Marriage and even children had made no difference: lapped by disorder, his orderliness had become entrenched. The dull morning light picked out the spine of a large book on his bedside table: *The Encyclopedia of Wildlife in Southern Africa*. He'd probably made notes.

Lifting the duvet carefully, I slid close, turning and stretching until my back was pressed up against his warm length. My limbs seemed to melt in the heat. The baby gave a little flurry of kicks high under my ribcage. Adam, still sleeping, moved closer, slipping a hand around me. I'd taken the following day off, I could relax, but a list flickered in front of my eyes even as the dark edges of sleep began to close around me. Coffee with Megan, a meeting with Mrs Philips, collect up the research papers to print off in case the Internet wasn't reliable in Botswana . . .

Surfacing into a bright morning, I saw Adam's face above mine. Side-lit by a narrow beam of early sun, the deep creases between his eyebrows were shadowed and faint traces of a flaking rash edged his hair.

'What happened last night that your registrar couldn't handle?' He bent to kiss me, his mouth tasting of toothpaste and coffee.

'Undiagnosed primip breech. Francesca panicked.'

Adam nodded and straightened to open the wardrobe. If we were still in France we would have woken up together and made love as the sun came into the room. I rolled to the side of the bed awkwardly and pushed myself up.

'What are you doing with your day off?' He looked faintly jealous.

'Meeting Megan for coffee, Mrs Philips after that –' I stopped. Alice had appeared and was standing inside the door, watching us. Zoë followed, pushed past her, held up her face for her morning kiss and ran out of the door again. I heard Sofia calling the girls to breakfast but Alice lingered.

'Hello, sweetheart.' She must have overheard her

teacher's name. 'Mrs Philips is going to give me your work for Africa today.'

'What happens if I get stuck on something when we're out there?' Her voice trembled. 'When we come back I'll be way behind the others.'

'You'll be fine, Ally, but if you're worried we can always get a tutor. What do you think?'

She nodded and disappeared.

'That's a great idea, Em.' Adam leant into the bedroom mirror, baring his teeth rapidly to check he'd brushed them properly. 'Told you she just wanted reassurance. The holiday in France did the trick.' He was whistling under his breath as he tucked his chin down, buttoning his shirt. Then he looked up. 'So, Megan, the new best friend. I wouldn't have thought she was your type, somehow.'

My type. Did he mean like me? I distrusted people like me: ambitious, complicated, careless. Megan exuded restful dependability.

I walked stiffly to the chair, leaning backwards, balancing the weight. I picked up my clothes, wondering if he minded. Were we competing for his secretary now? Though she was only part time, perhaps he resented our lunches or that she'd volunteered to pick up the girls on a Tuesday so I could finish my clinic without rushing.

'I like her, Adam. She's genuine. And kind.' I watched his face. 'Is it a problem?'

'Not to me. She loves being involved.' He put his arm round me, smiling. 'We really don't have to fight over Megan.' Then he patted my abdomen. 'He's getting huge.'

He? This was a girl, I was convinced. A tiny girl who moved in exactly the same way as Alice had; I felt as nauseous. She would look like Alice, too, a little dark-haired sprite. I hadn't scrutinized the scan, liking the edge of uncertainty, but all the same, I knew.

'Shouldn't we tell the girls?' He was bent to lace his shoes. 'Twenty-four weeks – they're bound to notice if they haven't already.'

'Kids don't look at their parents' bodies,' I replied, though sometimes I'd caught Alice's eyes scanning me with a quick flickering glance. 'Alice is anxious about her work. Let's wait a bit longer.'

He shrugged. I could tell from his face that his focus had shifted to the day ahead. He put on his jacket, kissed me again and clattered downstairs.

'Don't forget supper this evening,' I shouted.

He said something I couldn't hear. Then he called the girls to get into the car, and, after a few minutes, the front door slammed.

Two hours later I was waiting for Megan in the café. The smell of coffee, the background hum of talk, the crashing as plates and cutlery were cleared had become familiar over the past few months. Soon this place would be thousands of miles away. An unfamiliar dart of apprehension, like the echo of a contraction, went through me and was gone.

There was a little fluster of chairs moving. Megan was there, out of breath. 'Sorry I'm late. We'd run out of Andrew's meds and I had to dash to the pharmacy.'

'I ordered your cappuccino.' I watched her unwind a scarf, affection jostling with pity. Andrew seemed more like a patient than a husband.

'I've emailed my friend David in Gaborone.' She leant back as the waitress put a frothy cup of coffee in front of her. 'He should have some help sorted for you by the time the family arrives.'

I'd imagined working in a garden in the cool shade of a large tree, the baby sleeping by my side, the girls splashing in a pool or sitting next to me at a table doing their school work. A less cluttered life. Why would we need anyone to help? 'We'd have to get references beforehand,' I said carefully. 'It might be difficult.'

'David runs an orphanage.' She looked away, her cheeks stained with colour. 'All his workers have to be carefully checked.'

'How about we keep it in reserve for now?' I touched her hand and she smiled.

'The girls will be a help anyway,' she said. ' Have you told them yet?'

I shook my head. 'I'm still worried for Alice. Right now she's anxious she'll lag behind her school mates while we're out there; my pregnancy could be the last straw.'

'She seemed fine last Tuesday. 'We were talking about the trip. They can't wait. I hope Botswana lives up to their expectations.' Megan sounded oddly cautious, as though sounding a warning.

'But you told me they'd love it.' I stared at her, puzzled. 'Especially Alice – I remember your words.'

'Something happened out there that frightened me but it was a long time ago.' Her smile didn't reach her eyes. 'You'll be fine.'

She hadn't mentioned this before. Thinking back, we had never discussed her childhood, though I'd told her about mine, secret things I'd never told anyone before: how my father, blind with weeping, had turned the car over on the way home from the funeral, trapping us both inside, or how for years after that I dared not bring a friend home in case he broke down in tears. Now she was trusting me. 'You were frightened at a mission school? By the nuns, you mean?'

'I wasn't at the mission school. I boarded in South Africa, on a church scholarship.' A little frown appeared on her forehead.

'Tell me about it.'

She lowered her voice. 'It started because I looked

different. My mother made my clothes. I was fatter than the rest and my hair was red. There was a girl who told the others to leave me out – she was popular so no one spoke to me.' She paused, then finished in a whisper: 'After a while, I got the feeling that I wasn't real.'

The girl would have been slim, with a cruel smile. Perhaps she had golden hair. The scholarship would have paid Megan's fees but she would have still been poorer than the rest, with different clothes and different shoes. I pictured her standing at the edge of a playing field, stocky, red-headed, the last to be chosen for a team, and wanted to put my arms round her. 'Didn't you tell your parents?'

'They asked questions when they picked me up at the end of term, but once we got back, home took over.' She shrugged. 'They returned to the clinic. Mum was an obstetrician, like you.'

Not really like me, though I didn't say it out loud. I was planning something different. In a couple of months, Alice would be at the centre of our lives.

'What did you do?'

'I got into the habit of hanging around with the kids in the village. They let me into their gang.'

'That was lucky – that you were accepted, I mean. Obviously you were different from them, too . . .' I wasn't sure what I was trying to say.

'They didn't have rules. They didn't seem to notice I was any different. Dira kept an eye out for me.' She nodded slowly. 'She loved me.'

The woman at the table beside me knocked me sharply with her elbow. She didn't apologize. She was pulling apart the salad in front of her, her fingers glistening with oil. Her companion, neck bandaged with unnecessary scarves, was braying with laughter. The room suddenly seemed full of spoilt women wasting time. It would be good to escape to a culture where even the children had better manners.

'So Dira was like an adopted aunt?' It was time to go. I found a five-pound note in my bag and wedged it under the saucer.

'Dira was a witch.'

The unexpected word echoed in a hush that fell coincidentally, almost as though people had heard and were absorbing something frightening. Then the scarf woman laughed again and the chatter renewed. Perhaps Megan had been joking.

'Lucky you,' I said, as I groped with my feet under the table for the shoes I'd kicked off. 'I'd give anything for a few magic spells.'

'No, you wouldn't.' Her voice was tense. 'One of the girls from school went missing later, the popular one, the one who'd left me out.' She leant forwards, 'There was a nationwide search in South Africa but she was never seen again. A few months later, a bag of pelvic bones was found by the railway station near our home. They turned out to be hers.'

The words were grotesque; they belonged in one of those fairy tales Zoë loved to be frightened by.

'We were on holiday in England when it happened but friends wrote with the news,' she continued. 'There had been whispers in our village. People said it was Dira, because of her powers, but the police pinned it on a gang of rapists from South Africa. They were imprisoned for life. The girl's mother went insane.' Megan looked at me, her brown eyes empty of expression. 'Part of me still thinks it was my fault because Dira did it for me.'

The smallest Russian doll had been mashed to pieces. The bright flakes of china were all over the carpet. I leant to take Megan's hand. Deep inside the layers, the wife, the secretary, the friend, there was a badly damaged child. 'You said the school was in South Africa?'

She nodded, looking down.

'So how could Dira have had anything to do with a crime like that, hundreds of miles away in a different country? It makes no sense, Megan.'

She didn't reply. The café was quieter now: the women from the table next to ours had left and the waitress was clearing the plates. I had to go too. Standing and slipping into my coat, I touched her shoulder. 'My new registrar is coming to supper tonight. Why don't you join us? I'd like to meet Andrew.'

After a few seconds she looked up and smiled. 'We'd love to.'

I parked outside the girls' school, and hurried to the entrance across the playground. The low autumn sun shone through the trees, the long shadows cutting the tarmac into stripes of light and dark. How did Megan balance her faith in the brightly lit scientific world of her work, with dark beliefs that belonged to a shadowy, ancient past? I shivered, and rang the bell then pushed my cold hands deep into my pockets as I waited to be admitted.

In the classroom, Mrs Philips was in a hurry, slamming papers on desks. When she saw me at the door she nodded and walked rapidly to a cardboard box on her table. 'I've collected what you'll need – a copy of the curriculum, the syllabus and a weekly schedule, textbooks and a teaching guide for each subject.' She patted the box. 'It's all in here.'

'I'll do my best.' I tried not to feel daunted. 'Alice is worried about getting behind.'

Mrs Philips walked briskly back down the aisle, continuing to thump paper onto the desks. 'She's a bright child. Her grasp of languages is excellent. She's way ahead. In a way, that's her problem.'

I let that pass. If the school hadn't found a way to manage a bright child, it was a good thing she was leaving.

'Has anything else gone missing?' I asked.

'That seems to have stopped.' She walked back up an aisle, and as she came near she smiled. 'She seems happier now.' She watched me as I picked up the box. 'I expect she's delighted about the forthcoming addition.'

I didn't mention that I hadn't told Alice about the pregnancy; suddenly it seemed time that I did. I stowed the box in the car. It would have to wait till this dinner party was over. Tomorrow; I'd have time to tell her properly then.

# Chapter Nine

*Botswana, March 2014*

The jeep judders over ruts in the road.

Was Josiah's dog killed when he barked, in case he gave the abductors away? If Sam cries, will they kill him too? As I press the back of my hand against my teeth, biting skin, drawing blood, I remember maggots take time to hatch: the dog must have died two days ago, padding down the road, intent on adventure.

The village could be any village in Africa at night: no electricity, no streetlights. I'm quickly lost. The huts we pass are silent. I can't see where my clinic is. One hut by the road shows a lit square of window. I wrench the car to that side and, barefoot, step out into a warm puddle. Blood? Dog urine? I look down; my foot shines black. Engine oil.

I knock on the door, then bang with my fists. Behind me, in the car, Zoë whimpers. The door is opened by a young woman. A man stands behind her, his tattooed arms tightly folded, while an old woman hovers at the side, her fissured face wary. A boy in school uniform peers out at her side. Light from a paraffin lamp strung up behind them flickers over posters of cars on a dark green wall.

'I need to find Chief Momotsi. Can you tell me where he lives?'

The man pushes to the front, his arms spread to hold the doorframe. He jerks his head up, a soundless angry question.

'My baby is missing.' The obscene words make it true, the world sways giddily and the old woman steps forward, curls her cold fingers around my arm. Her grip is strong. Her eyes are bright under lashless lids; thousands of lines criss-cross her cheeks. Like a witch. Terror beats in my mouth. Then she smiles and reaches for the young woman, bringing her forward, to translate perhaps. The girl is very pregnant, probably a patient because she recognizes me and puts her hands across her abdomen, shaking her head – is she afraid my child's misfortune will contaminate hers?

Behind me in the jeep, Alice starts shouting, short, loud yells, like a car alarm that has broken and starts up for no reason. I turn, get back into the front seat and pull her to me. The yelling stops as suddenly as it began.

The old woman shuffles after me, the boy behind her. She put her thin hand on the top of the door; a delicate bead bracelet slides down over the bones of her wrist and hits the metal with a small clash.

78

'Kgosi Momotsi.' She points down the road. The boy nods as she turns to talk to him in rapid Setswana. He starts jogging, beckoning me to follow. I start the engine and the woman's hand slips off the door. Moving away, she becomes any old woman, tired and bent, going back into her house and her life, disconnecting from our catastrophe.

# Chapter Ten

*London, September 2013*

Francesca seemed too young to be a registrar. How could she have gone through medical school without so much as a line on her face? I'd forgotten how young, young was. Her husband, Gianni, was older and much fatter; grey hair crawled untidily at his neck. He stood close behind her, smiling and talking a little too loudly, as if to deflect from the age difference. Once in the sitting room, he dived for the smoked almonds and stood munching, legs wide apart, blocking the heat from the fire as he looked round.

It had taken two hours but the scum of papers and laptop leads had gone. The room gleamed with polish, and a bunch of white lilies stood in a thick glass vase, sending out their heavy honey scent. Cut crystal shone on the drinks tray, and a fire in the grate crackled and hissed. The room looked luxuriant and ordered; no one would guess that in a few days the papers would be back and the flowers would be dead. It worked for now.

When the bell rang again, Megan and Andrew were at the door. Megan looked different: her hair was swept up, the dimple in her cheek so deep it had its own little shadow. She'd recovered but Andrew surprised me: he was older than I'd anticipated or perhaps it was the disease. Gaunt and narrow-shouldered, he limped through the door, his face lifting at the sight of the open fire. I sat with him and Megan on the sofa, straining to hear as his speech came slowly and indistinctly.

Just before supper I slipped upstairs to settle the girls. Megan came with me: she wanted to say goodnight. Zoë had already fallen asleep on a heap of stuffed animals. I kissed her as Megan stroked her hair, her face tender. Caring for Andrew would fill the space where children might have been, but as I tucked the sheet round Zoë, I felt a pang of sorrow for the mother Megan would have made.

Alice was bent over her desk reading a textbook but she got up as we came in, staring at me as if I were a stranger. The hand holding her chair was clenched, her body rigid.

'Good news, darling, Mrs Philips said you don't need to worry . . .' I began.

'She said about the "forthcoming addition",' she whispered. I didn't understand at first. 'Why didn't you say?'

After all this time the news had come from

outside the family. I reached for Alice but she jerked away and stepped back against the wall, a small animal at bay. Megan stood silently behind me; she seemed to be holding her breath.

'I was going to tell you tomorrow,' I said. The words sounded inadequate, even to me. 'I thought you had enough on your plate, Ally, without worrying about a baby.'

'Why would I worry?'

'Sometimes children think a baby might mean they're less important.'

Her eyes were wide with fear. I took her cold hand – the fingers were ink-splotched, the nails bitten – and laid her palm against my abdomen. 'Feel. I'm relying on you to be my chief helper.'

I could feel her fingers trembling before she snatched her hand away.

'It's not going to make a difference to anything, sweetheart.' That wasn't quite what I meant but everything I said sounded wrong. As I searched for better words, Sofia's voice came faintly up the stairs, calling from the kitchen. She sounded panicked.

Megan stepped forward. She put her arms round Alice. 'Can I stay with you for a little while, Alice? I'd much rather talk to you than all those people downstairs.'

Alice's head nodded against her shoulder. Sofia's voice became louder.

'Thank you,' I murmured, and hurried out.

The kitchen was full of steam, the potatoes had burnt. Sofia had been laying the table and had forgotten about them. I measured rice into a pan and left it simmering.

In the sitting room, Adam was talking to Francesca. Gianni had moved to the sofa next to Andrew; I caught a few words about the Italian lakes.

I drew Adam aside. 'Alice knows I'm pregnant. That teacher told her about the baby. She's upset we didn't tell her earlier.'

'I knew it,' Adam said. His mouth had compressed into an angry line. 'I'll talk to her now.'

As he turned to go, Megan was at the door; she stopped him with a hand on his sleeve. 'Alice is fast asleep now.' She smiled up at him. 'She was exhausted. She had a little cry but then she cheered up when we talked about names. She's chosen one already.'

'I can't thank you enough.' I hugged her. 'Nothing I said was helping.'

'She guessed a while back but as no one said anything' – Megan touched my arm – 'she thought she must be going mad, imagining things that weren't there.'

'Poor Alice.' I felt sick.

'Thank you.' Adam bent to kiss her cheek. 'You've been brilliant.'

'I'm glad I could help.' Her blush was deep. 'I think it's all going to be fine now.'

I doubted it would be as simple as that but at least Alice knew the truth now. I took Megan's arm and led her into the candlelit dining room. The walls were dark red, the candles making little pools of light on the polished oak of the table. Sofia had set a small plate of thin pink ham, layered with crimson-fleshed figs and discs of mozzarella, in each place.

'This is so perfect,' Francesca said to Adam, drawing out a chair and sitting next to him.

'A bit womb-like, don't you think? Trust Emma to bring her work home . . .'

Francesca gave a tinkle of laughter.

I smiled and turned to Megan. 'What names did Alice come up with?'

'Samuel for a boy, Samantha for a girl.' Megan replied. 'She's reading *Lord of the Flies* in English. Sam was one of the boys in the good tribe. I suppose she thinks –'

'Of course,' I interrupted. I didn't want to admit I had no idea what Alice was reading. 'Samantha,' I repeated. 'I like that name.'

Sofia helped bring in the main course: a casserole of bubbling *bœuf bourguignon*. The rice steamed in its dish, sprinkled with parsley. There were little murmurs of approval. No one knew about the pan of burnt potatoes in the bin, and the meal looked perfect.

As we ate, the discussion turned to babies.

'I don't mind delivering them, but the thought of looking after my own is scary.' Francesca was skewering chunks of beef with her fork. She gave a small shrug, a little smile. 'Maybe I just need to be a bit older.'

'Oh, I don't know. I was younger than you when I had Alice and we managed to survive, despite the occasional scare.' An expectant silence fell. 'I was on call one weekend. It was quiet. Alice was a baby and I wheeled her to the corner shop in her pram.'

'Classic Em,' said Adam. 'She left her in the shop.'

'The hospital called me for an emergency; I went outside to answer my phone, then rushed straight there.' Why was I telling this story? It wasn't funny at all, but women like Francesca, play-acting helplessness, provoked the desire to shock. 'It wasn't till I was scrubbed in theatre that I remembered I'd left my baby by the freezer cabinet in the Spar.'

The silence was broken by another tinkling laugh from Francesca. Megan stared at the tablecloth; I'd upset her. She didn't know how strangely easy it was to be careless with your own children while you worried about the health of strangers. Or did she? An image came to mind of a child in the white heat of an African morning, watching her mother hurry away down the steps of a veranda, doctor's bag in hand. I wished I hadn't been so flippant.

'It was all right, as it happens,' Adam was telling everyone. 'Emma phoned me and I went straight round. Luckily the shopkeepers knew us or they might have called the police. Alice was sound asleep, safe behind the counter.'

Francesca was looking at Adam through long eye-lashes. 'So you saved the day?' Her short curly fringe reminded me of a calf.

'Since he wasn't tied up in hospital, delivering babies, I'd say it was a pretty straightforward job to wheel a pram home,' I said. 'More, anyone?'

Megan shook her head. Gianni nodded vigorously. Andrew's eyes were closed and, for a second, I thought he'd gone to sleep.

When I got up to fetch the pudding, Megan offered to help. She was carrying the white-chocolate mousse when she stumbled just as she reached the table. Time seemed to slow: the perfect white disc, rimmed with falling blackberries, turned over before it reached the floor. We stood quite still, look-ing down at the curdled mess of creamy white streaked with dark red. For a moment it looked like spilt blood.

There was a little flurry of activity around Megan, almost as if she had been hurt. As Adam swept it all up with a dustpan and brush, I quickly assembled the cheeseboard.

*

After everyone had gone home my face felt stiff from smiling. I took off my shoes and flung them into a corner. My uterus had been tightening off and on all evening. No more dinner parties until we got back from Africa. I didn't want this baby to come a moment before it was due.

# Chapter Eleven

*London, November 2013*

The baby came early anyway. It was a wet Sunday afternoon in November and Adam was on call. Alice had an English comprehension to finish while I worked on my laptop.

Zoë lay on the floor with a colouring book, crayons scattered around her. The driving rain against the windows isolated us peacefully from the rest of the world. The pregnancy was thirty-seven weeks; with the girls, I had gone full term, so I ignored the contractions when they started. When my waters broke, I stuffed a towel between my legs and carried on; I only realized I'd been groaning when Alice pushed the phone into my hand. 'Get Megan.'

'Sofia is here, Ally. Let's just . . .' I clenched my teeth. I'd forgotten what labour was like.

Alice stared at me, white-faced. 'I want Megan.'


'I'm coming round now.' Megan's voice on the phone was decisive. 'I'll take you to the hospital, the girls will come with us, and then we three will go shopping for supper. Andrew will be fine till we get back and they can sleep at mine.'

By the time we reached the hospital the contractions were more frequent and I was unable to walk. Megan found a wheelchair and pushed me to the ward. I could hear the girls' light footsteps skipping down the long corridors behind her.

An hour later Adam arrived, out of breath. By then Duncan, the senior obstetrician, had been called. The baby's heart was slow to recover between contractions. The pain was relentless. I hardly noticed Adam. I'd had epidurals with the girls – things had been better organized. It was too late now. All I wanted was a Caesarean but I didn't ask. I'd cope. I always coped.

*Other parents push around us on the platform looking anxious, but at least they are smiling. Dad just stares at me, his mouth turning down at the edges again. First term at medical school. Brown leaves curl on the train tracks.*

*He speaks so quietly I have to lean close. 'It's tougher than you think, Em. If you feel like giving up, remember –'*

*'Give up?' I laugh but my chest hurts. 'Watch me, Dad.'*

*He laughs too. We say goodbye. He is swallowed into the crowd, one head among many; he turns to wave before he disappears completely, still smiling.*

*How would you give up, even if you wanted to? Like how exactly? Do you let go? What do you let go of? What would it feel like? There is a poster on the wall opposite, advertising holidays: there's a train on a track, on a green field, leading towards a white cliff and sea. Would it be like falling off a cliff into water? Like drowning?*

Thirty agonizing minutes later, in a hot slithery rush, I pushed the baby out and lay back, sweat-soaked and gasping for breath.

'It's a little fella,' Duncan said. His tone carried the same serious delight as if he had been presenting me with an important award. A boy. How was that possible? I'd been so sure it would be a little girl. Adam squeezed my hand, his eyes full of tears.

Before I had time to stop him, Duncan had clamped, then cut the cord. I felt a moment of anger: all the papers I'd read on the timing of this showed it was better to wait. Then the baby was whisked to the bassinet to be checked by the young paediatrician. Adam followed closely. He'd been smiling broadly, but suddenly his face fell. My irritation about the cord faded. Something was wrong.

'What's happening?' I raised myself on one elbow, craning to see.

'Nothing. He's lovely, beautiful, fine,' Adam said heartily. The list was chilling.

'Then why –' Before he could answer I leant forwards and vomited into the cardboard pan on the bed. Even as I was retching, I was trying to see what was happening in the little huddle by the bassinet. 'For Christ's sake!' I lay back, feeling giddy, as the midwife took away the pan. 'Someone tell me what's wrong.'

'Here's your son.' The paediatrician put the baby into my arms.

A blotchy stain covered his right cheek, a brilliant strawberry map printed on perfect skin, the edge laced with indentations. I looked at the rest of him: well-shaped rounded head, a dusting of fair hair, tiny neat ears. Thin little fingers flickering next to his face. My eyes went back to the birthmark. The girls had been perfect, I hadn't expected this, I wasn't prepared. The paediatrician was a new registrar I hadn't met before.

'This looks like a strawberry naevus, unless it's a port-wine stain. Where's Mr Sutton?' An older paediatrician, he and I often worked together at difficult births. I wanted his gruff truthfulness now, not this nervous boy.

'His day off. I'm covering,' he said apologetically.

'We need to scan the lesion.' It was simpler to think of it as a surgical issue. If it was a port-wine stain, it might be linked with an underlying arterial-venous malformation that would need treatment.

'Of course, though I'm sure it's a typical strawberry naevus. It'll get bigger for the first few years, then fade completely.' The registrar paused and blushed.

'As you know. We'll keep you in for a couple of nights as he's three weeks early but there shouldn't be any problems.'

I tuned him out. As I brought the baby to my left breast, he turned his head inwards, the small mouth seeking the nipple. From this angle the red stain was invisible. He might have been completely normal.

Adam touched the baby's head reverently. 'It couldn't matter less about the mark, Em. You won't even notice it in a few days.'

My eyes filled with tears. Duncan rested his hand briefly on my shoulder. 'Time to do the repair work. Ready, Emma?'

The midwife guided my ankles into stirrups. A needle slipped into my bruised flesh like a bee sting and then the anaesthetic began to numb my perineum.

'John, after my father?' Adam cupped the tiny bloodstained foot.

'Samuel.'

'Where did that come from?' He bent to kiss the curling toes.

'Alice. She's reading *Lord of the Flies*. It was going to be Samantha for a girl.' But the faint image of a tiny dark-haired girl had disappeared, bleached out under the bright lights.

'What wrong with John?' he asked.

'Let's please Alice for once.'

'Samuel. Sam.' He walked around testing the name. 'I like it. I'm sure there was a judge in the Old Testament called Samuel.' He smiled. 'It means "heard by God".'

I was too tired to smile back – even my voice was thin with exhaustion. 'It's a name, Adam, not a biblical reference.'

A name Alice had got from *Lord of the Flies* for a boy who faced fellow tormentors, as this child might unless the mark faded before school. In the silence I could hear the squeak of thread as Duncan pulled it through the layers of tissue, the click as he cut the end. I closed my eyes and slept.

# Chapter Twelve

*London, early December 2013*

The front door opened downstairs. Silence followed. Adam's head would be tilted while he worked out where the screams were coming from. Four seconds passed, maybe six, then his feet came fast up the stairs. From the timing of the thuds, he was missing every second step. The bedroom door was flung open, letting in a rush of cold air. A light dusting of snow lay on his shoulders, His dismay seemed to fill the room and then he moved rapidly to the cot, pulling off his coat.

'Jesus, Em.'

The screams took on a downward, shuddering tone, Adam threw off his jacket, picked Sam up and began to walk rapidly backwards and forwards, cradling the baby against his chest.

I typed a couple more references. The digital clock at the corner of the computer read midday: feeding time, according to the chart I'd made the night before. I moved to the bed. Adam kissed the top of Sam's head and put him into my arms, then he sat down next to me, his face in his hands. The weight made the mattress dip and I half fell into him. He smelt of the cold, the tang of alcohol wipes, the hospital world.

Sam's wet face turned into my breast. As his mouth fastened onto my sore nipple, it was as though hot needles were piercing me. Adam, audibly wheezing, pulled out his inhaler and took a puff.

The small sounds of snuffling and swallowing seeped into the silence; I was too tired to explain that I'd been trying for a routine. The days and nights had blurred into a cycle of feeding and crying, an exhausting round, unlike anything I could remember. I probably wasn't producing enough milk.

Adam's voice was muffled in his hands. 'Can't you take a few weeks completely off just to settle him?'

'How much time have you taken "completely off"?' As I twisted round to speak to him, Sam was pulled off the nipple and started crying again.

Adam didn't answer. I settled Sam against me. Energy seemed to drain out of me as he sucked. The naevus was uppermost, the red skin shining where the tears had tracked. I looked away. From here I could read the results of the comparison paper on ventouse deliveries that were still on the screen. Somehow I had to finish editing it for next month's *Journal of Obstetrics and Gynaecology*.

Adam lifted his face from his hands, following my

glance. He got up, walked to the computer and picked up the little chart I'd made, with its columns and boxes. 'What's this?'

I didn't answer. He knew what it was.

'Breastfed babies can't be fed to a routine at four weeks.' He gave a little laugh. 'Think of the girls.'

'I am thinking of the girls. They were never like this – Sam cries for food after half an hour. I'm awake five, ten times a night.'

Alice had hardly cried. She'd been wakeful, but peaceful. I remembered gazing for hours at the minute perfection of her face and toes. I'd worked while she slept. Zoë had been predictable: she slept, fed, played. I used to pick her out of the cot, just to hold her. She'd smelt of new bread and baby soap.

Adam returned to sit next to me. I braced myself to avoid rolling into him, I hated him for that little laugh and didn't want to touch him, even by accident.

'I know it's hard.' Adam stroked Sam's hair. 'Do you think he could be extra hungry? He may need more milk than Alice or Zoë did. Boys are hungrier than girls.' He smiled.

Sam was smaller than the girls had been at this stage; he didn't need so much food. I pushed myself further away along the edge of the bed.

'I've been wondering if this could be, you know, some sort of postnatal depression.' Adam didn't look at me. His tone was cautious, almost apologetic. 'They say it's more common with babies who are premature.'

Sam had come three weeks ahead of time. That was all. I wasn't depressed, I needed to work and sleep, I was exhausted all the time. These facts didn't add up to an illness, but if I objected Adam would think he had a point. He might even ask our GP to come round.

He sighed and stood up. 'My clinic starts in twenty minutes. I just came back to check you were all right.' He looked out of the window at the falling snow, his hand scratching his neck, then he turned to me. 'I've got the answer. I'll get some bottles and milk powder after work. I'll give him a bottle at night. He'll sleep, you'll sleep. It'll all feel better.'

I didn't reply: if he thought the problem could be so easily resolved there seemed little point.

When he'd left, I put Sam back into the cot. He protested but I ignored him and he began to drowse. I started tapping in the results again.

It wasn't Adam's fault that he thought I was depressed. He was searching for something that made sense. Now that the scan had proved it was a simple strawberry naevus with no underlying lesion, he considered the problem solved. If I told him why I avoided picking Sam up, he wouldn't believe me. It would make no sense to him that every time I looked at that small marked face I felt the dull weight of failure.

I told Megan, though. She came early one frosty Sunday morning, her cheeks flushed with cold, carrying a basket of knitted toys. She handed Alice a tiny owl with round button eyes. Alice held it up to her face but in a few moments she'd left the room. She had retreated further since Sam's birth; she talked to Adam but answered me in monosyllables, slipping from the rooms that I entered. Adam said it was normal and that she just needed time to get used to the new, bigger family.

Zoë spent hours stroking Sam; it was as though she'd acquired a new pet. Megan had knitted her a baby zebra with deep mauve stripes and Zoë threw her arms around her, shouting with delight. Sam had a white blanket and a small grey elephant with leather ears which Megan tucked into my arms next to him.

'Take him if you like. He won't break.' I held Sam out to her.

She took him, her eyes wary. 'He's so light.'

'That's because I'm not producing enough milk, according to Adam. He gives him a bottle at night now.'

She burrowed her face into the baby's neck. 'He smells wonderful.'

'Baby sick and urine. Probably needs a nappy

change.' I was flipping through some papers at my side. It wasn't true. He had a scent like warm hay.

Megan shook her head, her hands tightening around his shawl. 'He's lovely, Emma.'

My eyes filled with tears. 'He's not, though. Look at him.'

She gazed fondly at Sam's face and her lips curved into a smile. 'If you're worried about the mark, how could it matter?'

'Maybe it shouldn't affect things but it does.' As a child at school, Megan had been rejected because of the way she looked. Of course appearances mattered, she must know that better than anyone. 'When I look at him, I want to cry,' I said.

'If I were you, it would make me love him more.' She kissed the top of his head. 'To me he's perfect.' She glanced at me. 'You have a perfect family, Emma. You're lucky.'

She gave me a warm hug. This was the nearest she'd come to admitting she minded not having children. It should have been me comforting her but all I wanted was to lay my head on her shoulder and cry.

After that Megan came round often. She organized a cinema outing for the girls and took the cat off our hands early, making good her promise to look after him while we were away. She never seemed to mind caring for Sam if I wanted to work or even sleep. Sometimes I wondered what I'd done to deserve such generosity. As she was leaving one day after dropping the girls, I asked her why she was so kind.

'You'd do the same for me.' She must have seen my doubtful face. 'I've never told anyone else that stuff from my childhood, but I told you. You listened. It felt like you really understood.'

I had understood; it wasn't hard. I knew exactly how the past can live inside you and for a moment my father's face was between us, with his down-turned mouth and tear-filled eyes.

As Megan turned to go out of the front door, she glanced back into the hall, which was strewn with toys, the pram and Zoë's scooter. 'And I love being with the children. It's you who's kind.'

A few days later, she saw me organizing papers on the dining table. 'Got your certificate?' she asked, rocking Sam in her arms.

I was printing the last documents I needed for my research. I caught the sheets as they shot out of the printer. 'Mine are done. The girls' last jab is tomorrow.'

Megan laughed. 'No, the certificate to prac-tise – you know, the Botswana Health Professions Council Certificate. I got Adam's a while back.'

'I'm going to work from home. That's the point.'

I stacked the sheets together and stepped back to admire the neat piles. 'There's enough here to keep me going for months.'

'If you want to gather more data or even observe a clinic you'll need it. Adam's came through quickly.' Sam's eyes were travelling rapidly backwards and forwards under drooping lids. Bending her head, she dropped a kiss on his nose. 'Just give me your CV, academic certificates and a copy of your passport and I'll sort it for you.'

A couple of weeks later she presented me with the certificate. Later that night I packed it into the case in my study along with my papers, grateful but convinced she had wasted her time. I glanced round the familiar space, the light in the corner, my father's desk, the piles of books heaped on its surface. I snapped off the light as I left, feeling a tingle of apprehension. Despite Adam's organization and careful planning, the maps, the books and the equipment, we were going into the unknown.

# Chapter Thirteen

*Botswana, March 2014*

The boy veers down a smaller track and through a gate, his long legs flickering in and out of the headlights. I follow, braking sharply when he dodges in front of the car before vanishing. The engine cuts out.

In front of us a rondavel is attached to a squat building, the tin roof glittering in the moonlight. Dark shapes huddle around a small fire. We get out of the car, the girls clinging to me.

'*Dumela.*' A tall figure moves from the shadows. 'Kgosi Momotsi.' He bows. Firelight flickers over a long, handsome face, as stern and still as if sculpted from stone. His grip is firm.

He leads me to a seat; a cup is pushed into my hand; Zoë burrows into my lap and Alice presses against my side. The people around the fire get up silently and disappear into darkness. Ginger beer burns a fiery track down my gullet.

'I was in the clinic, this afternoon. I work with Esther . . .'

He nods. He knows this already. He would have

known about us from the beginning; though we neglected to pay our respects, now we need his help.

'My baby was stolen today.' Will he believe me? 'He has a mark on his face,' I continue, circling my own right cheek, as if that would anchor my story.

'Who would do this?' Chief Momotsi asks quietly, his eyes intent on mine.

Who? Like a swarm of insects, the questions have been circling loudly, more closely: Teko, who loves him, whom I found crying in the corner? Josiah, who is old and kind? Elisabeth? She was there all the time. No one else had been around that day, apart from Kabo, and he'd been with Adam. A random criminal, then, but what could have been the motive?

'I have to go. The police might have come by now.'

'The elders will meet in the *kgotla* to discuss this.' He stands too. 'My son will drive you home now. Tomorrow my wife, Peo, comes to be with you.' He turns to indicate a tall woman at his side; she nods gravely.

Why would we need anyone unless they help us find Sam? But Chief Momotsi bows and turns away. The arrangement is already in place.

A tall boy steps close, his large spectacles neatly patched with tape. I drop the keys into his palm. The girls scramble ahead of me into the back seat and the jeep moves off jerkily.

Back at home, in London, the kitchen would have

been full of uniformed men in minutes, notes taken and information flashed between teams. Records would be checked even as cars were dispatched, sirens screaming down the roads. And then? There were babies in England who were never found; police were fallible everywhere. Sam could be just as lost, but at least everything would be familiar: I would know where to turn and who to call. Megan would be there, dealing with the children, making tea.

The headlights on the road pick out the twisted shapes of thorn trees at either side. Beyond, in the darkness, the empty land stretches for hundreds of miles.

# Chapter Fourteen

*In transit, London–Botswana, December 2013*

In the night sky five miles above Paris, the plane banked. Adam and the girls slept, while Sam dozed in my arms. Imagined horror played like a film in the back of my mind. A bomb explosion, mechanical failure, even a moment of inattention from the pilot, and we could all be spun down through space. Would Alice, deeply asleep, wake before she lost consciousness? Or Zoë, leaning against Adam's shoulder, snoring lightly, feel even a second of pain as the impact splintered the eggshell bone of her ear canals? Sam might survive a crash, being tiny and sheltered by me, but would perish in the fire that followed.

Hundreds of passengers slept. No one else was torturing themselves as I was – as I always did on planes. Adam usually held my hand but he was two seats away, head slumped sideways. He looked remote in sleep but in the last weeks he'd become remote anyway. He'd been staying late at the hospital preparing for the trip, whereas I got up early to finish editing the paper on ventouse deliveries. By the time he came home I was usually asleep. He'd settled on his diagnosis of postnatal depression: it was simpler for him to think my lack of interest in Sam was an illness that Africa might cure. We hardly talked any more. In a few hours we would arrive in a bright, different world but, contrary to what Adam thought, sunshine wouldn't cure anything.

Sam's head dropped backwards in sleep; his mouth slipped slowly off my nipple, pulling it as he went, raising a blister. The skin would burn and bleed when he latched on again. A thin skein of milk stretched from his lips and broke, trailing on my shirt. I lifted him to my shoulder. The flight attendant paused as she bustled past. Her eyes widened as she took in the birthmark; she saw me watching and gave a brief professional smile. She probably thought I was used to it.

I wasn't used to it. How could I be? How could I get used to a birthmark that spread like a stain, over the face of my child? I glanced around: the other parents looked so peaceful, sleeping alongside their children as they were transported through the dark skies. Somewhere in the world there must be parents like me, who didn't like the way their children looked, burying repulsion and burying guilt. Megan was the only one who knew how I felt, and now she was thousands of miles away. My thoughts, guilty and wretched as they were, would have to stay hidden.

The plane shifted, seeming to change course as it navigated towards Africa, taking us somewhere we had never been before. A tiny clutch of hope followed this thought, as if a hand had just taken mine. Something might be waiting for us that could change things beyond imagination. The warmth of Sam's body against me was hypnotic. In the dark I could pretend he looked completely normal. Despite my fear of the plane, the muscles of my face began to slacken and my pulse to slow as I slid into sleep.

The metal rail was hot as we stepped down the rickety stairway to the ground. Sensations crowded against my skin: heat, as if blown from an oven; light, thick and yellow as treacle; the scent of eucalyptus, fuel oil and dust. I wanted to absorb this moment of arrival, but my mouth tasted stale, my nipples were sore and Sam was wriggling in my arms. Adam was ahead with Zoë, Alice between us, half running after Adam. Beneath my shoes, the tarmac felt tacky. Around the airport, flat brown land stretched to a distant rim of hills. Next to the terminal there was an untidy sprawl of abandoned buildings and a wire fence, behind which two thin donkeys cropped a dusting of brown grass. Zoë's head turned to follow them as Adam guided her forwards.

Inside the glass-fronted building, white pipes

stretched upwards, birdsong and fluttering wings came from near the roof. I had imagined a low-ceilinged building humming with noise, not this cool cathedral. The woman who stamped my passport smiled and welcomed us to Botswana. The brilliant blue of an old woman's headcloth sang out in the crowds; red flowers in pots tumbled to the pale marble floor. It seemed we had arrived in an ordered, colourful world.

I bent to Alice. 'Does it feel good to be on the ground again, sweetheart? We're going to have fun here.'

She nodded and relief washed through me. I lifted her hand to my lips for a quick kiss.

Once we had collected our luggage, we stood together in the arrivals hall, the girls staring at a Christmas tree that listed unevenly to one side. It was Christmas in two days but my sense of the season had been dislocated. It felt as if we were starting our summer holiday. Those who had been on our flight were dispersing into the airport, swallowed into the sea of people. After a while there was a thinning out, a sense of quiet. Sam began to grizzle. Had we got the arrangements wrong? I wasn't even sure what they were. Adam was scrutinizing the crowd and began to wave energetically. Following his gaze I saw a large African man who stood shoulders above the throng; he was holding a placard with our name written unevenly across it in thick blue letters: 'FAMILY JORDAN.' A moment later he caught sight of Adam waving and hurried towards us. 'Welcome.' His voice was deep and seemed to echo in his mouth. He wore a crumpled white suit and half-moon glasses, which slipped down his nose as he bowed low to our little group. 'I'm Kabo.'

Adam had mentioned Kabo, his research assistant, bu I'd forgotten about him. Even before Sam had been born, details like this had got lost, drowned in background clamour. Perhaps it would be easier to hold onto things here. Kabo enveloped my hand in both of his and smiled widely.

'Thanks so much for coming to meet us.' Adam clapped him on the shoulder, then Kabo gravely shook the girls' hands in turn. He touched Sam's foot gently. There was no rapidly disguised pity or distaste in his smile, and some of the tension from the long night began to dissolve.

He had already found a couple of trolleys for our luggage and we walked past the pots of flowers into the blinding brightness of the car park, where long rows of cars glittered in the hot sun.

'Would it be a good idea for us to hire a car here?' Adam asked, pointing to a queue by a car-rental office.

'No need. I'm taking you to Kubung – I live not far from your house,' Kabo told him. 'And your cars are there already: a jeep for supplies and a four-wheel drive. You'll need them when it rains. Just don't forget to check them over – oil, water and so on. There's no AA here.' And he laughed, a deep chuckle that seemed to make the differences between our countries into a joke we could share. He gestured to dry beds of shrivelled flowers that ran alongside the road. 'The rains are overdue. They should have started in September. There is bad drought everywhere.'

I remembered that the yellow of the desert had seemed to cover most of Botswana in Alice's school atlas, the only break a tiny patch of green in the north-west by the delta.

Our luggage was loaded into Kabo's roomy car and then he helped strap Sam into the baby seat that miraculously appeared. The girls clambered in on either side of their brother and I sat with them, relieved to escape the heat. Adam took the front passenger seat. Kabo carefully manoeuvred round islands of straggling palm trees and desiccated hedges as we headed to the road.

'I hadn't realized it would be so hot,' Adam said, rolling up his sleeves. 'It hits you like a sledgehammer.' He gazed eagerly out of the window. I could tell the heat excited him.

'We pass a hotel with a pool on our way out of town,' Kabo said. 'We can drop by, if you like, no problem.'

'Great idea.' Adam looked back at me. 'What do you think, Em?'

'Not sure.' The prospect of cool water was tempting but I wanted to reach the end of the journey, settle Sam and sleep.

'We pass it anyway,' Kabo said. 'You can decide when you see it.'

The car gathered speed along a wide dual carriageway; Alice stared out of the window; Zoë's eyes were closing, despite the voices around her. Sam was drowsy, though he'd need feeding soon. Adam and Kabo leant towards each other, talking. I caught the words 'lymphoma' and 'AIDS'; already they seemed like a team. Outside, high-rise buildings flashed by, their blue-tinted windows gleaming. Kabo called out the names as we drove past: Diamond Terminal, Department of Health, Trade Centre. The roofs of smaller buildings were tucked among green trees; stalls stood here and there along the verge but we passed so quickly it was impossible to see what was being sold. A few people strolled along the edge of the road. This wasn't the Africa I'd been expecting: I'd imagined more poverty, milling crowds. Gaborone looked like any cosmopolitan city. It was hotter, different, of course, but the buildings, the people and the roads were reassuring. The children would be safe; I would be able to do my research. Things would work out.

After a couple of miles, Kabo slowed and pointed to a sprawling brick building ahead on the left. There were palm trees in the courtyard and an impression of green space behind; tall trees were visible over the roof. 'This is the hotel I told you about. Do you want to stop?' He turned to smile at the girls, as the car slowed. 'There are usually monkeys in the garden.'

'Monkeys!' Zoë echoed rapturously. She had woken and her head was already tilting so she could scan the trees.

Adam turned to me, eyebrow raised.

I removed Zoë's hand from the door handle. 'I suppose a quick dip won't hurt,' I replied.

Kabo drove into the forecourt, parking alongside a coach and a yellow minibus, which was covered with painted lions. As we watched, a stream of children descended from the coach and formed a straggling crocodile shepherded by two women in red blazers, clipboards in hand. A few seconds later they had disappeared into the hotel. Then the doors of the minibus opened, and ten much younger children clambered out, followed by an overweight white woman with piled blonde hair. They moved, an untidy little group, into the hotel. A tall African man in opaque sunglasses and a broad-brimmed cowboy hat brought up the rear.

'School outing?' asked Adam, as he unbuckled his seatbelt.

Kabo turned to look at him. 'Orphans,' he said, in a low voice. 'AIDS has removed a whole generation. These kids and thousands like them are brought up in orphanages.' He gestured towards the last child, who had run back for his dropped towel. 'They get taken for treats like this every so often. Hotels let them in for free when it's quiet – good for their image.'

I slid awkwardly out of the car with Sam, the girls scrambling after us. Adam put an arm round each of them; they leant against him, asking questions, their voices high with excitement. It was easy to forget how lucky we were. How would an occasional outing change anything very much in those orphans' broken lives?

We were greeted with warm flannels and glasses of juice; it was cool inside, and the cottony balls of a large bunch of mimosa on the front desk filled the lobby with almond scent. The damp cloth was soothing on my sweaty face. Kabo signed us in as visitors while Zoë twirled round and round on the shiny wooden floor in front of a Christmas tree, holding out the edges of her shorts. Alice was by the window at the back, studying the garden.

'They've got rooms available, Em,' Adam said. 'How about staying here overnight to break the journey? Kabo says it's at least two more hours to Kubung.'

Sam began to struggle and whine. The thought of stretching out in a bed after the night on the plane with Sam on my lap was compelling.

'Okay,' I said.

Zoe clapped her hands and the girl behind the desk smiled.

We found a table in the shade by the pool. Sam drank from his bottle as I sat with Kabo, a jug of fresh orange juice between us. The girls flung themselves into the water as Adam waited to catch them, Zoë shrieking with joy. The orphaned children stood together in silence in the shallow end, one or two jumping up and down cautiously.

'They seem so subdued,' I remarked to Kabo, 'not like kids in a pool should be.'

'They have no idea how to play,' he replied. 'Some of them have been in charge of families themselves or were found sleeping rough.' He shook his head. 'Orphanages aren't ideal, but the alternatives are far worse.'

The younger children from the minibus filed past us. No one was talking. As she walked by, the blonde woman glanced down at Sam, and her sunburnt face creased into a friendly smile. 'Beautiful,' she said.

Perhaps the birthmark was less visible to someone dealing with tragedy every day, but as her gaze lingered on his face I felt for the first time that a stranger was truly acknowledging him. The girls, as pretty babies, had garnered praise everywhere, but I'd been too busy to take Sam out, too tired to invite anyone in, too ashamed.

'That mark will vanish within a year, and then he really will be beautiful.' I could hear the eagerness in my voice. It could take nearer four years but it was hard to admit that even to myself.

'Welcome to Botswana. My name's Claire. Claire Stukker. Here on holiday?' She gestured to the hotel. Her South African accent gave her voice a hopeful, friendly edge.

I shook my head. 'Just overnight.' As Sam began to splutter, I stood up to wind him.

Kabo took over. 'We're setting up a joint research project to look at the risk of cancers in AIDS patients.' He nodded towards Adam and the girls in the pool. 'Dr Jordan's just arrived with the family from the UK.'

'Anything that could make a difference would be good.' She turned to me. 'These kids have lost everything.'

'Looking after them must be hard.' I watched as she glanced towards a couple of her charges tussling near the pool's edge. She seemed calm but vigilant, as she would need to be.

'We do what we can,' she replied, 'but it's not nearly enough. I have help, of course. My partner Daniel and a small team of girls. I couldn't manage without them.' She looked down at Sam again, and touched him lightly under the chin. 'You'll find people here want to help. I'd accept when you can. They love children and they need the money.' With a nod at both of us, she turned to go.

'Any more advice for us newcomers?' I didn't want her to leave.

'Depends where you're headed.' She looked back at me. 'Town or country?'

'Right out in the bush, I'm afraid,' Kabo told her, glancing anxiously at me. 'A few kilometres from Kubung on the Thamaga road.'

'In that case, snakes.' She started to walk away, calling over her shoulder, 'They hide in the long grass. Tell the children to wear shoes.'

Was that all? I'd hoped for something more. She'd reached the boys, who were now throwing punches, and was holding them firmly apart. I sat down again; I hadn't realized we would be so isolated.

Kabo smiled. 'Adam told me you were going to be working too. Tell me about your research.'

As we talked, I watched Adam in the pool with Zoë on his shoulders and Alice swimming beside them. The sun was still high; the air smelt of pine and herbs. If it hadn't been for the flock of children who stood waist deep, silently watching, we could have been back in Provence.

After a while everyone got out and the pool was

empty. I gave Sam to Adam, then changed and slipped into the water. I floated on my back for a while, resisting the temptation to start lapping – Kabo would think I'd gone mad. The blonde woman had stopped to talk to Adam as she waited for the children to change. Her hand was spread over Sam's head, her fingers absently fondling his ears. I wanted to get out, pull him away. I'd experienced the same unease when strangers had handled the girls as babies, but this was the first time I'd felt it with Sam. Obscurely heartened, I turned a somersault at the deep end and pushed myself into the depths of the pool. When I surfaced, the woman had vanished. Soon after that, I got out, and heard the buses noisily starting up in the hotel car park.

'Leaving already? Those poor children hardly had a moment to relax,' I said to Kabo, as I dried my hair with a towel. Zoë was squatting by my feet to inspect a small lizard that was basking on a flagstone.

'They're headed for a football match, packing a lot into the day. You have to admire the energy.' He smiled. 'She left her number and an address for you.'

Kabo handed me a scrap of paper. Inside she had written an address in Gaborone and a mobile number. 'Keep in touch' was scrawled in looping letters underneath. I'd forgotten how kind people could be to travellers. I tapped the contact into my phone.

Later, I showed Adam the note.

'A friend already.' He put his arm round me. 'Might be helpful.'

He was right. She'd been new to this country once; she looked after children; there could be hundreds of things to ask her.

Kabo was spending the night with his parents, who lived nearby, and he left, promising to pick us up at sunrise the next day. We walked around the garden. Banana and lemon trees were surrounded by velvety lawns. Tall gum trees stood in little groups. The spray from hidden hosepipes went backwards and forwards, darkening the papery trunks and releasing the warm scent of eucalyptus. Monkeys clambered through the branches and sprang onto the hotel roof, their young slung beneath them, clinging on with tiny fingers. Alice held Sam up, showing him the scampering animals. He seemed absorbed, reaching his hands towards them as if trying to touch them.

The next morning everyone slept on. The water smoked in the clear air and swallows dived low over the pool as I swam up and down. The scent of pine was already strong. After breakfast, Kabo came to collect us; once we were all settled in the car, he started the engine and the hotel receded quickly behind us. The swim had been restorative; it might be a while before we had another.

'Will there be a pool where we're going, Kabo?'

He peered at me in the mirror. 'Kubung is a poor

district,' he said carefully, pushing his glasses up his nose. 'Very dry. Water is precious. I don't think there is much to spare for swimming pools.'

I felt ashamed of my question but Kabo was continuing: 'The owner mentioned water behind the house. It could be a dam, I suppose.'

A dam would be perfect, better than a swimming pool. I remembered the images Adam had emailed. There might be shade, and grass round the edge for picnics. We could swim every day. As we picked up speed, I turned to tell Alice but she had already gone to sleep. I peeled off her cardigan and she hardly stirred. Zoë was staring out of the window, sucking her thumb, her eyelids were drooping. 'Sleep, baby girl.' I stroked her chubby arm and her eyes closed. I smiled, and glanced at Sam. His head was turned sideways in the padded seat. The naevus was uppermost: in the sun it seemed larger and shinier than ever. The sunscreen was in my bag. As I smoothed it on, his mouth opened and he seemed to nuzzle the padding on the chair. I leant back; my last conscious thought was that I hoped it was clean.

A complex fragment of a frightening dream slid away before I could grasp more than shadows. We had stopped, and the car was quiet. The window was filled with white sky, brown earth and green leaves. The girls were sprawled on the back seat, their eyes shut, breathing deeply, as if drugged. Sam's arms were flung wide – he seemed happy even in sleep. I slid past Alice and eased the door open. Ahead of us, on a rise in the ground, was a long, low, thatched building. Adam was under a tree, talking to Kabo.

The heat was ferocious; the skin on my face and arms stung. It was far hotter than it had been in Gaborone. Stumbling on tree roots in hard, reddish soil, I walked quickly to Adam. He broke off his conversation with Kabo and turned to me. 'We've arrived! You slept nearly all the way.' Then, turning, he indicated a young girl I hadn't noticed, half hidden by Kabo.

She stepped forward, and glanced down at her feet. They were bare and covered in red dust; her hair was tightly plaited; her face was smoothly composed. She seemed very young.

'This is Teko,' Kabo said. 'She's been waiting here for us. She heard about your arrival. She's come to look after the children.'

'Look after the children?' This child? Megan must have gone ahead with her idea, after all, but I felt irritation rather than gratitude. We didn't need a nanny – I thought we'd discussed that. I'd planned to spend more time with the children, working and playing together. I'd looked forward to bush walks collecting insects and plants, outings to wildlife parks, lying in the grass under the trees with our books. Bedtime stories. Adam's eyebrows were raised expectantly. I smiled and shook Teko's hand. It was rough-skinned. A working hand. Her face was pretty but tense; her eyes were older than her body looked. Although she wore no shoes, she was neatly dressed in a black skirt and crisp white shirt; there was a lovely necklace of blue stones round her slender neck.

'Our friend lived near here when she was a child. She said she'd find us help through a contact who runs an orphanage,' I told Kabo. 'I hadn't realized she'd gone ahead.'

Kabo turned to Teko and questioned her in rapid Setswana; she glanced at me as she nodded and replied briefly. 'She's come straight from the orphanage; her boss told her about your arrival.' He shrugged. 'This is normal for us. People can turn up for jobs, even without this kind of introduction.' Then he smiled, pushing his glasses up his nose. 'Teko was in charge of the babies and some older children. She's got a note.' He passed it to me. I read the few typewritten sentences about her responsibilities with the younger orphans. Her honesty was recommended. I handed it to Adam, who scanned it briefly and gave it back to her.

'Well, good for Megan for following through. We're very grateful,' Adam said heartily. He nodded at Teko. 'You've arrived in perfect time.'

'Like magic.' I turned to Kabo. 'How did she actually find us?'

'She was given the address by the boss at the orphanage. She got a bus to Kubung village, then a lift with a farmer going to Thamaga,' he answered, looking at her and nodding approval. She had managed a complex journey, his words implied; she must really want the job.

'So when do you want to start? Now?' Adam asked, with a smile. Teko looked back at him, the tight skin around her eyes relaxed, but she didn't answer.

'She can't speak English,' Kabo put in, 'but that's not a problem.'

Not a problem? How could we employ someone we couldn't communicate with?

'We need a tutor more than a nanny, Kabo, someone who can speak English.'

'I can find you a tutor, no problem,' he replied. 'But I think you might be glad of Teko's help all the same. She understands a few words. If you can just demonstrate what you want, she says everything will be easy to understand.' The glasses slipped down again.

Everything? Alice's anxiety? Zoë's exuberant demands for attention? Sam, whose routine was already shot to pieces? Would she mind the rumbling conflict between Adam and me? I doubted if anything in our family would be easy for a stranger to understand.

'It's not as if you won't be here all time in the background. It might give you a chance to work in peace,' Adam said. Then he was distracted by a bright blue bird that was bustling in and out of the branches above our heads. 'Blue starling,' he murmured. 'Fantastic.'

He flashed me a triumphant smile, like a small boy who has discovered hidden treasure. He'd read up about the birds here but, preoccupied with Sam, I hadn't had the chance to do the same. If I'd had time, I might have learnt some words of Setswana, or found out about the plants that grew here so I could show the girls. Even on the plane there had been no opportunity to leaf though the pamphlets about Botswana in the seat pocket in front of me. Bitterness began to rise.

'It would mean you could complete that research on cord clamping,' Adam continued, patting my arm. I pulled away, infuriated. He glanced at Kabo, who was inspecting the bird, whistling softly to himself.

The blue stones in Teko's necklace were the exact colour of Sam's eyes. As if sensing my interest, her hand fluttered up to touch her necklace; she smiled shyly. It occurred to me that if I refused her offer of help Kabo might think I was rejecting her because she was a local African girl. He might be offended. If we employed Teko, I could spend more time with Alice; even the woman by the pool had advised me to accept help if it was offered.

Kabo leant forward, putting an arm around Adam and me. 'Why don't you make up your minds later? There's no rush – have a trial run, if you like.' He smiled cheerfully. 'Come and have a look inside.'

The children were still asleep. Kabo had parked in the shade. I hesitated, glancing at the house, then Teko stepped closer to the car; her right foot dragged slightly. Childhood polio, perhaps, common in parts of Africa. It must have meant a difficult childhood. Perhaps work was tricky to find – maybe she'd thought this time she would be lucky. She nodded at me, she was going to keep watch while we went inside. Kabo was right: communication without words seemed easy.

'This is the country home of a businessman,' Kabo was continuing, as he led the way to a flight of stone steps cut into a dry earth slope. 'He built it in the traditional style for his family but now they all live in a grand way in Gaborone . . . Diamonds.' His gaze swept the gardens that surrounded the house: there was a large brownish lawn, with scattered beds of succulent plants and a group of gum trees at the far edge. 'He had three guard dogs,' he added. 'They were tied up in the day, but let loose at night. They're kennelled at Thamaga now. I could ask him to lend them to you. You're isolated here – it might be sensible.'

Huge animals, probably, panting fiercely around

the garden in the dark. What if the girls sneaked out to play on the lawn late one night? What might happen if Zoë tried to pet one?

Adam looked uncertain. 'Up to you, Em.'

'Thanks, Kabo, but I'm planning to be here all the time. Adam will be around at night. Besides, what kind of message would it send the community?' Rich whites, fearful of African neighbours. That's what the message would be, though I didn't say it aloud. *We're here to help, but we don't trust you an inch.*

Kabo took a breath as if about to argue, then obviously thought better of it. 'Let me know after you've had the chance to discuss it. It can be organized quickly. Come inside now.'

We followed him up the steps into the cool shade of the veranda. The room inside was dark after the brilliant sunshine. There was a scent of beeswax and cooking meat. A long sofa, covered with embossed velvet, stood in front of the window; a low table was piled with large books, striped cotton rugs lay on the wooden floor and a couple of heavy paraffin lamps stood on side tables. Shelves with more books reached to the ceiling. At a glance, they seemed to be about minerals and mining. A globe stood on the floor. The head of an animal with ridged, curving horns was on the back wall.

'Kudu,' Kabo said proudly, his eyes following my gaze. Once, this animal had been part of the landscape; now it was a decoration on the wall. I hoped Zoë wouldn't spot it too soon.

An iridescent reflection of water shimmered on the ceiling – it must come from the dam behind the house. As I walked towards the windows at the back of the room, my heart jolted: a man and a woman were standing silently against the wall, watching me. The man, with grizzled grey hair and milky irises, stood shoulders back, as if to attention. The woman was younger, neat-featured, plump. She wore a faded dress, a green woollen hat and battered plimsolls. Her eyes shone in the gloomy room. A second passed as we gazed at each other. As the shock ebbed, I managed to smile. She stepped forward, introducing herself to us in broken English; she was called Elisabeth; the old man was her brother, Josiah. He looked after the garden but spoke only Setswana. She was in charge of the house and the food. They worked for the owner and lived here, keeping the place going between his visits.

A gardener? A housekeeper? Servants had never been part of the deal. I'd thought it would be just us, together as a family; that had been the point. That, Adam's work and my research. An awkward guilt began to burn. It was easy enough to have help in England but I wasn't sure of the rules in Botswana and already it felt crowded, though I could hardly ask them to leave.

Then Adam was there, smiling and proffering his hand. Josiah took it with a little bow. Adam asked where his village was and how he managed his plot of land. Elisabeth, beaming, began to translate. Having taken his jacket off, shirtsleeves rolled up, Adam looked cool and at home. My linen trousers were rumpled and Sam had dribbled milk down my back. Plot of land? Adam had done his homework – he was better prepared than I was, ahead of me already. The bitterness began to return.

A distant wail rose above Elisabeth's quiet voice. Sam. His crying would have woken the girls and they'd all be frantic, not having seen where we'd disappeared to.

I ran, tripping over the rug and banging my shin on the table. Adam moved forward to help, but I was quickly outside and at the car; even as I was wrenching open the door, I could see that it was empty. I looked around, frantically scanning the garden and the drive before I realized they were right next to me under the tree, with Teko. She was crouching down and crooning in a low-pitched tone, holding Sam, her hand cupped over his left cheek as if to shelter the naevus from the sun. He was hiccuping, absorbed in pulling her necklace towards his mouth, the blue stones shining in his small fingers. Zoë was leaning against Teko's shoulder, one foot swinging back and forth to the rhythm in the tune. Alice, a little apart, jumped up and down, watching how the dust ballooned around her sandals. This was worth a thousand references.

Adam came breathlessly up behind me.

'You win. She can stay,' I said.

He hugged me, laughing. I noticed Kabo grinning, doubtless relieved that we were behaving like a normal couple. He probably thought my earlier irritation was because of tiredness. The rules that allowed us to slip between the roles of lovers and competitors were complex. Adam could win now: compared to the things we usually fought over, it seemed unimportant.

# Chapter Fifteen

*Botswana, 23 December 2013*

Once Kabo had gone, and the cases had been unloaded, Zoë ran up and down the corridor, her feet thudding on the floorboards. Adam whistled as he took out his books and stacked them on a shelf in the sitting room, pushing together a row of the owner's to make space. Alice walked about on tiptoe, opening cupboards, peering inside and closing them again. Leaving Sam with Adam, I stepped through the front door onto the wide veranda that ran the length of the house. A table and chairs were grouped in the shade. In front of me a vast sweep of brown land stretched to the distance, pierced by thousands of thorn trees and carved into uneven ravines. A line of mauve hills crumpled against the horizon.

I felt a prickle of apprehension. Despite Kabo's warning, I hadn't imagined we would be quite so alone. There was no sign of buildings or domestic life although some goats clambered among wild fig trees in a gully by the track. The sky was wider and emptier than any I'd ever seen. It was difficult to take in that thousands of miles away in England this high flawless blue would become a low, rain-smudged blanket of cloud.

Zoë joined me, wanting to explore. I remembered the shimmer on the ceiling and, longing to be in cool water again, I pulled out our damp swimming things from the overnight bag and hurriedly sprayed mosquito repellent onto Zoë's skin It hadn't seemed necessary by the pool yesterday but it was hotter here, much wilder. Zoë ran, whooping, down the scrubby slope behind the house; I followed more slowly, searching the ground for snakes. It wasn't until I reached the edge of the water that I saw there wasn't a dam after all. In front of us was a small circle of brown water crusted with green scum and invaded by reeds. The trees around the edge were looped with trailing creepers that reached down to the water's surface. A line of cup-like nests dangled over the pond, small yellow birds darting in and out. Zoë bent to slip off her sandals; we watched as the mud rose up between her toes, like small, brown slugs. Insects buzzed in hoof-prints around the muddy edge.

'I don't like it, Mummy.' She backed away, shaking her head.

'I made a mistake, darling. It's not for swimming. Let's put on your shoes, we'll go back.'

I wiped the mud off her feet with the damp towel.

She put on her sandals and ran back up the slope to the house. It had never occurred to me that out of the frame of Adam's lake picture there might have been patches of scum on the water, or insects in the puddled mud at the edge.

Zoë disappeared into her room and I began to explore. The house was a series of thatched rooms, on the same level, strung together with narrow corridors. The one at the end would be ours: it was large enough for Sam's cot; we'd put him near the glass doors that opened to the front garden, where he could watch the light moving on the leaves outside. In the adjoining room, Zoë was curled next to her zebra, the owl and the knitted lions; Alice lay alongside, holding Sam's elephant, one leather ear discoloured where it had been sucked so often. She was relating a story involving the rescue of a baby elephant from lions with the help of an owl. It had been a while since I'd seen them so close; I tiptoed away.

The kitchen was a dark, stifling room, tacked to the back of the house; a small fridge hummed in the corner, a forest of bottles balanced on top. A blackened stove crackled with logs. A door to the outside gave with a creaking rush and I stumbled into a back yard with a couple of sheds, a patch of straggling maize and some sunflowers. An old dog lying by the wall woke at the noise, and nosed towards me, sniffing at my feet. Close up, there were leaking scabs on his yellow coat. He lost interest in me, collapsing again in an ungainly heap. Under a thorn tree a goat backed away, straining at its tether, hoofs scrabbling on the hard soil. This was someone else's territory. I hurried back through the kitchen and into the sitting room, where Adam was walking up and down with Sam.

'Can you take him? Kabo wants to show me the study he rigged up in the garage. He's managed to get us online.' He smiled as he put Sam into my arms. 'Isn't this amazing? It's going to be such fun here.'

Fun? The dark room with its heavy upholstery and the monstrous kudu head seemed alien to me; through the window the harsh sweep of landscape was different from anything I'd imagined. How would we manage here, day after day? What would we actually do?

Later, Zoë came into our room while I was lying on the pillows, feeding Sam. Leaning against me, she stroked his head, watching how his toes wriggled as he fed. 'Is this really Africa?' she whispered, round the thumb in her mouth.

'Yes.' I hugged her with one arm. 'It really is.'

She stared at me for a moment, then disappeared again.

After his feed Sam's face crumpled. He pushed restlessly against my shoulder and weariness over-whelmed me.

Teko was sitting in the kitchen. 'Teko, could you look after Sam while I sleep for a short while?' She stood up, her hand darting to her neck to touch her necklace again, as if it were a talisman. She took him from me, frowning with concentration. I pointed to the back kitchen door and shook my head. 'Please don't take him outside.'

She nodded.

Lying on my bed again, Zoë's question reverberated; after the leave-taking from work and school, the vaccinations and the anti-malarials we had started to take, the packing and the long journey, was this really Africa? Could anywhere bear the weight of expectation we had built up? Where the grass was green and the sun was warm and we would all be happy. The underside of the thatched roof was festooned with webs as big as bird's nests. Spiders and other insects would be moving in the darkness above me. My last thought was a prayer that nothing would fall on my face as I slept.

When I woke, Adam was snoring lightly next to me and the heat from his body had drenched my shirt. My mouth was parched. The house was silent. The girls' room was empty, and so was the kitchen. Where were they all?

'Adam.'

He was breathing deeply, his glasses crooked, hair slicked into strands. He opened his eyes and glanced around. 'I'd forgotten where we were for a moment,' he said, looking amused. His eyelids drifted together again.

'The children have disappeared. So has Teko.' My voice was thin with panic.

He pulled himself to sitting, glancing out of the window. 'I saw them outside when I was in the garage,' he said cheerfully. 'They were heading towards the back garden.'

The reeds around the pond had been dank and tangled. Shoving my feet roughly into sandals, I pushed open the French windows, the heat a tight fist against my face. Running down the slope, I scanned the smooth surface of the water before I heard a laugh. It was so long since I'd heard Alice really laugh that I wasn't sure it was her.

'Ally? Zoë?'

The laughter had come from my left where there was a thick mat of flattened reeds. The muddy water bubbled between the tough strands. How much weight would they hold? The weight of a child, several children? As I pushed aside a clump of upright stems, a long insect landed on my wrist, orange wings whirring. I shook it off rapidly. There was a smell of stagnant water and decaying vegetation. Was it deep? Deep enough to be dark and silent at the bottom? Fear tightened like a band around my chest.

'Alice?'

The water closed above my feet. I pushed aside another thick wall of reeds, and glimpsed the red of Zoë's dress, then Sam's waving fists. He was lying in a shallow container made of woven plastic balanced on a mat of reeds, gazing at the branches overhead while his reaching hands opened and closed. Teko, crouching by his side, held the edge of the container; the girls squatted next to her. Water rising to my ankles, I stepped forward and snatched him up. He began to wail.

Alice scrambled to her feet. 'You're spoiling our game.' Her voice was loudly indignant, but she must have known it was dangerous.

'Come inside. Teko, I asked you not to take the children outside.'

Teko's face was expressionless as she picked up the basket and followed me silently. Zoë began to cry.

Later, Sam settled to sleep; I tucked the edges of his mosquito net under the cot mattress and sat for a while, watching his birthmark fading, blotted out with shadow as the room darkened.

Adam was reading a story to the girls in the sitting room, Zoë on his lap, Alice's hand on his shoulder. He glanced up. 'It was ingenious in its way, Em,' he said. 'They were playing Moses in the bulrushes –'

'It was a ridiculous place for Teko to take them.'

Sam might have tipped from the basket, sliding without a sound under the brown water. He could have drowned immediately. 'We ought to ask her to leave.'

Alice winced; Adam put his arm round her. 'I talked to Elisabeth just now,' he replied. 'Teko misunderstood Alice. She thought you'd told the children it was all right. The water was only inches deep where they were playing – I've checked. No harm done.'

A baby could drown in inches. Through the window, the pond glowed in the sunset; above, it was as if a great fire was burning in the sky, shot through with yellow, crimson and scarlet flames. A single long-necked bird streaked past, black against gold. My hands on the windowsill were trembling. Adam came up beside me, and we watched, side by side, in silence. The sunset didn't last long and in minutes the sky was black.

I lay awake for a long time, staring into the dark outside. We'd come thousands of miles to a different world. It must be because we'd travelled so quickly that I felt I had lost all my bearings.

When I woke next morning, my uncertainties had melted away. The sun lay across the bed in bright yellow stripes. Adam stirred beside me, the warmth of his body reaching to me. We hadn't made love since

Sam was born and it was as if we were meeting again after a long time apart. When he realized he wasn't hurting me, he pushed more and more deeply inside. We had to be quiet – Sam's cot was next to the bed. As he moved faster, Adam put his hand across my mouth, muffling my cries. This morning it was his turn to be in charge. After sex, after showering, we became our daytime selves. If Adam had told me what to do then, I would have been incensed.

We had breakfast outside, Sam sitting peacefully on my lap. He seemed happy after sleep, his blue eyes shining as he watched Zoë chattering. Streaks of sunlight lay across the bushes; chuckling birdsong came from the gum trees. 'Kingfishers,' said Adam, without looking up from *The Rough Guide to Africa* as a brilliantly coloured little bird appeared, flashing though the branches.

'How did you know what the bird would be, Daddy?' Alice demanded.

'I bought a CD of African birdsong, played it in the car on the way to work again and again until I knew it off by heart,' he replied seriously. I laughed.

There was warm homemade bread, guava and paw-paw for breakfast; the air smelt freshly of trees and grass, and a deeper, dustier scent that came from the bush in front of us. In the clear air the gnarled shapes of the thorn trees stood out sharply.

'I don't like this melon. It tastes of sick,' Alice said suddenly.

'It's not melon, Ally, its paw-paw. I'll have it if you don't want it.' I tried to take the thin sliver of fruit, but it fell through my fingers to the ground.

'Christmas tomorrow,' Adam said. There was a little silence as we all stared at him. Despite the trees at the airport and the hotel, Christmas didn't feel close or even real.

'Let's plan something fun.' He flourished his book. 'There's a game park not too far from here, with giraffes and rhinos and zebras, we could explore those hills over there or maybe we better go and say hello to our neighbours in the village.'

'I want to see the animals!' shouted Zoë, jumping up and hanging round his neck. 'Please, Daddy!'

'Can Teko come?' asked Alice.

I nodded – she might enjoy it. As I leant to study a photograph of rhinos in Adam's book, soft footsteps shuffled past just below the veranda: Josiah with the dog at his heels. With his hoe, like a rifle over his shoulder, and a khaki hat pulled low, he looked like an old soldier turning up for duty. He turned to nod but, catching sight of Sam, his face expanded into a wide smile; he gave a little wave before walking on, singing to himself in a low, rumbling voice. Zoë hung over the veranda railings to watch the dog as he lumbered after the old man towards a bed of flowering cacti.

By my feet, a seething heap of black ants was obliterating the scrap of paw-paw, a dark trail already marching up the steps. How had they arrived so quickly? Alice, face averted, stepped over the boiling mass, but Zoë squatted, peering closely. Soon the paw-paw would vanish completely.

The next day, Christmas morning, we left at sunrise, Zoë clutching the knitted hippo from Megan that I'd stuffed into her stocking the night before. A purple paper hat was wedged over her fair hair, her T-shirt already smudged with chocolate. She climbed into the back next to Teko and Sam, asleep in his car seat. Alice sat silently on his other side. Adam switched on the radio and carols filled the car. He and Zoë began to sing along. A sense of wellbeing spread through me: we were spending Christmas in this new country on a gap year all together. I felt lucky again and leant to give Adam a kiss as he drove. He smiled and caught my hand in a brief grip.

We passed through a small village a few kilometres down the dirt road. Men were already sitting in the rim of shade by their huts, the children gathered at the fences, staring, as we drove past. The children were thin, the roofs ragged, with gaping holes in the thatch. The yards around the huts were bone dry and mostly empty. Kabo had been right about the drought and the poverty. The lucky feeling thinned; this was a different Botswana from the prosperous capital, a darker, sadder place. Once the car was on tarmac we went faster, the dried verges glittering with rubbish; a dead donkey lay at the side of the road, its neck stretched out at an awkward angle.

The sun was high by the time we drove through the metal gates of Mokolodi Nature Reserve. Two smiling rangers appeared as we drew up, but when Teko saw their battered, open-sided truck, and realized she would have to sit in it, she shook her head and backed away, holding Sam. The outdoor restaurant was cool and empty, apart from a young waitress by the counter wiping glasses. I put Sam into his seat on the table; he was awake now and gazing around. I bought Teko a drink and sandwiches and gave her Sam's baby bag with his bottle of water and my mobile, scribbling Adam's number on a paper napkin. The waitress drew near Sam, shyly twiddling her fingers and smiling at him. We left, promising we would only be gone an hour or so. Adam took a photo of Teko and Sam on his phone and showed her. She touched her neck uncertainly and didn't smile.

The truck lurched rapidly from side to side on the track. It would have been difficult to have kept Sam safe. Scrabbling for my hat by my feet, I caught a bunched movement of brown muscled skin and a flash of horns between the trees as a kudu bolted from the track. The dark eyes of a giraffe by the trees turned to follow us. After half an hour of heat and bumping and glimpses of grazing impala, the driver stopped the car, pointing to rippled dinner-plate-sized prints in the dust. 'Rhino,' he announced.

Climbing down with his gun, he motioned for us to follow. The cicadas scattered to either side of our feet as we walked after him in the scorching heat. Twenty minutes further on, he stopped to kick apart a pile of damp dung. The broken clods were alive with scuttling green beetles. We were near. He pointed to large grey boulders beyond the sparse foliage. Closer, they became two rhinos under a thorn tree, a mother and calf. The animals moved together, ears flicking, their breath peaceful in the hot air as they watched us with deep-lidded eyes.

In the car going home, we were all quiet; Sam fed hungrily.

'What's the point of all this fuss about animals?' Alice's sudden question made me jump.

'To preserve them, Ally.' I swapped Sam to my other breast and she looked away, a revolted expression on her face. 'To stop them being poached.'

'Why?'

'So they don't become extinct.'

'What difference will it make to anything if there are no rhinos?' Her face was pink under her cotton hat.

'We have to look after wild animals. Rhinos were here thousands of years before us.' I put my arm round her awkwardly, Sam still on my lap. 'They have as much right to be here as we do.'

'But rhinos aren't like people.' She pulled away. 'They're not important.'

Sam started crying, his fists punching the air. The naevus seemed to pulse in the heat. The surface was wet with milk and sweat. I wiped it as I sat him on my knee to wind him. 'There are millions more people than rhino, Ally. Fewer people wouldn't matter. Fewer people would be good. No one would notice. There's only a few hundred rhino left. Losing even one would matter.'

'Why?'

'Wouldn't you want your children to see them?'

'No.'

Adam met my gaze in the mirror and winked, but I felt worried as I twisted to strap Sam into his seat. Alice's response seemed unusual. Was she finding it difficult to order all the different images we had seen, the vast diamond-trading centre, the magnificent animals, the thin barefoot children and the tattered roofs? How does this hierarchy work, she might be wondering. Who should come first?

'She's entitled to her point of view,' Adam said that night, as he came out of the shower, wrapping a towel around his waist. 'It would be difficult to see how animals fit in when there's so much poverty.'

'I agree, but she ought to realize that rhino are worth preserving.'

'How about fewer oughts?' He leant over me on the bed, his wet hair dripping on my face.

I pushed him away. 'Don't be such a hypocrite. You're totally driven by oughts.'

'And you're not?' He bent lower and kissed me. I shook my head, laughing, giving up the attempt to keep dry – the air was as warm as an oven.

He was right, though: I was driven by oughts. The word had run through my head at medical school like a chant, muted yet continuous, underlying everything . . .

*I ought to study.*

*I ought not to go to the pub, stay up late, drink, smoke, have sex.*

*I ought to come top, be first, win prizes.*

*I ought to send him good news, make him smile, keep him safe.*

I studied, I came first, I won all the prizes. Winning became addictive. If the costs seemed high, the pay-off was higher, and always in my head the picture of my father on the poolside, smiling. Even after he died, he watched me. Even now I had to make him smile.

Later, as I fed Sam, rustles of unfamiliar nightlife in the garden outside came in through the window.

The sky was full of different stars. I watched Sam as he drifted to sleep on my lap. The rhino would be finding their way to water, drinking in the dark, the female quietly on guard. It was comforting to think of the large animal standing calmly in the night, looking after her calf.

# Chapter Sixteen

*Botswana, March 2014*

The boy stops the car at the top of our drive; the house is dark, the door wide open. Have other thieves come in our absence? There is nothing left to take; how could it matter?

The boy gets out of our car and runs off. A light goes on in the house. Kabo stands on the veranda.

Adam stumbles towards us. In the headlights his hair is plastered to his skull. A patch of scum is smeared on his sleeve. He smells of sweat and stagnant water. His face is wet against my cheek. He shakes his head, his thoughts following mine. No, Sam wasn't in the pond.

He lifts Zoë from the car. Alice slides out and runs up the steps into the house. Teko appears silently from the dark kitchen; Alice goes towards her, then turns to give me a deep, blank stare. She looks ill.

'It's all right, Ally.'

Her eyes close. She knows I'm lying.

'I'm going to drive Adam to Gaborone police station.' Kabo's cheeks are streaked with tears and dust, the knees of his trousers caked with mud. He must have been crawling under bushes. He puts an arm around my shoulders. 'The police haven't arrived, so we're going to them. Teko's coming too. They'll need to ask her what she saw.'

'Has anyone talked to her yet?' I catch Adam's hand but he shrugs: he doesn't know. I turn to Kabo. 'Has she said anything?'

Kabo shakes his head. 'She's too shocked. The police will know what to do.'

Kabo speaks to her but Teko stares back at him. Her eyes shift to mine, then slide away. I want to scream at her but guilt fights with rage. If Teko should have been at Sam's side, so should I. I am his mother, she a stranger.

The men disappear out of the door – Kabo touches my arm as he passes. Teko slips past me and follows the men into the night. Elisabeth appears from the kitchen and guides the children from the room.

There is silence. The stub of candle on the windowsill that someone lit gutters in a pool of wax, then goes out.

I put my hand against the wall. There are two realities. I can switch between them, on and off. On: this is a normal Wednesday evening – the girls have gone to bed, and in the room further down, Sam sleeps in his cot, breathing quietly, his small chest rising and falling in the moonlight. Off: he is not here; he is

outside in the night somewhere, being held by someone I don't know. He is screaming because his ear is
hurting. I don't know what they are doing to him.

I am not sure how I will survive from moment to
moment.

On: he is here. Off: I am falling, tipping, turning
into darkness.

# Chapter Seventeen

*Botswana, January 2014*

Africa suited Adam: his rash had vanished; he even looked taller. One evening I was startled to the window by an unfamiliar noise. Adam, back from work and standing outside with Kabo, was doubled up, laughing a bellowing laugh I hadn't heard before. There were beer bottles on the veranda table. On the desk behind me, his papers had been left in spilling piles, the pens dumped in a mug. Something had loosened. I rested my forehead against the cool pane; my own life was coiling so tightly around me that I could hardly breathe. After the excitement of the first days, the world had contracted to the darkened house, the curtains always drawn to shut out the sun. Sam was fretful in the heat and the Internet failed frequently in the garage office. I slept badly: the house, cooling at night, seemed full of creaks and whispers.

How had I got it so wrong? The wide landscape had shrunk to the dimensions of a cage. There was nowhere to go. I was working, two review papers were done, but for once I didn't feel triumphant. Adam seemed to be heading towards some other, secret, goal – I played with possibilities: results that he was keeping to himself? An affair? When I asked him outright why he was so happy, he laughed the new noisy laugh and told me it was because we were having sex again. In more sensible moments I knew he would never be unfaithful, that the heat and inactivity were distorting my vision. Megan would have restored my sanity, but she wasn't here. On my own, I couldn't get beyond the conviction that I was missing out.

In the hushed early hours of a Friday morning, half asleep and feeding Sam, I caught sight of Adam through the bedroom window: he was sitting on the veranda outside the sitting room. His stillness snagged my attention: his shoulders, outlined against the sky, had the austerity of a statue.

I settled Sam back in his cot, and walked out of the bedroom, along the corridor and through the sitting room to the veranda. 'Adam?'

There was no answer. I walked behind him and put my hand on his shoulder. He reached his up to cover mine, sliding his warm fingers under the cuff of the old shirt I wore in bed. 'Hello there.' His voice was slow and sleepy. 'Why are you up? It's early.'

'Why are you?' He had no book in front of him, no laptop, not even a cup of coffee.

'Sit here and see.'

'I ought to get going. The Internet works best first thing and Simon's coming early. He wants Alice to sit a mock maths exam before it's too hot.'

He didn't relinquish my wrist. I sat on the chair next to his; the dew-damp edge of roughened plastic bit into the back of my thighs.

'This is my favourite time of day.' He gestured to the faintly glowing sky. 'The feeling of space before the heat narrows it down. The smell of the bush before it gets burnt away.'

'I'm impressed you've noticed. You're normally too busy to see anything.'

He shrugged, smiling. 'There's less to do here.'

What was it that seemed so different? His hair was longer, curling to the collar of his pyjamas. His skin looked less lined. Maybe it was just the relaxed way he was sitting, his long back curved against the seat.

'You were always busy, especially when there was less to do.' In the quietness my voice sounded brittle. 'Think of weekends.'

Weekends had been almost worse than weekdays: Adam had sorted emails and international calls. In the moments between, he'd rushed to squash, Zoë's ballet, Alice's Mandarin lessons.

He nodded. Adam never usually agreed.

'Being here has allowed me off the merry-go-round,' he replied. 'Different things seem important.'

'What, for instance?' He might have escaped his normal routines but, despite help, I felt trapped. The girls were settling in but the walks I'd planned hadn't happened: the landscape was too vast, too barren, too hot. They followed Teko rather than me. I was free to study but I was jealous. I'd thought jealousy would disappear here but it was stronger than ever. Adam's work allowed him to escape, and explore beneath the skin of this country. It made it worse that I knew I was being ungrateful; that here, in Africa, I should be revelling in the peace and wilderness around us.

'I saw a woman yesterday.' Adam gazed towards the gum trees at the lawn's edge, still folded in shade. 'Coughing blood. Ulcers in her mouth and vulva. Her lymph nodes were the size of golf balls. She was dying of AIDS. There was nothing I could do to help her.'

'People die in England too.' I felt irritated. 'We didn't need to come here to feel helpless about death.' In the gynaecology ward at the Royal Free, there were women with inoperable ovarian cancers and disseminated uterine tumours. They wouldn't recover either.

'It's not just about death. It's how they die.' He

turned to face me. 'Most of my patients don't have electricity – they can't get a cold drink or clean sheets when they need them. It's like a furnace in a tin-roofed house, worse at night as heat comes back up from the ground. In the rainy season the palliative teams struggle to get to the villages.'

'Palliative teams?' I had an image of the hospice in Barnet, with its hushed corridors and cheerful counsellors. 'What about family?'

'Dying people need access to pain relief and hygiene.' Adam sounded angry. 'It's difficult to get that here. I'm raising this at the AIDS conference in Gaborone in a couple of months.' He pushed back his chair and got up. After a while he spoke more quietly. 'But, yes, family is crucial. Everyone pitches in. Even without illness, babies are shared. Mothers give children to sisters who have none.'

'Sounds ideal if you want to offload a child . . .' He was supposed to laugh, but his eyebrows drew together, and the moment of silence lengthened. 'I'm joking, Adam.' Surely he could tell. 'Though, emotions aside, you have to admit it has a certain logic.'

'How can you put emotions aside? What do you think it would feel like to give a child away?'

The rim of the sun appeared behind the hills and the cicadas started. He stretched. 'I must get dressed. Kabo will be here soon.'

Footsteps sounded in the sitting room, then the

door to the corridor shut quietly. If it was Elisabeth, she might have overheard my glib words about giving children away but, hurrying to look, it was only Teko, carrying a pile of clean bedding. Even if she'd heard me, she wouldn't have understood. Alice was by her side, staggering under an equal load.

'You're up early, Ally. Let me help you.' I reached to take the sheets.

'No!' Alice shouted, as she twisted away, clutching the linen. They walked together down the corridor, Teko leaning towards Alice so their heads were almost touching. I watched them as the little shock settled, listening to the rising sounds of insect and birds coming into the house through the open windows. Alice was asserting her independence, that's all. Sam began to cry. I turned away; another hot day was beginning. Later, from the garage, I heard Simon's car arrive and waved from the open doors as his lanky frame unfolded from the driver's seat. His face split in a wide grin as he looked towards me, returning the wave. Simon was Kabo's friend, a maths graduate, as intent on teaching the girls as if he were their university tutor. Even Zoë was learning more than she would have done back in Reception; she could count to a hundred already and was beginning to grasp simple addition. Simon bent over Elisabeth while they exchanged the rolling African greetings; Alice's excited tones and Zoë's high voice sounded in the background.

Then the front door slammed and it was quiet again, apart from the endless shrilling of the cicadas and the quiet hum of the electricity generator.

*Delayed cord clamping . . . increased blood volume . . . decreased anaemia.* I looked up from the paper in front of me through the open doors to the brown lawn and the hills in the distance. The outcomes of this research could be useful here: special-care baby units must be few and far between. It seemed a simple way to help a newborn baby thrive. I spent an hour processing the outline proposal for another trial, attached it to an email for Francesca and sent it. Nothing happened. I tried once more. There was a little clang as sending failed again. The Internet had gone down. I'd lost count of the times this had happened.

By now the heat was reaching inside the stone walls of the garage. I walked outside and up to the window of the house. Standing on tiptoe, I could see Simon and Alice through the window, sitting close together at the table. Alice was writing, Simon pointing to the page, talking and smiling. Zoë was lying on the floor, absorbed in stacking bricks into little piles. Sam lay on his rug next to her, watching her closely. Teko was nearby, ironing, her head tilted towards the girls. They didn't need me. I stepped back, not quite sure what to do. I walked quickly round the house, pulled a hat from the cupboard and hurried down the drive to the gate.

Once outside the grounds, the sense of distance vanished into a close world of grey and green, the smell of dust and animals was pungent. The silence dissolved into the humming of insects and the bleating of goats. I walked down the rutted track, relishing the air against my skin. Wire glinted behind some scrubby bushes, and, beyond that, a group of thatched huts framed by green, like a picture-book version of a medieval English country village in spring. I walked nearer, my feet crunching on grass. Close up, there were holes in the thatch and a pile of broken machinery; goats were bleating from a makeshift pen. A woman was sweeping the ground, her muscled arms were roped with veins; a boy leant against the door playing with a puppy on a string. The peace in the small yard seemed to beat in time with the rhythm of the broom.

The heat was fierce now. I turned back on the track and in a moment the huts vanished from view.

When I got home, Simon's car had gone. Across the lawn, the children were with Teko under the trees, Sam's seat pushed into the shade. Josiah was digging, and Zoë crouched next to his feet, a shoebox by her side. Alice and Teko were sitting on the rug; from here it looked as though they were laughing. I walked quickly towards them.

Zoë ran over to meet me. 'Me and Josiah found a frog and a baby lizard,' she said. 'Come and see.'

Teko scrambled to her feet as I neared. 'It's fine, Teko, don't go,' I said, but she slipped past me. Alice got up, took Teko's hand and together they walked towards the house. Sam woke and began to cry. Before I could reach him, Josiah had hurried over and, dropping stiffly to his knees, began crooning at Sam in a quavering voice. Sam stopped crying, staring into the old face near his. As I approached, Josiah pushed himself up and touched his hat. I smiled my thanks and, holding Sam, let Zoë lead me to the box. Tense with excitement she lifted the lid. Inside a small green frog palpitated under a handful of grass. The lizard was in a corner halfway up the side, limbs splayed, motionless. I congratulated Zoë, though my mind was on Alice. She had seemed so close to Teko but it was as if I was watching at a distance, from the other side of a fence.

When Kabo dropped Adam off that evening, I told him about the problems I'd had with the Internet.

'I'll get an engineer to call out, but it could take weeks,' he warned.

'I can't wait weeks.' I passed him a cup of tea. 'I'll go crazy.'

Through the window, Zoe was with Josiah and Adam under the gum trees, surrounded by a roll of chicken wire and pieces of wood. The sound of hammering came across the garden. Alice stood with Teko, who was cradling Sam.

'You were quite right about Teko. She's been a godsend,' I told Kabo. 'But I have more free time than I'd thought; there must be something useful I could do for a few hours a day. I'd like to help.'

'There's the health centre in Kubung.' Kabo sipped his tea thoughtfully. 'It's not grand, but they're often short-staffed. I'll ask.'

By the time I walked with him to his car, the sun had left the garden and the children had gone inside. Thin red clouds lay across the darkening sky but Kabo was gazing into the shadows under the trees. 'What about those dogs?' he asked, opening his car door. 'You said you'd consider it . . .'

'We've got one – didn't I tell you?' I gestured towards the back of the house. 'He belongs to Josiah.' I didn't tell him Josiah's dog was old and spent his days sleeping. He'd be able to bark if anyone came, and Elisabeth and Josiah were always around.

At bedtime, Zoë was drowsy. I moved aside Megan's hippo to kiss her face.

Alice was propped on an elbow, reading a wildlife encyclopedia, the page open at a picture of a rhino. 'Teko says they're really dangerous,' she burst out. 'She says she'd be glad if they all died.'

Teko couldn't possibly have said that. I smiled, although my heart sank. An image of the broken dolls came into my mind, and the box with the stolen items. Why did Alice still need to lie? 'They're only dangerous if they're frightened, Ally.' I kissed her. 'Like everyone, I suppose.'

'Why would Alice say Teko spoke to her?' We were in the sitting room later; the paraffin lights were lit but the room was full of shadows. 'I didn't want to confront her tonight but it was clearly untrue.'

'Maybe they talk in Setswana.' Adam was looking out of the window. The darkness was more intense than usual; clouds had been gathering for days. Everyone hoped for rain. 'Does it matter? At least they're communicating and she's found a friend.'

'She should understand we can recognize when she's lying.' I sat down on the sofa. 'How else will she know when to stop?'

'She's a clever girl.' He glanced at me. 'She'll work it out for herself.' He turned back to the window. 'Remember that orange glow from traffic and streetlights at home? I love the pure emptiness of the dark here, knowing there's no one else for miles and miles.'

He bent forwards, peering intently through the glass. I didn't tell him I missed the orange glow. I missed people and streets; I even missed cars. When I woke to feed Sam at night, the darkness didn't feel empty to me but full of unnamed menace. In the mornings when the sun rose, flooding the world with light and warmth, my thoughts seemed childish even to me.

The next day, the Internet was still down. I scrolled through my phone contacts, looking for Francesca's number, and came across Claire Stukker's. She'd been friendly. She'd told me to keep in touch. Perhaps she was lonely sometimes. I could drive over and we would have lunch. She might even know about jobs.

*Hi, hope you are well. We're settling in.* My fingers hesitated. *I'm looking for a job! Maybe you could advise? Would be good to meet up, Emma.*

Her message came back in seconds: *Will keep my ear to the ground. Good luck!*

I read it several times, trying to make it say more than it did; at least she'd replied. I put the phone down and walked to the door, looking up at the sky. She must be run off her feet with so many children. The clouds were larger than usual, grey-streaked and heavy. Perhaps I was simply missing Megan. We'd emailed and texted but it wasn't the same. I walked back to the table, pulled out my box of papers and sat down to read, glad now I'd printed them out.

The next day Kabo phoned. They were short-handed in the clinic at Kubung: a nurse had gone on maternity leave. Did I have the right documents?

I found the certificate I needed jammed in with

other papers in a box under the table in the garage. As I smoothed it out, I had the feeling that if I turned quickly enough I might catch my father standing in the shadows, smiling at me.

# Chapter Eighteen

*Botswana, February 2014*

The garage doors were wide open. From here I could see Josiah as he worked near the pram, singing in his growly voice. The dog lay close, greying muzzle settled on his paws. From time to time Josiah put the hoe down and pushed the pram a few times backwards and forwards, nodding. I could hear the answering coos from several metres away.

Alice lay on her stomach on a rug, surrounded by books. She pushed her homework into Simon's hands every day as he arrived, flushing with pleasure when he congratulated her. I'd noticed how close she sat to him; and how she followed him to his car. If she had a little crush on Simon, it was harmless, part of growing up.

Zoë was running about with jam jars, catching cicadas for the reptiles in her zoo. My eyes flicked automatically to the girls' feet: I hadn't forgotten Claire's warning about snakes, but we'd seen none so far.

The rains had finally arrived, and the garden was

glistening, the scent of grass reminding me of England, though there would be a different sort of rain at home: a cold drizzle might be falling from a dark sky; there would be muddy lawns and bare branches.

From: drjordan32@gmail.com
To: meganhoward@gmail.com

*Hello*

*The Internet is working. Finally!*

*How is Andrew, and work? More difficult or easier without my husband?*

*Things have improved here. I'm working. Clever Megan, you knew. I'm doing a nurse maternity locum, in Kubung, part time. The full-time nurse, Esther, tells me what to do and I comply. Most of the cases are straightforward: kids with diarrhoea or chest infections . . .*

Should I tell her about Baruti? Would she be able to put Esther's story into some kind of perspective? Baruti had come to the clinic with a chest infection. His mother had brought his twin, Ibo, as well; they were six years old and had hacking coughs. I'd advised antibiotics and review, but she'd brought only Ibo back and refused to discuss Baruti. Later I'd gone to find Esther, who was tidying the box of bandages in her lunch break. 'Mrs Munthe didn't bring Baruti back with Ibo. She wouldn't talk about him.'

'That's because she doesn't know where he is,' Esther had whispered, glancing around. 'A neighbour asked him to help search for some donkeys two weeks ago and he never came back.'

A young child missing for two weeks in England would have caused uproar, but I'd heard nothing. 'What do the police say?'

'No point asking them. It's election time.'

'What have elections got to do with a missing child?'

'They get taken from the bush,' she murmured, eyes darting to the door. 'You know ... for medicine.'

'What on earth are you talking about?'

She put down her bandages, got up and closed the door, then pulled the window shut. 'Power,' she said quietly, sitting down again. 'Politicians and businessmen buy medicine for power. The police do nothing. They're frightened of the *boloi*. Everyone is.'

'*Boloi?*'

'Witch doctors, the worst kind.' She pulled her chair closer to mine and her voice sank to a whisper: 'They make medicine from parts of a child – eyelids or hands or testes. Arms and legs.' The words poured out in a compressed rush, water through a broken dam. 'The screams make the medicine stronger.

They take the child out in the bush before they start the cutting. It has to be an open place, or the magic doesn't work so well. Then –'

I stood so quickly my chair fell backwards. Esther's hand went to her mouth: she hadn't meant to tell me this; it couldn't be true. Barbarism happened in wars, not deliberately, for money. This must be a fairy tale like 'Little Red Riding Hood' or 'The Babes in the Wood'. The content of fairy tales was irrelevant. Everyone knew that. The real story here was about the importance of children or, perhaps, the power of belief.

Esther left the room. I picked up the chair, the clinic started again and we didn't talk about it any more. I wouldn't involve Megan – there seemed little point. It might stir up the dark sediment from her own past.

*The children are fine. Sam is putting on weight. You'd hardly recognize him now. He smiles constantly . . .*

His face seemed to melt when he saw me. I'd think about that smile all day and hurry through the house to find him, making up for lost time. I didn't like the mark, but it didn't get in the way any more. When I looked at Sam now, I could see him properly.

*The girls live outside. Zoë is in her element. She loves everything. Alice*

Teko had come out since I'd been typing, and was lying on the rug next to Alice. She had brought a little bag of dried pods with her and they were threading them on a string to make a necklace.

*Alice is happier.*

Was that true? She followed Teko everyhere and lived for her sessions with Simon. She helped Zoë with the zoo. I watched her smiling at Teko as she held up the growing necklace. I tapped quickly:

*Much happier, picking up Setswana . . .*

She was shy of trying it out in front of us, but she talked to Teko, in whispers so we couldn't hear.

*You wouldn't recognize Adam. He's almost normal. His desk is a mess!*

Just then Kabo's jeep came up the drive. The best part of the day was about to begin.

*All in all this is turning out to be a very good gap year.*

*Love to Andrew, lots to you from all of us,*

*Emma x*

Adam and Kabo came into the garden. The evening

ritual began; covering his eyes, Adam started counting down from ten loudly and slowly. Zoë squealed and ran to hide under the mass of red bougainvillaea around our window. Alice slipped behind a tree.

'. . . three . . . two . . . one. Ready or not, here I come.' Adam threw his jacket onto the grass, took Sam from Teko and, holding him tightly against his chest, strode theatrically around the garden, bending low to look under every bush.

Elisabeth came out of the house, balancing bottles of beer on a tray. 'Join us, Elisabeth.' I took the tray from her. 'Have a beer.'

She shook her head and hurried back into the house. A warm smell of curried chicken drifted into the garden. Kabo drained his bottle and joined in the hunt on his knees, growling loudly as he approached each tree.

The children were flushed out of their hiding places and rushed, shrieking, across the lawn. I took Sam from Adam and went inside to run water into the basin in our bathroom. He was almost too big to fit and laughed his chuckling laugh as I nuzzled his tummy while his soapy fingers clung in my hair. He fell asleep quickly after his feed but I walked about the room for a while, holding him against me.

Kabo stayed for supper; his wife had taken her mother to the doctor; they would have a long wait and would return later.

'Where's the surgery?' There seemed so few in Botswana.

He shifted in his seat. 'No surgery, just a small hut. He's a traditional doctor, herbs and roots and so on. Most people go to them for help.' He pushed his glasses up his nose. 'If I get a stomach ache, I go along too – it always works. My wife went last week for a charm. She's worried that the neighbours could be jealous because I have a good job and wanted to keep us safe.'

Kabo, an educated scientist, believing in charms? He nodded at me as if he could read my thoughts and was agreeing with the paradox.

'How do witch doctors fit in?' I kept my voice quiet but the children had already moved to the sofa and were listening to Adam describing owls; he was demonstrating their swooping flight with Alice's knitted one.

'There's a whole spectrum of doctors here,' Kabo replied. '*Ngaka ya setso*, the good healers at one end. At the other, the boloi.' His voice lowered. 'They are the ones who make terrible spells . . .'

Zoë's head turned at the familiar word.

'Kabo's been telling me a fairy story.' I stood up. 'So, babies, how are we going to find some owls for Daddy?'

Later we played Monopoly on the veranda; the swallows shot past us, skimming so low that Alice ducked and Adam laughed. Kabo smiled as he gathered up his winnings; he was getting very good at this game. It was hard to remember the weighty texture of life in London now, the rushed evenings and the exhaustion at the end of the day. Finally we were living the life I had imagined.

Gradually the shadows crept across the lawn and the mosquitoes began to bite. We stacked away the game, picked up our glasses and, shepherding the girls ahead of us, went inside and shut the door.

# Chapter Nineteen

*Botswana, March 2014*

Adam had got up early and was folding clothes into a case for the AIDS conference in Gaborone. He would be away for a couple of days.

Birdsong came through the window, Sam was snuffling in the cot next to me. I opened my hand wide in a patch of sun: back-lit, the edges of my fingers were translucent, as though light were trapped inside. I leant from the bed to stroke Sam's hair, it was thicker now and stuck up in glossy twists. I'd always thought happiness belonged to children or the faintly stupid, that it was pointless to strive for something so illusory; I must have changed or been changed. Now it seemed that the silky texture of happiness was just within my reach.

Teko was waiting in the kitchen. I had grown fond of her. She had hardly learnt a word of English but it didn't matter: she seemed to know what I wanted before I told her. Though I invited her to join us at meals she always refused, seeming content to be on the edge of things, watching. Perhaps life had taught her to be wary.

She took Sam and bent her head to his face. She was close to him, that was all that mattered.

Elisabeth's plimsolls made a soft slapping sound on the wooden floor as she stepped backwards and forwards while sweeping the sitting room.

Adam caught my expression. 'What's the problem?'

'Just . . . guilt. Elisabeth does everything.'

He poured coffee from the jug into two mugs and passed one to me, the steam curling in the morning air. 'She seems content. She's paid for the job she does.' He took a sip of coffee, his gaze following a blue starling as it waddled on the lawn. 'Does she really need your guilt?'

How could I not feel guilty? Sitting down as Elisabeth worked around us felt wrong, though when I offered to help she shook her head, looking away as if embarrassed. At work my guilt intensified: most of the illnesses were due to poverty, but at the end of the clinic I walked away to plenty. I drove home wondering whether I was helping the patients I saw, or helping myself to an illusion; since my conversation with Kabo I realized most of my patients saw traditional doctors as well.

Oddly, with Josiah I felt none of this conflict. After work I lay in the hammock under the gum trees, Sam hiccupping and wriggling on my stomach. Josiah worked nearby, his eyes resting on Sam, his battered hat pulled low, the faithful dog somewhere near. I'd watch the smooth swing of the hoe hitting the ground and I wouldn't feel guilty at all.

As if my thoughts had conjured him, Josiah walked past the veranda, giving the children a little salute.

'His dog's not there,' Zoë announced, with surprise, as she hung over the balustrade, her legs in the air. She was right: for once there was no lolloping animal at his heels. I watched the old man walk slowly towards his shed, a small bag of biltong strapped to his belt. I'd seen him share the strips of meat with the dog: he wouldn't be far away.

'Asleep, I expect, Zoë. Put your feet down, darling, or you'll fall off.'

'He's yucky. I hope he's gone and never comes back,' Alice muttered.

Adam put down the paper he was reading and looked at her. He must have noticed the dark smudges under her eyes at the same moment I did. 'Do you need a fan at night, sweetheart? You look as if you've hardly slept.'

She stared at him. 'It was you who kept me awake, creeping around, banging into things.'

'Did I?' Adam pushed back his chair. 'Sorry, Ally.'

'You were breathing outside my door. I heard you whispering.'

'Sorry.' He dropped a kiss on the top of her head. 'I don't remember. Maybe I got up for a drink – or perhaps I was sleepwalking.' He winked at her, but she turned away.

'What do you mean the dog's yucky?' Zoë's eyes filled with tears. 'He's nice, I want him back.'

Alice shrugged, got down and walked out without answering.

'She's only teasing.' I wiped Zoë's eyes, wishing Alice wouldn't exert her power over her sister; it was so easy to reduce Zoë to tears. 'I'll ask Elisabeth – she'll know what's happened.'

Kabo arrived after breakfast. As he waited for Adam to gather his things, he leant against the door to listen to the radio. Local elections, diamond trading, new rural roads planned. 'That would be good, if only I could believe it.' Kabo sounded resigned. 'The roads are worse than ever.'

His grumbling was good-natured. It was hard to imagine Kabo upset about anything. His bulk matched his kindness. Even Alice relaxed with him, trying out her Setswana, laughing when he teased her about her accent.

The men left, Kabo's head bent to Adam's as they walked, studying the sheet of results for their presentation. Adam swung round as they reached the car to wave at the girls, who were straddling the veranda. Zoë waved with both hands. Alice nodded. They jumped down, Alice running swiftly to the zoo, Zoe following slowly, stopping to inspect the ground as she went.

In the kitchen Elisabeth's hands were deep in soapy water. I put the tray of breakfast things by the sink. 'Josiah's dog wasn't with him just now.' I began to unload bowls and cups. 'Zoë was worried. Do you know where he is?'

'He wanders off into the bush sometimes,' Elisabeth said. A look of mild exasperation crossed her face as she shook her head. 'We never know where he goes but he'll come back when he's hungry.'

Today Simon was earlier than usual. On work mornings I'd have left by the time he arrived. I offered to call the girls, but he shook his head. 'I came early to catch you,' he said.

I sat with him in the sitting room, conscious of the minutes ticking by. Behind his pebble glasses, Simon's brown eyes were anxious. He cleared his throat. 'Alice has finished the syllabus in maths already, and Zoë understands addition.'

I watched his larynx move up and down as he swallowed; he pulled his fingers until the knuckles cracked. 'They're doing well. We're grateful, Simon –'

'I have to hand in my notice,' he said quickly. 'My wife has just heard she's in the running for a new job further away. Our son is only six months old . . .'

'I see.' My heart sank.

'I'll sort out a replacement. A colleague is looking for extra hours, and has a degree in biology. I could ask him.'

'When do you have to go?'

'Tomorrow will be my last day. We didn't know until last night and she needs to prepare.'

'The girls have got so used to you, especially Alice,' I said. His forehead shone with a fine film of sweat: he felt bad enough already. 'But congratulations, of course. Your wife must be excited.'

'She is.' His hands relaxed. 'She's standing for election as secretary of the village development committee in Serule. It's important for her, the first rung on the political ladder.'

Just then Alice pushed open the door, her face alight. Zoë followed. I said goodbye. Zoë would be fine, but I dreaded telling Alice.

On the outskirts of Kubung, an old woman walked across her yard as I drove past, a couple of small children staggering in her wake: AIDS orphans. How could I worry about Simon leaving? It was a tiny blip in the children's lives. There were so many broken families here.

Mmapula was the first patient in the antenatal clinic, her pretty face distorted with pain; on examination she was in early labour with a breech presentation. She shook her head when Esther translated my offer to take her to Thamaga maternity unit immediately: her boyfriend had a car, she would call him right now. She disappeared quickly. Two hours later, when I phoned the unit to check, she hadn't arrived. Glancing at Esther's worried face, I gathered a delivery pack – forceps, gloves, syringes, needles and anaesthetic. Together we hurried down the steps, Esther panting directions as we ran.

The concrete hut was half hidden behind a large thorn tree. As we ran across the yard, chickens scattering from our feet, I could hear groans coming from the door of the hut. Mmapula was lying on a mat just inside. Her face was wet with sweat; she was writhing in agony. Gazing wildly at us, she gasped a few words. Esther, translating, shook her head angrily: the boyfriend had been drunk, asleep in his hut. She knew the man – he was always drunk.

We asked Mmapula for permission to examine her. Even without a torch I could see the tiny buttocks at the introitus. Esther listened to the baby's heart with a Pinard stethoscope; it was slow, there was no time to move her. She held Mmapula's hand while I tore open the delivery pack and wrenched out gloves. I washed the vulva with disinfectant soap from a sachet and injected local anaesthetic. I cut down rapidly, then eased in forceps and tugged, sweating, with each contraction. A few tense seconds passed. Suddenly a tiny male trunk slithered out, the head and shoulders still trapped inside. I loosened the cord around the neck, repositioned the forceps and pulled. On the third tug, the head came free. A little bloodstained boy lay blue, motionless and unbreathing in my hands.

I heard Mmapula ask a question, and Esther murmur a reply; I lifted the silent child with one hand, thumb over the chest and rummaged for the aspirator, elbowing my hair from my eyes. Suddenly, unexpectedly, the tiny chest heaved and the familiar cat-like cry filled the hut. Shocked, reprieved, eyes burning, I lifted him onto Mmapula's abdomen. Her hand came down to rest on the small back and her eyes closed.

When the cord stopped pulsating, I clipped and cut it, glad the research would benefit this little boy; Esther delivered the placenta and then we helped Mmapula stagger across the room into bed and gave her the wrapped baby. While Esther held the torch I repaired the episiotomy. I had no more local anaesthetic to give her but Mmapula lay completely still, gazing at the tiny boy in her arms.

Esther left to start the lunchtime tuberculosis clinic. I stayed on to check the blood pressure. Mmapula and her son slept. It was dark and quiet; the labour ward in my hospital had high lights, humming machinery, bleeps and drips, scalpels. Masks. I hadn't known my patients' names. They'd trusted my skill but not me: they hadn't known me. Here, that separation didn't seem possible. The baby mewed. I leant to check his pulse; the tiny fingers curled round mine, holding tight.

The hut began to fill with neighbours, a can of hot sorghum was produced, cups of tea, ginger beer. When Esther returned, Mmapula was still sleeping and I hurried back for the afternoon clinic.

It had started raining by the time I drove home; the old woman and the children I'd seen earlier had disappeared. The village looked a different, grimmer place. The ash under the cooking pots was dark with water. There were no families sitting in the sun, no children playing in the dust.

It was quieter in Adam's absence. I noticed more things. Alice moved everywhere with Teko, helping with Sam. They talked in whispers; I couldn't hear what they said but I wouldn't have understood anyway. It was time I learnt Setswana – it would be helpful in the clinic. When I took Sam from Alice at his bedtime, her anger surprised me. 'Why are you putting him away?'

'I'm not putting him anywhere, Ally. It's his bedtime. He needs a routine.'

'You mean you do,' she said loudly. 'I know you don't want Sam to be part of the family.'

What had triggered this? I tried to put an arm round her but she shrugged me off. Her words echoed in my head as I fed Sam by his cot. She was partly right – I did want a routine – but she was also wrong. He was loved, even if I hadn't shown it from the start. I touched his birthmark gently. As he drowsed to sleep, I stared absently at the white walls, noticing that dark fingerprints had appeared near the glass doors. The children should take more care: it was our house on loan only. I turned the key in the door and put the keychain in a drawer, then settled Sam and found the girls in their room.

'Ally, Zoë, remember to wash your hands when you come in from the garden. There are fingermarks all over the wall by the doors in our room. I've locked them now, the keys are in the bedside drawer in case of emergencies.'

'What emergencies?' asked Zoë, jumping off her bed. 'Will lions come in our room, or elephants?' Her voice shook with excitement.

'Fire, stupid,' Alice muttered.

Zoe looked crestfallen. Tears welled.

'Elisabeth says the dog's gone off on his own little adventure,' I told her quickly. 'He'll be back soon, you'll see.'

Zoe had recovered by supper and as we sat together over Elisabeth's pumpkin stew I told both girls that Simon was leaving us, explaining that his family had to move. I was watching Alice as I spoke but I was still unprepared. She pushed her plate away, knocking over a glass of bougainvillaea flowers. 'It's all your fault!' she shouted, then ran to her bedroom and locked the door from the inside. She refused to open it; in the end Zoë had to sleep in our bed.

'Why is Ally so cross?' she whispered, as I tucked her in.

'She's upset because Simon's leaving,' I whispered back. 'She liked him.' It was more than that. For the first time a teacher had responded to who she was, taking her seriously. Had I neglected this? Trying to understand her emotions, had I forgotten her mind? But emotions were part of this too – she'd adored Simon.

I took the mobile phone outside. The darkness was dense with moisture. I called Adam. His phone went to voicemail. I tried the hotel and was put through to his room. He picked up immediately; he'd forgotten to recharge his mobile.

'I'll see if I can come home early,' he said, when he heard about Simon. 'We'll do something nice this weekend – a camping trip?'

'I won't say anything yet.' He might be held up but, with luck, this would make a good surprise, just what Alice needed. 'I miss you.'

He said something in reply, which was lost in a storm of background noise, and then the connection had gone. Flashes of lightning lit up fragments of the hills miles away; I'd never before told Adam I missed him. It had been hard to admit, even to myself, that I needed him. I'd waited in the kitchen in London drumming my fingers on the table with irritation if he was late, wondering what he was doing or achieving. It was simpler now. I just wanted him here with all of us.

Noises began to percolate through the silence – rustling in the bushes, a sudden flapping of wings and sounds like quiet breathing, as though, in the darkness, the land had become alive. I stood up and went inside.

Zoë had spread her arms and legs across our mattress so I had to lie awkwardly along the edge of the bed, my arms itching with bites. I didn't sleep well. Much later I thought I heard a door opening and closing, then Alice's footsteps running down the corridor and, distantly, the kitchen door closing. She must be raiding the fridge, having left her supper unfinished. I drifted off, hoping there was something left for her to find.

Even before I left the next day, I was hurrying to get back. Sam woke crying and pulling his right ear. Teko held him: she was worried, her free hand hovering over her necklace as I inspected the eardrum with my auroscope. The tiny branching blood vessels over the thin skin were dilated, the early sign of an infection. The red skin on his cheek felt hot. I gave him a spoonful of our precious Calpol and found his little elephant. The small fingers closed tightly round the knitted body and he started chewing a leather ear.

The sitting room looked like home now. Alice's jigsaw lay on the table and Zoë's paintings were tacked to the wall. My cardigan was flung over the arm of a chair. Teko had hung the necklace of dried pods from the antlers of the kudu, and the cushions had been plumped up. The phone rang as I picked up my bag. Simon. Lightning had struck a mopane tree where the dirt track branched off the main road from Gaborone. A team was coming to clear it away but in the meantime he couldn't reach us. He was sorry, especially as this would have been his last day. Alice should continue with her maths exercises; Zoë was to learn ten new words beginning with W and draw pictures in her alphabet book. He would email more work, and look for another tutor for us; in the meantime could I say goodbye to the girls? He rang off, apologizing.

'What kind of words?' Zoë had arrived, first for once; she sat down and looked at me sideways through fingers spread like a star across her face.

'Worms, Zo-Zo, whales, wasps. Warthog?'

'Wobbly jellyfish?' She grinned, one of her front teeth had begun to grow at last.

Alice had come in silently; she was sitting at the table by her books.

'Simon can't get through because the road is blocked. He asked me to tell you to carry on. Are you all right, Ally?'

Her face was bleached of colour, the dark marks now like bruises under her eyes.

'Is it Simon?'

The hand on the book trembled. Tears seemed near.

'I'm so sorry, sweetheart; I know how fond you are of him. I like him too. I'll stand in till we get someone else. I heard you last night – did you find something to eat?'

She didn't answer. Was she missing Adam? 'I don't like Daddy being away either. He's looking forward to –' but Adam's early return and the camping trip were to be a surprise – 'seeing you when he gets home.'

She didn't reply and my heart ached for her; she would forget Simon, though she didn't know that yet. She would enjoy the trip. I kissed her cheek. It was getting late. I had to leave; I couldn't find my sandals so I slipped on my old flip-flops by the door.

The road was puddled and I drove carefully, expecting to see more fallen trees, but the storm here hadn't amounted to much, or perhaps it was still to come.

By chance, it was a morning for children and old women; tomorrow could be a day for old men and pregnant women. I liked mornings like these. I liked the children, their shy dignity, the way they stood bravely, chests pushed out, waiting for me to sound them. Ibo should have been among them. When I mentioned this to Esther at lunchtime, she put her half-eaten sandwich back in her Tupperware box. 'Mrs Munthe's gone to Francistown, taking him with her.'

'And Baruti?'

She shook her head and got up to lay fresh paper on the couch. Baruti's name was left floating in the room.

The afternoon moved slowly: three men from the same family with food poisoning after eating boiled goat left to stand at a wedding, ringworm, chronic back pain, vitamin deficiency. When Esther left on her scooter, it was nearly time for Sam's evening feed. I pulled the heavy iron doors behind me, hearing the lock catch. The sun was lower now, and the feathery tips of the maize in the small plots around the huts by the clinic were hazy with trapped light. I hurried to the car, but when I turned the key in the ignition, nothing happened. I tried again. The lights worked – there was enough petrol showing on the gauge. I opened the bonnet under the gaze of a gathering crowd of children. Enough water, enough oil. Adam's phone went to voicemail again, still uncharged. He would have left the hotel by now. I tried the house phone but it was dead: someone had left it off the hook.

Picking a cotton hat out of my bag, I nodded to the watching children and set off down the road, arms swinging. This was an adventure, I told myself, the word Adam had used to lure me here in the first place. As I walked past the last hut of the village, I thought back to the moment he'd first told me about Africa, how worried I'd been about my work, how angry. Looking back, it was as though I was remembering a play I'd seen once, about a woman in a story I'd almost forgotten.

# Chapter Twenty

*Botswana, March 2014*

The hot evening closes around the track; the rasp of cicadas dense. My feet crunch quietly on the stones. Walking seems as easy as breathing; my thoughts loosen and drift in the warm air.

Adam will be sipping beer, happy; that new word . . . Zoë, maybe under the trees with a lizard in her hands. Alice will be near Teko, reading, dark hair sweeping the page, calmer than this morning. The scent of supper diffuses into the garden; Elisabeth puts flowers in a glass.

A crested bulbul startles up from the track, his staccato call tearing the peace: *be quick, be quick, Doctor, be quick*. The gold light darkens between the trees; a desert flower flares red in the shadows, and then it's dusk.

Supper time. Bath time. Sam might be crying.

Another bird answers the first and another, then all the trees are full of their broken sounds. The darkening air feels thick as cake in my mouth.

In front of my feet a thin snake slithers lightning fast across the track and disappears into a gully. I want a drink with gin in it. I want Adam to be impressed I made it home on foot – sorry he forgot to check the car, sorry he didn't charge his mobile.

The gate is shrouded in shadow by the time I reach it, though the wood is still hot under my hand. It swings back with the familiar two-tone whine. The frogs have started their night-time belching in the pond behind the house. When I kick off my slimy flip-flops, the dust is soft under my feet. Relief at being home blooms like a pain under my ribcage and I round the curving sweep of the drive, impatient to see the first lights pricking across the scrubby lawn.

It takes seconds to register that all the lights in the house are blazing, that torch beams are moving jerkily across the lawn. Adam is shouting, his voice a low-pitched bellow, like an animal in pain. He's over by the trees. When I start running, his face turns towards me, glimmering white through the dusk. Zoë, inside, stands against the wall, crying quietly. It's not her, then. Alice squats in the corner, she sees me and stands with fluid grace. It's not her either.

And then I know.

The shadows in our bedroom flicker differently: it takes me a second to see that the curtains are torn, and moving a little in the slight wind. A glittering pile of glass lies in front of the window on the carpet, a few jagged shards still lodged in the frame.

The cot is empty.

# Chapter Twenty-one

*Botswana, March 2014*

Kabo's car roars down the drive, slows, stops at the road, and pulls away, the noise fading to nothing. It will be two hours before they reach the police station in Gaborone. Kabo will be talking, not Teko. Adam will be silent, hoping, as I am, that Sam will be at the police station: lost property, handed in. But people don't hand in babies, not ones they've just stolen.

The house is quiet, but the kitchen has a life that turns on its own. The stove roars. Thin strips of meat for Josiah's biltong are hanging from hooks in the ceiling, stirring in the hot air. Elisabeth sits at the table, pushing at a lump of dough. Josiah feeds wood to the fire, staring at me as if he doesn't know who I am. His eyebrows are drawn low, wrinkles deeply furrowing his forehead, eyes sliding to the sides of the room, confused. If he doesn't understand what has happened, I don't either.

'Tell me what happened, Elisabeth. You were in the garden?'

She nods. 'Teko was inside looking after Sam.' She glances at her brother. 'Josiah was sleeping, in his hut.'

Catching his name, he turns his eyes to her trustingly, like a child.

'Teko made a noise,' she continues. 'We ran in. Sam had gone.'

'Where have you looked for him?'

'Everywhere.'

'Everywhere?'

'All the rooms.' Her hands begin to work the dough again. Her voice lowers. 'In the cupboards.'

A small body could be bent to fit into a tiny space, pushed deep into a dark recess. The fridge in the corner hiccups and starts a deep whirring. I've hardly looked at it before. Never inside. I stand up and pull the door open; the movement startles Elisabeth to her feet with a little cry. There is almost nothing on the shelves. A little butter, some milk. Green leaves tied together. Elisabeth's dismay hovers in the air. Josiah wipes his hands across his face and goes out of the door, shutting it behind him.

'I'm going mad,' I whisper.

Elisabeth is silent. She puts the dough into a tin by the stove, covers it with a cloth, and begins to sweep the floor.

'The chief's wife is coming tomorrow.'

She nods without looking up.

'I found Josiah's dog, Elisabeth.' I get the words out quickly. 'He's dead.'

She looks at me then, shaking her head, as if what I am saying fails to make sense.

'He must have been hit by a car. The body was in a ditch. I'm sorry. I'll tell Josiah.'

Her mouth tightens; she glances at the door. 'I'll tell him,' she says.

I leave the kitchen. It will come better from her. For a moment I picture the small yellow puppy he must have once been, racing and tumbling in the garden, sleeping under his master's bed. Then Sam's face fills my mind again. His mouth is open, his cheeks shiny with tears, his body in a stranger's grasp. Somehow I have to wait out the hours until Adam gets back. Kabo will go home and tell his wife. Soon all our neighbours will know. Our disaster will ripple outwards further and further, seeping into other lives.

The late news on television shows men shouting on a platform, holding banners, crowds. Elections. I turn off quickly, my head ringing with fear.

The wine bottle in the cupboard is half full; I drink two glasses quickly before I notice the telephone cord has been severed. They used a knife – the cut is clean. I back away as though the cord is dangerous.

Zoë is lying asleep on her side, but Alice is awake,

eyes wide in the moonlight. She turns her face to the wall when I tiptoe in. I lie beside her, hoping my presence is some comfort. An hour passes before her body softens into sleep.

In our room, the bedspread is smooth. They didn't have time to sit down. They had bent, reached into the cot, lifted and turned away in one curl of movement. Deft. Maybe practised. The pile of towels and the stack of nappies next to it on the chest of drawers are undisturbed. Why didn't they take those? It would have been better if they had, a sign of kindness, a plan to keep him alive.

His right eardrum will be bulging by now, the thinly stretched skin smoothly red. He will be screaming with pain but they won't understand. Will they punish him? I slide down the doorframe and sit, rocking, on the floor, my head bent into my hands.

*I surface. He shouts from the boat, telling me to move my arms and legs.*

*I sink again. It's silent and dark under the water.*

*The water fills my throat. I am drowning.*

The minutes hang, like meat from the hooks in the kitchen, lengthening silently.

I finish the wine. Sleep, when it comes, hits like a truck.

# Chapter Twenty-two

*Botswana, March 2014*

'*Dumela.*'

The light hurts my eyes. Wedged between Adam's chest and the cushions of the back of the sofa, I can hardly breathe. His shirt has ridden up. The damp flesh pressed against my face smells of alcohol and sweat.

A second later, despair rolls back, bringing a memory of Adam lifting me from the floor and falling with me onto the sofa. He'd slept immediately; his body heat had been narcotic and I'd slept again or, rather, was tipped back into unconsciousness.

'*Dumela.*' The quiet voice repeats the greeting.

A tall woman comes into focus, her body bent towards me, hands clasped together. Peo, the chief's wife from last night. Her slanting eyes are sombre, her mouth unsmiling. Questions scramble in my head as I nod to her. Will she be able to help? Will she find Sam for us? I won't be able to offer words to her or to anyone else; as if she can see my thoughts on my face, she disappears from view and the kitchen door closes quietly.

I am in yesterday's clothes. The clothes in which I kissed Sam goodbye, saw patients, ran home. Sliding past Adam, I put my feet to the floor: he groans and mutters, slipping back into sleep. Questions jostle for space in my mind.

*Was it a man or a woman who came? Both?*

The sitting room looks different: the floor feels colder underfoot. The chairs stand in a semi-circle. We've never sat like that. Perhaps we should have done. Would that have been better? Would Sam have been safer if we'd been the sort of family who sat in semi-circles to talk, rather than leaning against the door on the way out, or in the car, remarks thrown over the shoulder, from the front seat to the back?

*It may be that when they came and he started to cry they put a hand across his face, blocking his mouth.*

Through the window, the spectacular landscape has condensed to scrubby wasteland. Somewhere out there the hot air shapes itself around my baby. Someone knows where he is.

I should be outside, looking in the thickets and down by the gully. Do I wait for the police, or run into the bush and search behind each tree?

As I stand, my head tingling with indecision, Zoë's voice comes in from outside; through the window I can see she is sitting at the veranda table. Alice is opposite. Two women are with them. The older has a hand on Alice's back. The rings of a young, round-faced woman opposite flash as her long fingers pick over a pile of marula beans. Teko isn't with them, she'll be sleeping, as Adam is. As I step outside, the women look up and fall silent. The hand slips from my daughter's back.

'*Dumela.*'

My voice sounds different, even to me. Zoë looks startled, Alice wary. Both have been crying. The older woman inclines her head. Dark moles are scattered untidily over her cheeks as if someone had thrown them at her face. The younger one is pretty; her full lips painted a brilliant pink. She looks across the garden, tapping purple fingernails on the table, a flush on her high cheekbones, embarrassed.

Zoë slides off her chair and runs to me. 'Have you found Sam yet?'

'Not yet, Zoë.'

Bending to Alice, I whisper, 'Thank you for being sensible, darling. Daddy and I are going to work out the best plan. I've got to go back in and talk to him now.' I kiss her. Her lips tremble, then set in a tight line.

Adam is still asleep. He half wakes and tries to sit, but slumps again, a hand over his eyes. On the table next to the sofa, clean clothes have been laid out for me: a coloured skirt, with blue and orange circles, and a red shirt. Elisabeth or Peo: someone who knows that the act of choosing clothes to put on would have been impossible. The kindness makes my eyes sting.

*It is also possible that they hit him, knocking him unconscious to silence him, as they crouched over him in the dark, hiding in the corner of the room.*

I strip and shower, shuddering in lukewarm water, then dress in the clean clothes. In the mirror my puffy face and shrunken eyes look back at me, alien.

Adam is sitting up, though he's still half asleep.

'What's happening?' I grip his arm, unable to wait any longer. 'What are the police doing?'

He puts his hand on mine, his fingers are hot, slightly sticky. 'They've put blocks on the major exit roads and sent a team to the airport.'

I should have driven straight to Gaborone airport instead of Kubung: I could have waited by the departures lounge, looking at each baby in turn before they were taken out of the country.

Adam runs his tongue round his lips. A small glass of cloudy water has been left on the table; I hand it to him, he drinks quickly, then carries on talking. 'They're searching locally as well. Two officers are coming here this morning. No one must leave. They want to question everyone.'

So the police are coming at last. 'What happened when you got there last night?'

'They saw us quickly.' He lies back on the sofa. 'I was called into a room with two officers. Kabo stayed outside. It was his turn afterwards. They treated us as suspects. They kept asking the same questions over and over, trying to catch us out. It was as though they thought I'd done something to my own son.' He looks around the room, frowning, as if he were back in the station, being questioned like a prisoner in a cell.

'They must have known it couldn't be you. When Sam was taken, you were on your way home from the conference. Teko's account must have tallied with yours.'

'They'll talk to her this morning.' He nods towards the door as if he expects her to appear, on cue.

'Why didn't they take her statement last night?'

'Perhaps because she wasn't there?' He talks slowly as if to a child.

'How wasn't she there? She left with you.'

'She got out of the car when we stopped at the end of the drive.' Adam seems puzzled by my question. 'She started crying, so we let her go. Kabo thought it would be easier for her to answer questions with Elisabeth for support. Didn't you see her?'

Before he has finished talking, I'm hurrying through the sitting room into the kitchen, where Elisabeth, watched by Peo, places a pink cloth on a tray, the gentle colour glowing in the dark room. She stares in surprise as I run past into the corridor beyond. In Teko's room there is a mattress on the floor, nothing else. Not the smallest scrap of paper.

The room is windowless; I snap on the switch but the light doesn't work. I've never been in here. Shame licks along with the surprise and fear. Was this how she lived, in the dark, in the same house where we had electric light, furniture, books and clothes? Laptops, plentiful food? What kind of resentment would build?

'She's gone.'

Adam has followed me in, staring into the corners as though she could be there, pressed invisibly against the walls. Is that why she left? Because she felt invisible?

'What does this mean?' He looks bewildered.

I know what it means. It means she could have taken Sam. That's good. Back against the wall, the bare concrete feels cool under my fingertips, a little gritty. Good, because Teko will be easy to track down. I liked Teko, trusted her. Fury starts to swell but I push it away. I need a clear mind. She will return to the orphanage she came from: that's where we'll find them. She'll keep him hidden in her bedroom until she works out what to do with him. Has she taken him because she loves him, or because she hates us?

'She's got him, Adam.'

He nods wordlessly.

Peo and Elisabeth have put the tea-tray on the table in the sitting room; now they are outside with the other women and Alice and Zoe. Their voices make a gentle noise, like a song on the radio, background music.

This is why Peo and her friends are here. They are doing the talking for us, the walking and the living. Keeping the house alive. The bitter tea has the green-brown taste of raw leaves; the heat penetrates deeply.

We drink our tea still standing. I put my cup down, misjudging the saucer. It tips over and a small brown circle bleeds outwards on the pink linen.

Adam's eyes are red-rimmed; a dark pink rash edges his hairline.

'Wait for the police,' I tell him. 'I'll go to her orphanage. That's where they'll be.'

He shakes his head. 'I'll go. The police have questioned me. They'll want to question you next.' He replaces his cup. 'I'll need the address.'

'Is it connected to the hospital in Molepolole?' I stare at him, as my fingertips begin to sting with panic. 'Or a mission centre somewhere?'

He shakes his head. He doesn't know. We've never known. We had accepted Teko at face value with no address and no references beyond the flimsy piece of paper we gave back to her. I always checked references; the au pair agency in England was renowned for its safety.

Outside, the scrubby lawn stretches to the road.

The trees glitter. In England there would be pale almond blossom by now, primroses in wet green banks. Was it because we are in such a different place that we'd ignored the rules or thought they didn't apply? Had I been so frightened of giving offence that I put my own child's safety at risk?

'I'm leaving now.' Adam is at the door. 'Let's not tell the police about Teko yet. If it gets out that she's got Sam, they'll go after her, then the media will latch on. She could be frightened into vanishing for good. I've got to get there first.' His lips stretch in a grimace. 'Once we get him back, she can disappear for ever, for all I care.'

'How will you find it?'

'I'll find it.' Adam's face looks different, as mine did in the mirror. The slick fit of his eyeballs in their sockets seems to have loosened so that his eyes look bigger, less defended; the dry crease between his nose and his mouth has deepened. His shoulders have rounded overnight. For the first time I can imagine him as an old man.

I'm shivering, though the heat is already hammering at my skull. Are there images crowding in Adam's head, as there are in mine? Images that I'm burying beneath a picture of Teko smiling at Sam. The picture slips. I see cut bodies, severed hands.

'Say goodbye to the girls for me.' Adam unhooks the keys. The metallic jingle summons a memory:

Adam coming in through the door in Islington, putting his keys down, smiling, lifting Sam from me. Was I smiling, too, or was my face tense because I'd been with the baby all day and would rather have been at work?

Adam leans towards me, his hand on my shoulder. 'See what Elisabeth can tell you about Teko. Any fragment could be vital.'

I follow him to the veranda. He runs down the steps, but turns at the car and shouts back, 'Try Megan. Phone me.'

Megan? Muddled with fear, it takes me a few seconds to remember that it was Megan who asked her friend to organize help, which was how Teko came to us in the first place. We should be able to track Teko down through Megan. Even her name makes me feel better, bringing with it her calmness, her thoughtful eyes, her kind voice.

Adam opens the car door. Even from this distance his shirt looks creased and sweaty. He's forgotten his hat and in the humid air his hair is already sticking to his forehead. The engine starts and the car speeds down the drive, stones spinning from the wheels.

# Chapter Twenty-three

*Botswana, March 2014*

Megan doesn't pick up. Clumsy with haste, I text instead, making mistake after mistake, leaving damp smudges on the keys. Zoë runs from the table to loop her arms around my waist, glints of mauve and green sliding along each strand of blonde hair. I've never seen Sam's hair in the sun. We kept him covered up and parked him in the shade to be safe. Women here strap their babies to them, even safer. Regret and fear mount. Zoë presses her face tight against my skirt. 'I want Sam.' Her voice is muffled. 'Where is he?'

'Daddy's gone to look for him now, Zo-Zo.' My voice sounds casual, implying Sam might be down the road under a tree, or in a garden sleeping, perhaps waving to the figure bending over him, in the new way he's discovered, his chubby arms moving jerkily up and down.

Zoë nods, as though I had answered her question, wipes her nose with the back of her hand and clambers back on to the chair. 'Look at my beans, Mummy.'

We could be back in Islington and this an ordinary

Saturday morning. Zoë could be drawing at the kitchen table, wanting my approval, Adam fetching Alice from her Mandarin lesson. Sam would be on the table in his seat, close to Zoë, smiling when she looks up and grins at him. Safe. I would have been on the phone to my registrar, talking her through some problem, and absent-mindedly tickling Sam's tummy.

'Look.' Zoë's voice is insistent.

I've forgotten what I'm supposed to look at. 'Clever girl,' I say automatically. The green heap in front of her shines and swims.

Alice turns her head away when I kneel by her chair.

'Daddy's gone to find Teko.'

Her face whips round. 'Why? Where is she?' she asks, her voice thin with surprise. 'She didn't tell me she was going anywhere.'

Tell? I put an arm around Alice. The outline of her shoulder blades feels sharp. Teko could have told her anything and I can't confront her about lying, not now.

'I don't think Teko planned ahead, Ally. I think she left because she was upset about Sam disappearing, a spur-of-the-moment thing.'

It wouldn't have been like that, though. Teko must have planned this very carefully. I can guess exactly what happened. Having settled Sam in a car, she would have left her accomplice to wait out of sight;

then she must have gone back to collect some last-minute things. When Adam returned unexpectedly early, she would have been trapped. The driver would have had to leave without her but, tiptoeing away in the early hours and hitching lifts, she would have caught up now.

'We think she'll be with the people she knows at the orphanage,' I whisper, though I don't tell her we think she has Sam with her. 'She might be able to tell us something.'

'What kind of thing?' Alice searches my face, her hands are tightly clenched.

'She might have seen or heard something. She was the first to find out he'd gone.'

She turns away and stares straight ahead; the bright bulge of a tear slides down her cheek.

'Just before Teko discovered Sam was missing, Ally, did you see anything unusual in the front garden?'

Alice is motionless, as if she hasn't heard me.

'We were round the back,' Zoë blurts out in the silence.

'The back? By the pond? But . . .' How could it matter now that I'd told them never to go near the pond again?

I turn to take Zoë's hand. 'Did you hear anything then, Zoë? A noisy car, maybe?'

Maybe there was no car. Maybe they came on foot,

silently. In my head there are two, one reaching into the cot. Sam might have smiled at him. The other would have gone to the corridor and listened. They would be thin, hats pulled low, bare feet. Would they look cruel? Amused? Or intent, doing a job, wanting the money? Teko must have saved up for a long time to entice them to help her.

Zoë is shaking her head. 'We banged drums. It was a concert – Elisabeth had a ticket.'

'Was that Teko's idea, to make a loud noise?'

'Ally said about the concert.' Zoë sounds confused. 'Then Teko shouted something from inside.' Tears are gathering in her eyes. 'So Ally and me went and Sam wasn't there . . .' She bursts into noisy sobs.

Alice puts her fingers in her ears. I kiss Zoë and stand, resting my hand on Alice's head. Her hair feels burning. I find her hat in her room, and hurry back while trying Megan again. She picks up as I reach the veranda.

'Yes?'

'Megan, it's Emma.'

'Emma!' Her voice lifts. 'I've just woken and seen your message. We're an hour behind you so I thought I'd just get Andrew up, then –'

'Sam's gone. He was taken yesterday.' I walk down the veranda steps to be out of earshot of the girls but my legs give way and I half collapse on the bottom step.

'Taken? What do you mean, taken?' She sounds confused. 'Where to?'

'I mean abducted taken. Someone broke in through the windows and took him. We were at work. Teko was supposed to be looking after him, but she's disappeared too. We need the name of the orphanage she came from.'

'What are you saying?' Her voice is hollow with shock. 'I don't understand any of this. Sam, abducted? I don't understand . . . I can't take it in. Who is Teko?'

'The girl your friend found. We have to trace her.'

'Where are the police? Shall I –'

'The important thing is the name of the orphanage.' I don't care if I sound frantic – I am frantic.

'But I don't know. David never said. It was always just "the orphanage" in his Christmas cards.'

'What's the address, then?'

'I don't know.'

'How come you don't know anything?' I shout. 'You arranged it all.'

'I emailed him originally asking him to look for someone.' Her voice is trembling. 'He emailed back, promising to help. After you told me you didn't need anyone, I phoned but his housekeeper said he was in hospital. I left a message for him but he didn't ring me back. I lost track. It must have gone ahead . . . Oh, Emma, I'm so sorry, it's my fault, then. . .'

'No, I'm sorry . . .'

It's not her fault. David must have set it up before he went to hospital. It's not his fault either: it's ours for not checking, mine for employing someone I didn't know at all.

'I can find out where she came from,' she says quickly. 'I'll phone David right now. I'll get back to you as soon as I can, it may take a while, sometimes he doesn't pick up for days.' She rings off.

There is a sudden flicker of colour on the ground. A great snake is gliding towards me from the darkness under the steps. A snake here, after all this time. The skin is bright with bars of orange on grey. The scales shine as if greasy; a streak of orange-red tongue slithers in and out.

It stops as I pull my feet away. The triangular head lifts, darting to and fro. In a second it twists and disappears into the grass.

Claire warned me; she knew. I start fumbling through numbers on the phone; Claire runs an orphanage. She'll know the orphanages in Molepolole and who runs them.

'Yes?' The South African voice is businesslike.

'Claire, it's Emma. I texted you a while back, you'd said to keep in touch . . .'

'Yes?'

'My son's been kidnapped.' There is a shocked silence. 'The girl who looked after him has vanished.

Adam's gone to look for the orphanage she came from but we don't know its name, so –'

'Where is it?' she interrupts.

'Somewhere in Molepolole. If you can give us a list, I'll phone him . . .'

'Molepolole? God, I'm sorry. If it had been an orphanage in Gaborone, I'd know. Molepolole is way out of our area.' My heart falls but she is continuing: '. . . not a large place, it won't take him long. Would it help if I came over?' The words are kind and I almost weaken.

'Maybe later. Thanks, Claire.'

Though she can't help us now, the thought of her on our side is something to hold on to in the midst of roaring panic. The sun is scorching. The air above the empty drive shimmers, like the start of a migraine. The door opens behind me. Elisabeth comes out of the house with a tray, holding a water jug and glasses; she walks slowly, her head bent. She comes down the steps, takes Alice's hat from me and goes back up to the table. The hat is put on, and there is a moment of gentle laughter from the women round the table.

'Elisabeth.' I climb up the steps and put a hand on her arm as she walks back towards the door. 'Did Teko tell you where she was going?'

'Teko didn't talk to me.' She shakes her head slowly.

I've never seen them talking, but I'd imagined they

might chat at night round the table, swapping details from their lives.

'Do you know why she left?'

She stiffens slightly. I am treading too close for comfort. Then, smoothing the skirt of her apron, she leans towards me. 'She told Josiah, and he told me.'

Josiah would make a good listener; he would nod and smile. He wouldn't judge.

'She is frightened,' Elisabeth confides, in a whisper.

'Frightened?'

'She thinks people will say it is her fault. She is worried she may go to prison, so she says she will run away.'

*And ask Teko why the fuck she wasn't with Sam this afternoon. She should have protected him.*

I feel an unexpected stab of pity for Teko; I see her stumbling from the house in the dark, frightened by my words, crying for Sam, scared of blame.

'Did she ever mention where she came from? She won't get into trouble, but she may have clues that would help.'

Elisabeth's head bowed in thought. 'I ask her once,' she murmurs. 'Teko say nowhere special.' Then she makes a little movement with her hands, taking in the house: she wants to go back, continue with the tasks of the day. Life has to carry on, though life has stalled. Food must be prepared, rooms cleaned, curtains pulled against the sun. I put my hands together.

'Thank you, Elisabeth, I'm grateful.'

She nods, and walks away.

*Megan doesn't know which orphanage Teko came from. Try all.* I text Adam. *E says T left because scared of blame. Maybe T not involved. Be careful.*

I walk up and down, up and down the drive, pushing through the scorching air. The truth is somewhere; I just need to reach it.

*I surface for the second time. My father leans over the edge of the boat, hands stretched out.*

*Move, child. Move your arms. Kick your legs.*

*I bang my arms into the water, scissor my legs, dip below the green surface, swallow water, come back up.*

The sun is at its height, the heat baking the scent from the little yellow-green bushes that line the drive. The cicadas' grating noise fills the air: like thousands of tiny saws. Twenty hours have passed now. My breasts ache with unused milk.

It makes sense that Teko ran away out of fear. Why would a young girl want someone else's baby when she could have one of her own? A black girl with a white baby would attract attention. She would need a network of friends. Teko didn't have shoes when she arrived; she doesn't own a phone. How could she organize a kidnap? If Teko was involved there would have been no need to break the windows, she could have opened any door to her accomplice. Who has him if she doesn't? Esther's story slips free of its mooring and floats in front of my eyes. Perhaps he is dead already, murdered in the minutes after he was taken. Was he maimed first?

I sit on the steps again, huddle over the phone, rocking backwards and forwards, conscious that the low keening I can hear is coming from the back of my throat.

A hand touches my shoulder. A cup of tea is set down on the stone next to me. Soft footsteps retreat. I look round but the front door closes quietly.

The tea slips down, scalding my throat. Peo knows how a kind gesture can halt the slide into darkness.

*Tread water.*

*Survive.*

Josiah is digging at the back of the house. His hat is pulled low, dusty feet wide planted on the soil.

'Josiah, did Teko tell you where she was going?'

He shakes his head; he doesn't understand. There is a mound of soil by his feet, a rough cross at one end, two sticks tied with string; so he went to the ditch last night, found the remains of his dog and brought them back to bury.

'I am sorry.'

He looks away. The skin beneath his eyes is

sodden. Loss swells in the space between us, and the question about Teko dissolves in the air.

As he picks up his spade again, I describe the snake, writhing my hands together. He follows me round to the steps at the front of the house. I point out the place it disappeared. He stoops to peer into the grass, fingers tightening on the spade. At that moment a white car with a thick blue stripe swings into the drive and a couple of policemen get out. Josiah disappears. The taller man looks around as he walks and, like one half of a comic act, almost bumps into a tree. The shorter, thick-set man strides purposefully; he holds an Alsatian tightly on a leash, the animal slinking close to him, as they approach the house.

# Chapter Twenty-four

*Botswana, March 2014*

The policemen stand as if to attention. The room shrinks and darkens around them. The younger man's face is cavernous; his skin tightly stretched over sharp bones. He drops a large case to the ground, then straddles it, hands behind his back. His colleague, a narrow-eyed bulky man, shakes my hand. He introduces himself as Detective Goodwill; his partner is Officer Kopano. I am to call them simply by their surnames.

'Thank you for coming.' The floor tilts as I speak. I haven't eaten for a day, maybe two. 'Please sit down.' Gesturing to the chairs, I sit quickly.

'I regret the delay today.' Goodwill eases himself into the leather chair; he takes out a handkerchief and wipes his forehead.

Elisabeth opens the door from the kitchen and brings a tray of yellow juice, ice clinking in the jug. His eyes follow her closely as she bows and walks softly from the room.

He fills and drains a glass, then settles again with a

sigh. 'We questioned your husband last night. He has phoned today to say he has gone to recall a servant. He will tell us more this afternoon.'

'I'm glad you have come. I know–'

He holds up a silencing hand. 'Do you wish to hear what is happening in the search for your son?'

This man has the power to find Sam: I have to let him order the conversation any way he wants.

'There is surveillance operating on all main roads.' He is watching my face; am I meant to thank him? Could there be some protocol for this conversation that I am failing to follow? It is taking all my strength not to fall to my knees and beg, weeping, for help.

'There are police officers in Kubung, calling at every house. There are men at the airport and the rail stations. Interpol and the consulate have been informed.'

'Thank you.'

They will find him. Missing children turn up close to home. The headlines of the newspapers that I used to read in the coffee room between operations detailed kidnapped children found in the next house or down the street. The police might walk into a hut in Kubung at any minute, and Sam could be there, sleeping in a cot in the corner.

'There has been a press release.' He has to say it twice.

'Already? I'd thought, somehow . . .' That they would find him so quickly it would be pointless to involve the press. He holds up his hand again. Beads of sweat glint along the creases of his meaty palm. 'The media has to be involved. It's important that the public know a child is missing. It can make all the difference.'

Less than twenty-four hours ago Sam was asleep yards from where I sit. I kissed his cheek before I left; his skin had been hot. He'd belonged only to us. Now his image will be shared with the world. We should be grateful.

'We will take any reported sightings very seriously indeed,' Goodwill adds. He sounds angry.

Will a stranger remember Sam, should they glimpse him in a pram in crowds? Would they bother to tell the police? My fingertips push against each other, as though in prayer.

'If members of the press get in touch, I'd advise you to pass them on to us. We will talk to them as necessary. Tomorrow you can speak on television. It will help.'

What happens to those parents, once they have stumbled out of the limelight? There must be armies of broken mothers and fathers, people we pass in the street unknowing. I drink a glass of juice, then another.

'We will need to examine the room your son was taken from, then all the house and the grounds.'

'The entire house?'

Goodwill stares at me, expressionless. In that silence I understand; in case I or Adam have hidden him. Killed him and concealed his body. I make myself meet his gaze; he is eliminating possibilities. I don't care. I don't need him on my side, just on Sam's.

Kopano bends to his case, pulling out a camera, overalls and gloves. I lead him down the corridor and he aims his lens from the door of our bedroom, the shots exploding like gunfire. Then he puts on white overalls and steps in on tiptoe, graceful as a cat.

In the sitting room Goodwill, hemmed by his chair, leans awkwardly to the table, and presses the button on a small recorder. His presence absorbs the energy from the room. The furniture, the rugs, even the walls fade into the background. His face is the only thing I see and his narrow burning eyes. He asks me about my work. How often do I go to the clinic? Who comes to see me? He takes Esther's phone number, my certificate to practise, my doctor's bag. Does he think I have drugs? That I would drug my son? The sweat collects around my neck as he frowns over his writing. His gaze skims my body when he asks me about my pregnancy, the birth and afterwards. Postnatal depression? Crossing my arms tightly, I tell him I've been happy, that Sam was loved from the moment he was born. What difference does it make? The complicated truth would snag his attention.

He asks if there are problems between me and Adam. As I look outside at the sun on the trees, my mind slides between us whispering in bed and shouting from the door, between love and its opposite. I turn back to Goodwill and shake my head. No problems at all. He turns off the recorder.

He wants photos. As I scroll through the images on my phone, Sam appears unmarked: his photos were always taken from the left. Goodwill uses the passport instead. I feel shame that the only complete picture of my son is an official one.

'Very fortunate to have this little mark,' he says. 'It will help.'

I want to kiss him for those words. I want to thank God in prayer for the mark. Goodwill pulls himself out of the chair with a grunt, and goes into the kitchen to talk to Elisabeth and Josiah, Peo and her friends. There is no message yet from Megan. I text one to her instead: *Has David replied?*

The children come to wait with me. Zoë sits yawning on my lap. Alice is on the floor next to my feet. I turn the pages of Zoë's fairy tales but there is no story without death or witchcraft at its heart, so I read from the encyclopedia instead about weaver birds, hyenas, warthogs and giraffes:

'The sparrow weavers of Africa build apartment home nests in which 100 to 300 pairs have separate flask-shaped chambers . . .

'Hyenas are predominantly nocturnal animals, sometimes venturing from their lairs in the early morning . . .

'The warthog derives its name from the four large protuberances found on the head, which serve as a fat reserve . . .'

Facts, plain as water, though my voice trembles as I recount how a mother giraffe, never straying, defends her babies to the death.

Goodwill comes back to question the girls. He pulls out a notebook but they have little to say. Zoë tells him about the concert. Alice stares and shrugs. He scribbles a few lines and they return to the kitchen.

'What do you think has happened, Goodwill?'

He bends to stare closely at his shoes. A moment passes. He looks up. His eyes are guarded. 'Would you prefer to wait until your husband returns?'

'Adam will be late. I'd like to hear now.'

The leather creaks as Goodwill settles his bulk more deeply.

'Sometimes the cause is found in the home – one parent taking the child to punish the other, for example. The child may be moved quite far.'

On the lawn four days ago Adam lifted Sam from

my arms, kissed me and kissed him. In the early evening, the garden was saturated with gold; I shake my head, unable to speak.

'The abductor can be someone known, very close to the family, who is driven by jealousy. A relative or a close friend.'

'We have no relations. Both sets of parents are dead.' There has never been time for many friends, apart from Megan. It's been family and work, always. When my mother died, my father was there. Later Adam and the children filled my world.

His eyes shift from mine. 'Someone may come across the baby during the course of work. A delivery man, for example, or a gardener. A man repairing the roof.'

'Josiah does all the repairs and the gardening. No one delivers here. Josiah can't drive so Adam takes Elisabeth to Kubung for supplies once a fortnight.'

'Then there are women who become desperate . . .' His voice rumbles on calmly. He could be discussing the weather or a shopping list. 'Childless women, who take children belonging to others.'

Years ago a baby disappeared from my hospital. A deranged woman who'd miscarried was accused. But we're too remote for a random snatch. Besides, Adam said people here share babies. There would be no need to steal ours. Goodwill's speculation isn't helping.

'I must warn you that there are other cases, even more . . . challenging.' He is watching me closely and his voice has a sharper edge. 'Finance is involved.'

'We have savings, a house . . .'

'Kidnapping for ransom is one possibility, but we must consider others. Trafficking generates large funds, ransom isn't usually demanded.'

Trafficking? My mind stalls. Fragments of his speech come to me through a roar of panic.

'. . . evil trade . . . porous borders . . . sold like loaves of bread . . .'

Sold? Who buys babies? Why? His lips frame more words but I can't hear them. Inside my chest a space opens into which my heart seems to fall. His eyes move over my face, assessing damage.

'We should wait for your husband. Tomorrow there will be time to answer more questions. Now we need to make a thorough search of the premises.' He stands, walks to the door, then turns back. 'The press will phone. Keep them on your side but at a distance.' Goodwill pushes his hand away from his body to demonstrate; the wide fingers are identically scarred over four knuckles.

The room is silent after he leaves. The girls are eating in the kitchen; their pale faces swivel towards me. Peo hands me a bowl of warm sorghum but I'm unable to swallow any food. Zoë leans her head against my shoulder, yawning. Afterwards, I express milk into the basin, watching the tiny tubes of thin white liquid hit the metal, then dribble uselessly down the drain. My breasts feel bruised but lighter.

Later the men hunch over the broken doors, scrape walls and furniture, then remove the phone with its cut flex. They fingerprint everything.

As the girls drowse in their rooms, Goodwill's warning reverberates: trafficking conjures immigrants packed into lorries, men forced to work, women held in cellars. Sam could be jammed with others into a tiny space, roughly held, semi-conscious with hunger and heat. I pace and sit, pace again, shaking my head but the images don't shift.

The cot is dismantled, the mattress wrapped and taken to the car. Sam's little elephant has disappeared. Perhaps they took it with them. My heart lifts fractionally at the thought. Later, Goodwill brushes the ground beneath the doors of our bedroom, collecting fragments of glass and soil. He doesn't reply when I point out the imprint of a toe. I sense he dislikes my hovering presence.

Zoë wakes from her nap and we watch from the window as Kopano puts on waders, entering the pond with a wide, sweeping net. She exclaims as the dog bounds in and out of the water, barking and shaking its heavy coat, the spray glittering like diamonds. If we had followed Kabo's advice we would have had dogs like this on hand, dogs who might have barked at the men who came or, better still, attacked them.

The dog jumps from the water, a small grey rock lodged in his jaws. Kopano follows, holds out his hand and the dog drops it into his palm. Kopano puts the object into a transparent bag, then slips it into his pocket.

My mobile rings. 'Adam?'

'*Botswana Gazette* here. Can you tell me with whom I am speaking?' The woman's voice is nasal.

'Mrs Jordan.' How did they find my number?

'I'm sorry to hear that your four-month-old son disappeared from your home yesterday . . .'

Yesterday? Is that all? It feels as if he has always been missing, as if I've been waiting in this room all my life.

The woman continues firing words like bullets from a gun. 'So you are doctors, working locally, I believe. How does it feel –'

'Thank you.' Why thank her? There is nothing to be grateful for. I cut the call. They have been in touch sooner than I expected.

The mobile rings again.

'This is the *Ngami Times*, ma'am. Am I speaking to the lady of the house?'

'Yes.'

'Can you confirm that while you were out your baby son was taken from his cot?'

While you were out, while you were not watching.

'Please contact the police,' I reply.

Goodwill said to keep the press on my side but it feels as though insects are hovering in a stinging cloud, drawing blood. There is another call but I let it ring until it stops and then turn the mobile off.

Goodwill knocks to let me know they are leaving, that they will return tomorrow. They have finished with our bedroom, he says. We can use it now, though the window will need boarding. Kopano pauses to collect his case; the dog is back on the lead.

'What did the dog find in the pond, Kopano?'

He pulls the bag from his pocket and shows me. Sam's little elephant is inside, the body looks a little larger as if it has absorbed water. One ear is missing, perhaps torn by the dog.

I hold out my hand, my fingers trembling, but Kopano slips the bag back into his pocket. 'Evidence,' he says.

# Chapter Twenty-five

*Botswana, March 2014*

Hours later, Adam still hasn't returned. Peo's friends have gone back to the village and the house is quiet. I fall asleep on the sofa but am woken by dragging footsteps outside, fumbling at the handle. My mouth dries. There will be weapons I can use in the kitchen: a knife on the draining-board, a bottle in the fridge. Before I can edge halfway across the room the front door opens and Adam stumbles in. His bloodshot eyes stare blankly at my face, as if he doesn't recognize me. He sinks heavily into a chair; my heart slows as I kneel next to him. He shakes his head. His cheeks are the colour of putty; even his lips look bleached, like those of a patient who has been bleeding for a long time.

After a few moments, Elisabeth brings warmed-up food and a glass of water; she must have been waiting patiently in the kitchen all this time. Adam balances the plate on his lap as he explains what happened.

'Finding the hospital was easy.' The hands on the knife and fork tremble; I doubt it was easy. The roads would have been difficult to navigate, the signposts few and far between.

'The deputy manager told me the mission had been discontinued. She remembered Megan's parents and the younger man, David, who worked with them.' Adam pushes food around his plate and swallows a mouthful of water.

'When they died, David took charge of an orphanage but she had no idea which one. There were three. I went to them all. A disused church, a bungalow and some huts, just out of town. None of the staff in any of them had heard of Teko. I ended up looking in cafés and shops, showing Teko's photo to everyone I could. No one recognized her.'

People would have been discomfited by a wild-eyed European, begging for information. They might have even been frightened.

'I got your text about you scaring Teko away.' He puts his plate down and stares at me. 'Were you that angry? I don't remember.'

'I was furious. We'd trusted her. If she'd been with Sam, he would still be here.'

Was that fair? Would I have been hovering next to the cot all the time? The attackers might have broken in and stolen him in seconds, while she made a cup of tea.

I shouldn't have shouted, I see that now. 'According to Elisabeth, she was terrified she might go to prison.'

'So she ran away,' Adam says slowly. 'I can understand that.' He gets up and pours wine at the sideboard. He drinks quickly and sits down on the sofa next to me, his face paler than ever.

'We still need to find her, Adam. Even if she's innocent, she could know something. She might have seen a car, heard voices or glimpsed a figure.'

Adam leans back without replying and closes his eyes. His face slackens and he starts to breathe heavily. Behind him, through the window, sheet lightning flashes green in the blackness. It's been one and a half days since he had my milk. I dig my nails deep into the skin of my arms. Megan hasn't got back to me yet – what the hell is taking her so long?

Megan.

The name scribbles itself across the darkness of my mind, and images start to unfurl faster than thought: Megan's glance as it rested on the photo of our family the first time she came to the house, the hand open on the table; I'd thought even then she was waiting for something. The way she looked at Sam.

*It could be someone known to the family . . . driven by jealousy . . .*

Did Megan envy me the handsome man she worked for, the beautiful children she saw in that photo? Or did she want to punish me, the competitive wife, a mother whose daughter was unhappy, the careless woman who left her baby in a shop? She'd suffered for her appearance: had my response to Sam's birthmark lit some vengeful flare? The tumbling mug, the falling mousse: trivial retribution compared to what she might have been planning.

I crouch beside Adam, twisting memories into new shapes: Megan persuading me to come to Botswana, then offering to find us help. Had she begun to plot even then? Did she deliberately procure someone young, distractable, smoothing the way for thieves to creep in unnoticed and steal our son for her? She organized my certificate: it would be easier to steal a baby whose mother was at work.

'Adam, wake up.'

He is deeply asleep, snoring heavily.

'It could be Megan.' I shake his shoulder.

His head jerks upright and his eyes snap open. He looks confused, glancing round, as if she might be in the shadowy corners of the room. 'Megan?'

'She could have planned the whole thing. She might have Sam now.'

'What?' He rubs his face rapidly, as if trying to rub away my words. 'Have you gone mad? How do you make that out?'

'She lived in Botswana before. She has contacts here. She could have organized the whole thing. It makes sense.'

'No, it doesn't.' His eyebrows draw together. 'This is crazy talk, Emma. You need to calm down.' He stares at my face closely. 'Have you eaten anything today?'

'You don't know what happened to Megan in the past.' I stand then and pace back and forth, twisting my hands as needling suspicions light up other thoughts that had been buried in darkness.

'She knew a witch.' Adam looks blankly at me as my words tumble out. 'The girl who bullied Megan at school was murdered, and they found the bones. Megan said the witch did it for her sake. The same witch could have Sam now.'

'Witches and bones,' Adam repeats incredulously. 'Emma, this is insane. How could Megan possibly do this? Why would she? She's a friend, she's very fond of us –'

'Of you.'

The first time I'd seen her, scented and groomed, the thought had flashed through my mind. At our dinner party, her hand had rested on Adam's sleeve. She had blushed when he kissed her.

'That's it, of course. She's in love with you.'

'What can you mean?' The lines between Adam's eyebrows deepen. 'Megan's married to Andrew.'

'That's the problem. They have no children.'

*. . . women who become desperate . . . childless women who take children belonging to others . . .*

'She'd want a child. Yours. It all fits.'

'I can't listen to this any more.' Adam's voice is

flat. He pushes himself out of the chair. 'I need to sleep.'

'She got the certificate for me on purpose. That way I would be away from the house.'

'How the hell would she smuggle him abroad?' Adam interrupts, as he walks to the door. 'If we're going to find Sam we have to remain sane.' He disappears into the corridor.

The kudu head stares into the distance. The necklace of dried pods has vanished. Unadorned, he looks wilder, the horns capable of carnage.

Adam's words percolate through the silence. Could he be right? Am I going mad?

In the quiet I can feel the throb of my heart as it slows, and after a while the pictures in my head shade into others: I see Megan's head bowed as she listens to my worries; I hear her voice consoling me. I remember that she trusted me, sharing her past. She'd stepped in to look after the girls; she'd read them stories. She'd knitted toys for them, looked after me and made me rest. She'd told me to love Sam. She got through to Alice when neither of us had been able to. Her sanity had kept me going.

Which set of memories tells the truth?

I find Adam in the bedroom, sitting on the edge of the bed, unlacing his shoes.

'Maybe you're right. Maybe I'm mad to think it's Megan. I know she's my friend, it's just that . . .' It's just that there's roaring emptiness where we need answers. There's an answer somewhere; someone has Sam, even if it's not Megan. 'There's something else.' I speak to his bent head. 'Something worse.'

He straightens. His face, flushed and swollen from bending, looks unfamiliar. His eyes search mine impatiently. 'What?'

'Goodwill mentioned trafficking.'

'I don't think babies get trafficked,' he replies. 'Men, women, children, yes.' He pushes his boots off and lies back on the bed. 'Not babies.'

'Goodwill wants to give both of us more information about it tomorrow.' I lean against the door, too tired to move. 'He wouldn't tell me much. He thought we should be together.'

'I won't be here,' Adam says, closing his eyes. 'I phoned the consulate – I've got an appointment.'

If I went, too, it might dull the anguish for a few minutes. I might feel I was doing something useful.

'You need to stay here,' Adam continues, guessing my thoughts. 'The girls . . . the police . . .'

He's right. Even without those responsibilities, a knock on the door might come at any time and Sam could be there, held out to me by the stranger who found him by chance. Sam, bouncing with eagerness, his mouth wide open in a smile. My throat aches with longing.

'I told the police about Teko on the way home. I

sent them the picture of her that I took at the game park on Christmas Day.' Adam's voice slurs with tiredness. 'They'll find her . . . ' He falls asleep again, in mid-sentence.

The window bangs, followed by the soft, rushing sound of rain. After a moment, the scent of wet earth leaks into the room. Then I catch the sound of footsteps shuffling along the veranda. It could be someone returning Sam, just as I'd thought. I run back down the corridor and into the sitting room. I struggle with the heavy front door, twisting the handle this way and that. Finally it swings open.

The veranda is empty.

Rain blows in my eyes; a blurred figure moves into the circle of light from the door. It's Josiah on his nightly round; keys glint in his hand. He nods, pulls his hat lower and steps into the darkness again.

I crouch; my hand spread out on the wet wood. The rain pours onto my back, but I stay where I am, bent over the space where I'd imagined my son to be.

# Chapter Twenty-six

*Botswana, March 2014*

When Sam was newborn, I brought him into our bed every night. He'd burrow against me, nails softly scraping, face pushing into my breast, small mouth latching on while I drifted in and out of sleep. It was easier that way, though the health visitor disapproved. Sometimes I'd wake later to find him moving on my abdomen, wriggling and elbowing as if he were still inside me. As I wake on the second morning without him, my skin feels the imprint of his body, as though he had just that second been lifted away.

Adam is up already, his pale face empty of expression as he downs coffee in the kitchen. He hasn't shaved; his hair is still flattened on one side by sleep. Today he will recount our loss to strangers and may have to listen to horrors we haven't thought of. Megan's name isn't mentioned. My suspicions have faded in the night, taking on the quality of a nightmare, disturbing but unreal, sliding away into the shadows.

Before he leaves, I tell Adam that Sam's knitted elephant was found in the pond.

'Who could have done that, Adam? Why would they?'

He stares at me, as if he's forgotten that Sam even had such a toy.

'It could have been there for days,' he replies after a few seconds. 'Dropped in the garden, then kicked into the water by accident. Zoë drops toys all the time.'

But Zoë picks her toys up – they're precious to her; and, apart from that concert, the children knew not to play near the pond again. Adam shuts the door, without saying goodbye, and my thoughts circle round and and round, going nowhere.

I take the girls with their books and a rug to the lawn under the trees. Alice hunches over her maths, but her eyes are closed, her hand rests on the cover. The book remains unopened. Zoë lies on her stomach beside her, sighing. She opens a nature book, settles tracing paper over the outline of an elephant and makes a start, breathing deeply. Peo sits close, hemming a green linen cloth, her long legs tucked under her skirt. Her eyes move constantly, registering Josiah sweeping the veranda, the van that flashes white through the trees as it passes, and the way the shade falls, so that the children keep inside its grey edge.

Sam was there, under the tree, three days ago, the day before he was taken. The leaves had been reflected in the blue of his eyes; his arms and legs were moving. He was intact. Leaving the children with Peo, I walk back to the house, my heart banging, eyes and throat burning. I feel ill, as if anguish itself were a virus, growing and multiplying in every cell.

Megan still doesn't answer her phone. Sam's image springs out at me on the screen when I bring up the news on my laptop. His passport photo has been magnified, the birthmark clearly visible, a brighter scarlet than it is in reality. I touch it through the screen. His eyes meet mine, their gaze hopeful but solemn. The text is garish.

*Baby Sam, only son of English doctors on a mercy mission in Africa, has been missing for forty hours. Torn from his . . .*

*Dr Jordan returns from doctoring to find her son Sam has vanished . . .*

*Successful couple robbed of only son . . .*

*Tragedy for Brits . . .*

The media industry recycling our despair.

None of the articles mentions trafficking. When people read these pieces, will they think to look in the places where traffickers hide their goods? I take the laptop to the window-seat, the better to watch the girls in the garden. Alice is kneeling now. Zoë has rolled over onto her back and is holding her tracing paper above her face, waving it about.

The rewards for traffickers must be vast to make the risk worthwhile. Who has the money to pay them? 'Politicians,' Esther had said, and businessmen buying power for the price of a pot of medicine. *Eyelids or hands or testes,* she'd whispered. I lean my face to the window, smearing the glass with sweat. *Arms and legs.*

Outside, Alice is standing on the rug, as immobile as a little statue. I start tapping quickly: *Human medicine.* The page comes up immediately, as if searching for this could be something people often do, like looking online for a dress you might need, or where to go on holiday.

> ... *taking of human beings to excise body parts to use as medicine or for magical purposes in witchcraft ... since 1800s, increase in times of economic stress ... topic of urban legends ...*
>
> *In 1994 in Mochudi, Botswana, a fourteen-year-old, Segametsi Mogomotsi, was selling oranges by the road to raise money for a school trip. Men bought all of them but had no change. She waited all day. They came back, gagged her, dragged her into the bush, and cut her into pieces ... No one was charged ... police corruption suspected ... student riots ... Scotland Yard involved.*

The horror seems to leak from the screen into the room until the air vibrates with it, so it takes a while for the shouting outside to reach me. When I look through the window there are only two people on the rug instead of three. Peo, standing, with Zoë by her side, is calling loudly for Alice.

I push my laptop onto the seat and run. All the rooms are empty. Behind the house the pond is coin-flat, reeds untrodden. Pounding down the drive, I glimpse cars in the road through the trees As I round the last sweep, Alice comes into view, facing towards the gate. Sick with relief, I slow and walk towards her as a man leans over the bars, calling to her, micro-phone in hand. Surrounding him are vans, satellite dishes and a forest of tripods. Dozens of cameras click in unison. Where has all this come from?

The man's head jerks in my direction as I approach: he has white skin stubbled with growth, brown hair frothing at the neck of a T-shirt and small eyes that dart over me. Next to him, a young Motswana girl lifts her camera in the air, aiming it at me. There are others behind her, a mass of faces, brown and white, looking towards me. I turn Alice round very gently and we start walking back. Loud voices call after us.

'What happened, exactly?'

'What did you see?'

'How are you coping?'

'Where's your husband?'

'Who do you think did this?'

'How do you feel?'

I want to shout that I feel like dying; that death

would be better than the torment of wondering every second if he's suffering, screaming. Dying. That I want the earth to open and swallow their cameras and the cars, their terrible, intrusive questions.

Zoë flings her arms around Alice, crying noisily. Peo pats her head, then folds the rug, collects the books and her needlework, and they walk back to the house.

We need these journalists. We need anyone with a camera, a microphone and a notebook. I return to the gate. Speaking above the flurry of clicks and questions, I force myself to thank them for their interest and tell them the police will let them know more. Cards with numbers and email addresses are pushed through the bars; more questions surge up the drive after me.

The silence in the house lies like a cool sheet. Elisabeth takes the girls into the kitchen, the door closing quietly on the scent of baking. Five minutes later, Kopano and Goodwill arrive. They emerge from their car looking calm; they must have negotiated their way through that scrum with no effort. They do this all the time. Kopano strides into the garden, but Goodwill follows me inside. Wedging himself into the same seat, he pulls out his notepad. He flicks it open and looks up, unsmiling.

He has read the email Adam sent him about Teko, and wants to know everything about her. I explain that we think she absconded out of fear, not guilt, though we don't know anything for sure.

'Where does she come from? Surname? Family? Village?'

I know none of the answers. She has slipped away like a shadow, as insubstantial and silent as she'd been when we met her.

I trace the train of events that brought her to our door: Megan, David, the orphanage that Adam couldn't find. Goodwill takes Megan's number and goes outside to phone her. He comes back, his mouth set. So he can't reach her either.

'It is important that we find this Teko,' he says, sitting down with his notebook. 'She may have seen something. Experience tells us, however, that young girls do not commit these crimes. It is unlikely she was involved. She didn't disappear with your son, which I would have expected, and someone had to break in through the doors in your room. If she'd been helping, she would have unlocked them.'

'She didn't know where those keys were. I'd removed them,' I told him. 'But the front door is unlocked in the daytime. If she'd been helping an accomplice, she would have shown them in that way.'

'As I said, I think her involvement is unlikely.' Goodwill sounds irritated.

The criminals must have crouched in the bushes, watching the room as Teko stood, stretched, yawned, walked out to the kitchen maybe. It would have taken only moments to shatter the glass and snatch Sam.

'Where is the key now?' Goodwill asks. I find it in the bedroom drawer where I left it and drop it on the table. He looks at it, nodding. 'Why did you lock those doors in the day but not the others?' he asks.

'There are marks on the wall by the doors. I thought the children had made them . . .' Then I get up quickly and hurry to the bedroom. Goodwill follows but the marks have gone. Elisabeth is summoned. She cleaned the walls, she says, looking frightened. Four days ago. She thought the children had made them dirty.

'She is doubtless correct,' Goodwill says, sitting down in his chair again. 'Is there anyone else who works for the family,' he asks, 'who might also accidentally have slipped your mind?'

'You've met Josiah and Elisabeth.' Then my eye is caught by Alice's exercise books, still neatly stacked on the table. 'There is someone else or, rather, there was. Simon Katse. A tutor for the girls. He left before this happened.'

'When?' Goodwill starts writing in his notebook. 'Why did he leave?'

Why did he? For a moment I can't remember when or why he went, or even what he looked like.

Goodwill waits, tapping his red pen against his teeth impatiently.

'He left because of his wife.' It comes back to me gradually. 'She has a new job in Serule, so they had to move. They have a child so he –'

'When exactly did your Mr Katse leave?'

'Monday. The day before Sam was taken. Four days ago.' Another lifetime.

'And the new job that is so important?' He is writing quickly now and doesn't look up.

'Something to do with a development committee. Simon told me she was up for election . . .' The word seems to hang in the air of the sitting room.

'We will need to speak to this Simon,' Goodwill says slowly. 'Have you an address?'

'No. Kabo knows where he lives.'

'Anyone else?' He clears his throat impatiently. 'Anyone at all you have met or been in contact with since you arrived in Botswana?'

I've hardly met anyone since we've been here. Esther's frightened face floats across my mind's eye, Claire's broad one. The smiling rangers at Mokolodi. Esther will be scared, Claire could be annoyed, but Goodwill may find his way to them anyway. While he is writing down their contact details, I text Esther and Claire a rapid message, hoping they'll understand. *So sorry. Police checking all our contacts; might even visit you.*

Hearing me text, Goodwill frowns. Does he think I'm warning my friends? He closes his notebook and walks out, closing the door behind him. Soon he is striding up and down the veranda, the phone clamped to his ear.

Simon is a good man, but what might she be willing to do, his ambitious political wife?

Kopano appears in the doorway. 'The cages,' he says.

A statement or a question?

'They belong to the children, for their zoo.' How could this be important?

Zoë must have been listening from the kitchen because she comes into the room at this moment, walks up to Kopano and holds out a bowl of plums. He takes one from her, but puts it down on the table. 'It's a zoo, for lizards and a frog.' She tilts her face up to his, a dark ring of chocolate around her mouth. 'There are two lizards, called Josiah and Simon. They're best friends. There's only one frog so far. We call him . . . Sam.' She flushes and, glancing at me, lowers her voice to a whisper: 'Because he hiccups.' Then, putting her bowl down, she runs quickly to me, burying her face in my skirt.

Kopano looks at her, then at me, his deep eyes flickering with an emotion that is difficult to read, though I register unease. Loosening Zoë's fingers, I take her back to the kitchen; and am caught for a moment by the ordinariness of the scene in front of me, the colour in it: orange nasturtiums in a green glass, a plate of mauve plums besides Alice, who is reading a book at the table. Elisabeth puts a blue-striped mug beside her, the steam twisting up. Zoë takes a muffin from Peo. I want to stay for a while, watching, unnoticed, but Alice has noticed, she slides from her chair, the book in her hand, and, still reading, shuts the door in my face.

Kopano touches my shoulder; he wants me to accompany him outside. We hurry down the steps. Alice is grieving; I mustn't mind. Kopano takes long strides. It's hard to keep up. She doesn't hate me: this is simply her way of coping.

The thin shade under the gum trees is aromatic, a relief after the glare on the lawn. Kopano points to the cages: all the doors hang open. Have the children let their animals go? As I get nearer a loud buzzing comes from the largest cage. Inside, a glittering mass of flies clusters in the corner towards the back. Kopano stretches his arm past me, and flicks his fingers above them. The noise swells into an angry crescendo as the flies rise, uncovering a small heap of glistening muscle. It takes me a few seconds to realize that the little frog has been skinned.

# Chapter Twenty-seven

*Botswana, March 2014*

Kopano and Goodwill carry the cages to the car. I tell Alice and Zoë that I've freed the lizards and the frog; kinder now that neither girl is allowed in the garden on their own. Both accept this silently, a small loss swallowed by the greater, but the mystery haunts me. Who skinned the little frog? Why? Where are the lizards? Are random hooligans gathering, hyena-like, attracted to devastation? Despite the penetrating afternoon heat, I feel chilled. It seems like a warning, but one I can't read.

Goodwill comes to find me: he has prepared a statement he wants me to read.

*Three days ago our four-month-old son Sam was taken from our rented house near the village of Kubung in western Botswana. Sam has a large red birthmark on his right cheek, fair hair and blue eyes. Please report any sightings.*

*His nanny, Teko, went missing the next day. She may have important information and anyone with any knowledge of her whereabouts should come forward immediately. Teko is in her late teens or early twenties, medium height, slight build. She has dark hair, which is often plaited, and a slight right-sided limp.*

*When last seen, she was wearing a necklace of blue stones.*

I fill jugs with water from bottles in the fridge and, with Goodwill beside me, carry a tray of stacked glasses down the drive. A young woman takes the tray with a little bow. A group gathers and the jugs are quickly emptied.

Goodwill guides me to a line of microphones; facing the journalists and several large cameras mounted on tripods, I begin to read: 'Three days ago, our four-month-old son . . . our son Sam . . .' The writing blurs. 'Please help us . . .'

I back away from the microphone and the paper falls from my hands. Goodwill picks it up and continues. 'Sam was taken from the house where his parents live near Kubung village. He has a large red birthmark . . .' His voice fades as I walk away up the drive.

Before he leaves, I ask Goodwill about trafficking again. He simply shakes his head.

Adam returns in the evening, grey-faced and quiet. He has been tailed by the press on the way home, then surrounded by the group outside. He drove through but now lies exhausted on the bed. His body seems to take up less space than it did, as though grief and stress have diminished him already.

'Interpol are now co-ordinating international teams,' he says. 'Though they think it unlikely he's already left the country. The searches at border controls and airports have been stepped up.'

It would be difficult to smuggle Sam: he'd be too visible. The mark will protect him.

'They're tracking all the known cross-border criminal organizations,' he continues.

But borders must be irrelevant in the deep bush, where there would be no one to stop a gang walking across a wild stretch of land from one country to another. It would be impossible for any police force to monitor miles and miles of desolate countryside.

'I talked on Skype to a German anti-kidnapping agency,' Adam says. 'If we're contacted by the abductors anywhere we should involve this agency. Never agree to transfer money.'

Against this glimpse into global crime, the horror of the destroyed cages and skinned frog seems to fade a little.

'It could be local kids,' Adam says when I tell him what has happened. 'Egging each other on. They might think we'd be off our guard so they could get away with it.'

They have got away with it. The shadows cluster under the trees where the cages had stood; it would have been easy for children to hide there at night, quietly performing their cruelty.

Zoë runs into our room, clambers onto the bed and rests her head against Adam's chest. He puts an arm around her, his face relaxing. A few seconds later he's asleep. She edges down and runs out of the room again.

No one talks at supper. Zoë yawns repeatedly, Alice leaves her food and so do I. Adam eats half a plateful of okra stew.

Once the children are settled, we continue the conversation in the sitting room.

'What did they say about trafficking babies?'

'You were right. It does happen,' Adam replies.

My heart plummets. I don't want to be right.

'But it's rare. Botswana is more of a staging post for children who are being taken from other countries and on through to South Africa.'

'Why?'

Adam turns away. He goes to the sideboard, opens the cupboard and pours a drink.

'Why are they trafficked, Adam?'

'For illegal adoption, which may mean slavery, and that means forced labour or the sex industry, then . . .' He stops talking and drinks some wine quickly.

'Go on.' Each of these is worse than the last.

'Organ trading and . . . witchcraft,' he finishes, very quietly.

For a while neither of us speaks. I don't even think. In my head there is a crackling sound, like a radio that's stopped working properly.

'Simon's wife is facing elections,' I tell him, after a while. 'Did you know politicians use medicine made from human body parts?'

'Not Simon,' Adam replies quickly. 'He's a teacher, rational, intelligent. He couldn't believe in witchcraft.'

Reason and intellect don't drive belief though; it comes from some deeper darker place. Kabo believes in charms. Once I believed that if I swam faster than everyone else, it would protect my father. That nothing was more important than keeping pace with my husband. Adam must have believed that if he laid his pencils in a neat line on his desk and kept his papers neatly stacked, he would be safe.

I move closer to him. 'I read on the Internet that in Tanzania albino children are used for witchcraft. It's thought their body parts are especially powerful, so that might mean a white baby –'

'It's children who are used mostly,' he cuts in, as though he's repeating a mantra. 'Children. Not babies.' He walks to the window and pushes it open, with force.

Side by side we stare out to the dim shapes of the gum trees. Perhaps the men who took Sam didn't have a car. They could have carried him instead. I see them moving across the lawn, stepping over the fence, then walking through the bush. There was a moon that night. While I was driving to the village to find him, men with our baby might have been walking deeper and deeper through the silvery trees. Sam might have slept, lulled by the rhythm. They would have reached their destination, a hut on its own or an old cattle post. Someone, waiting, would have opened the door to them. But I can't see inside the hut. It's as though the door has shut in my face.

'You're right,' I tell Adam. 'Simon wouldn't take Sam. He's our friend.'

'We need to let them make their enquiries all the same.' He nods, as if to himself. 'Simon will understand they need to be thorough.'

This must be how witch hunts started in medieval times: fear kindling suspicions that run counter to common sense. Already the image of our tutor is shadowed by his darker twin.

My mobile rings, breaking my thoughts. This could be a kidnapper, getting in touch. I've decided, in the seconds it takes to pull the phone out of my pocket, that I'll agree to anything they ask, despite what Adam said, but it's a reporter from America, careless of time zones, wanting information.

'*Washington Post*. Am I speaking with Dr Jordan?' At least he's polite; that makes it easier. Adam is immediately by my side. I shake my head. This isn't news. It's not a kidnapper either.

'I would like to extend my sympathies at this difficult time, ma'am.'

'Thank you.' My eyes fill with tears. Scripted compassion but still powerful.

'Could you let me know how the case is progressing so I can share it with the millions of people who are following your story?'

Millions? I'm caught as I'm meant to be. Are millions of people following our story? I look up, half expecting to see faces pressed against the window, figures thronging the garden.

He continues, undaunted by silence. 'There are so many people who are feeling for you right now, Dr Jordan.'

'Everyone is doing all they can to help us. The police have been very kind.' My answer is scripted too. 'We're hopeful.'

Hope is inaccurate. Dread would be nearer.

'Any leads at present?'

'We . . . I . . .' They mustn't know about Simon. Not yet. 'Please ask the police. Thank you.'

I turn off my mobile.

A pale-winged moth flies through the window, so large it could be a bat or a small bird. It flaps silently to the ceiling then around the room, hitting the walls with a muted crashing sound, settling on an edge of a curtain. I shut the windows quickly.

Adam goes to check on the children. Zoë has left the bowl of plums on the table. I draw it towards me and take one, but even as I curl my fingers around its comforting shape and softness, I drop it back. It occurs to me it is the size and weight of a baby's heart.

# Chapter Twenty-eight

*Botswana, March 2014*

A loud knocking on the door shakes me awake. My eyes open onto the dull light of early dawn. Wrapping my dressing-gown around me, I hurry down the corridor, heart banging with hope and fear.

Elisabeth has got to the door ahead of me: the bulky figure of Goodwill stands in the dark sitting room as I enter, my hands fumbling at my dressing-gown cord. Elisabeth pulls back the curtains and disappears. I hear the clump of the kettle on the stove, followed by the rasp of a match.

Goodwill's gaze is faintly hostile. He is immaculately dressed, despite the early hour. It flashes through my mind that I have no idea how long it takes him to bump over the rough roads to see us.

'We have found a lead. One of your workers.'

They have discovered it was Simon, my worst nightmare coming true.

'We will make an arrest shortly.'

'Shortly? But . . .' Simon and his wife might be on their way to another country. Shouldn't the police have arrested them by now? Adam comes quietly into the room behind me. 'They're going to arrest Simon,' I whisper.

Goodwill looks up. He has heard what I said and his eyes narrow. 'This is not to do with Simon Katse. We located him yesterday evening along with his wife and they will be questioned later today.' He pauses, glancing round for his usual chair, then lowers himself cautiously into it. So, is Simon a suspect? Or are they questioning him merely to exclude him? In either case, they should hurry.

'This is about your gardener, Josiah.'

'Josiah?' Gentle, friendly Josiah? 'There must be a mistake.'

'Why do you suspect him?' Adam asks, scratching his wrists. His nails make a loud rasping noise on the dry skin, sandpaper on wood. 'He wouldn't hurt a fly.'

Goodwill peers down at sheets of paper on his lap, as if to remind himself why they suspect Josiah. 'We obtained his fingerprints from the cages that we took.'

'But he made those cages. Of course his fingerprints will be all over them.'

Goodwill's thumbs circle each other continuously; they flicker at the edge of my vision. 'These are recent fingerprints, very recent,' he says.

'He has been feeding the animals recently. I haven't

allowed the girls out on their own since Sam was taken.'

Adam's hand drops lightly on my shoulder. 'He will have his reasons,' he says quietly.

Goodwill nods. His expression is benign but, from the glance he gives me, I know there is something more. He pushes himself up, heading for the door. The conversation is over. We hear him talk to Elisabeth in the kitchen; then, minutes later, he walks past the window with Josiah at his side, Elisabeth following. As usual there are no shoes on Josiah's feet, and without his khaki hat, his face looks defenceless. I want to run to him and explain that we know he's innocent, but Adam holds my hand, shaking his head. 'Anything is possible,' he says.

Next to Goodwill's vigorous bulk, Josiah looks as delicate as a skeleton. He might be held for hours, days even. Grabbing a bottle of water from the fridge and bread from the pile under muslin on the table, I hurry down the steps, but the car is beyond the gates, already disappearing into a cloud of dust. Elisabeth walks straight past me, back towards the house, her eyes unseeing.

'I'm sorry, Elisabeth.'

She stops as if waiting for me to say more, head lowered. I want to add that this arrest is not of our doing, but of course it is. If we hadn't come here, Josiah would be peacefully setting about his day in the garden, perhaps with his dog at his side. Though, of course, if we hadn't come here, we would still have Sam. In the clear morning light her face seems thinner, the skin withered. She looks old.

'I was too late to give him these.' I hold out the bread and water, and she takes them, then climbs the steps slowly and disappears into the darkness of the house. Kopano is already in the small shed that is Josiah's sleeping place. The white shirt of the policeman shines in the dark room as he moves, gloved hands wreaking havoc.

'Please be careful.'

If he hears, he takes no notice. Each drawer in the small chest is hanging out. I glimpse a carefully folded shirt, a small, ragged towel.

Kopano lifts the mattress from the bedstead, then pulls it to the floor. He stands looking at what he has done but whatever he was expecting to see isn't revealed. He shrugs and walks past me towards the door; his deep inward gaze avoids me.

Josiah didn't look at me either: his eyes never quite met mine though they followed Sam everywhere. A pulse of uncertainty begins to beat, along with the worry about Megan. She hasn't phoned back – it's over twenty-four hours now. Could my suspicions about her have been right, after all?

Back in the house, there is no sign that the police have been. The girls must have breakfasted already – they're helping Elisabeth to wash bedding in a tub on the front lawn. Alice and Zoë are squeezing water from a sheet, which they twist between them. Elisabeth takes it, pegging it into the tree, where it hangs like a sail, blindingly bright against the leaves.

In our room, Adam is buttoning his shirt, a piece of bread pushed into his mouth. He is wearing the thick shoes and close-weave trousers he packed for the safaris he'd planned. He wasn't to know he would wear those clothes to track his baby son. Today he looks calm and moves purposefully, as though this were the start of one of those expeditions. Yesterday he drew a twenty-kilometre circumference around the house on a maps he'd printed before we came, then divided it into eight segments. He plans to walk a diagonal every day. Perhaps cutting the space into slices reduces it for him, but the lines are illusory: what have they to do with miles of untracked bush? The distance will be the same as searching Scotland single-handed. The task is impossible.

He walks past me as he swings his rucksack to his shoulder; it travels in a small arc through the air, catching the side of my head. The pain unleashes fury. 'Do you ever ask yourself if this could all have been avoided?'

Adam stops in the act of reaching towards me, his

face puzzled, then, in an instant, wary. 'What do you mean?' His eyes track my face for clues.

'Has it occurred to you that if you hadn't made me come with you on this fucking trip, we would still have our son?' Warmth trickles down my face: the buckle must have torn the skin.

He is staring at me with no expression, as though he hasn't even heard my words. Zoë's voice outside the windows sounds happy. Birds are singing, the rasp of cicadas is relentless; the backdrop to normal life, though life is no longer normal at all.

Then his face darkens; his eyebrows knit together. 'I didn't plan to come here with a baby. You were the one who got pregnant in secret, remember?'

By the time he has finished the sentence his voice is raised, and he's breathing quickly. We haven't argued for months but we're immediately at war.

'You were the one who's always bloody wanted another child,' I shout.

'You should have fucking waited until after the trip,' he shouts back, 'instead of going behind my back.' He flings the rucksack roughly onto the bed; it hits the bedside lamp, which falls to the floor, the force shattering the bulb and the thin wood of the base. Footsteps come down the corridor. They stop just before our door and drawers are opened. Peo, gathering clean linen for the beds from the chest outside our room. We stare at each other, both panting.

The drawers are closed and her footsteps retreat, fading to silence.

He moves towards me: close up he smells of ammonia, like a horse; he hasn't showered for days. The stubble on his face is dark. He kicks at the door, and the violence of that movement makes my heart jump even as my fury mounts.

'What the hell are you doing, Adam? Open the fucking door.' I try to push past him but trip over his feet and fall onto the bed. Adam leans over me, pinning me down. I can't move.

'You didn't really want another baby, did you? You're normally so bloody careful. Am I supposed to believe it was an accident?' He's holding the sides of my head, speaking into my face. His eyes are red and so close I can see that the tiny blood vessels are engorged. Has he turned into someone else, or become more himself, the surface layers stripped away?

'Somewhere along the line, you decided to use me. How do you think that felt?'

'Don't be stupid. It was a mistake. I told you.' As I struggle to free my hands, I can see his thoughts play across his face, which is inches from mine. I can tell what's coming next. We've fought in bed before but that was playing. This is real. What if I let it happen? Will it displace the torment for a moment? Will it burn away what I did to him? I see him registering my hesitation, deciding to read it as permission. He pulls away fractionally to unzip his trousers and in that moment Sam's face floats between us, innocently smiling, Sam who was conceived in a moment of love and abandon, despite what Adam thinks.

I try to twist from under him but he pushes up my dressing-gown and, though I struggle, he is quickly inside me. It hurts, but after a second, I don't care. I'm taken up in the blaze of his desire and I want this too. Everything that isn't this becomes blotted out. For a few moments I think of nothing but the feel of Adam, pounding angrily into me; even the crushing weight of his body on mine feels right. When I open my eyes, his face looks wild: his mouth is distorted. I close them again, but in those seconds the frenzy has passed completely and my desire, if it was that, vanishes. I wait for him to finish. In a few moments, he shudders and cries out, then pulls out of me, rolls off my body and lies beside me.

Gradually the birdsong seeps back, as do the children's chatter and the distant sounds from the kitchen. Adam's head is turned away, his shoulders shake; he is crying. The voices get louder. The children are coming back into the house. I twist away and push myself off the bed, strip and shower, letting the water flow over my body until it runs cold and I'm shivering. By the time I come out Adam is gone.

I fetch a dustpan and broom for the shattered lamp

and, as the fragments of glass and wood clatter into the pan, it's as though I'm sweeping up the remains of a broken weighing machine, the balance mechanism smashed beyond repair.

# Chapter Twenty-nine

*Botswana, March 2014*

The morning crawls by. It hurts to move, as though I've been mugged. Sam stares at me from the screen with the same hopeful solemnity; the words beneath his image are exactly the same as they were yesterday. My eyes burn so I close them. I know those words by heart.

Peo brings me tea; she places her hand on my head for a few seconds. The heat of her palm goes through to my scalp. Can she read the signs? Does she know what's happened? Do I? The violence and the tears, his and mine, echo in my mind, but exactly what took place is blurred, the events becoming black background already. The trauma of this morning expands the trauma of what was there already; the weight I am carrying is heavier and much darker.

Walking in the garden with the children before noon, I feel chilled, though my skin burns in the sun. Forgetting everything, I forgot sun block, though Peo has put some on the girls. At the gate, the crowd of waiting journalists seems to have swollen; there is the curl of smoke from a bonfire, a drifting scent of cooking. Shouts and laughter; the air of a carnival. Adam would have walked through them this morning: did they try to talk to him? What would he have said? They see me: lights flash, my name is called. I should go down to them but I have no energy to make words. We walk slowly to the back of the house and sit on a rug near the pond. Zoë's head is in my lap; Alice lies completely still, closing her eyes.

After lunch, the children sleep on their beds; the house feels wretched. I choose the deep shade of the veranda. There are new images on the screen now, a small one of Adam, blurred as if walking fast, the backdrop the trees and our gate – taken this morning, then, and already beamed around the world. Scrolling down, it takes me a second to recognize myself addressing the television cameras yesterday; I look like my mother did in the days before she died. They missed the main story: there is nothing about Josiah. Although he was driven through their midst, the old man in ragged clothes had been invisible to them.

A lizard lies on the floor, motionless, a small splash of green paint on the wood; when my mobile rings, he vanishes without seming to move.

It's Megan. At last; I know she has bad news from the length of the pause after she says my name. There's a protocol for breaking bad news; it takes longer and involves warnings. In the seconds before she speaks, the thought runs through my head that she's about to confess she has Sam, that he's been spirited out of Africa at her bidding but that she's changed her mind now and wants to hand him back. I'd forgive her, I'd forgive her everything if she gave Sam back to me.

Another beat of silence. 'I'm so sorry for the wait. The housekeeper left and it's taken two days to track her down. It's not good. David passed away four months ago. Cancer. I knew he'd gone to hospital but I'd no idea . . . I wish he'd said . . .'

Passed away: passed where, exactly? As if dying is a gentle wafting from life into some better world, not the brutal tip into the void I've seen so often on the wards.

'Emma, are you still there?'

'Did he have a wife?'

'She died a long time ago in a car crash on the road to Francistown.'

A car crash. Brief words, like 'missing' or 'stolen', containing a world of wreckage and suffering. 'So does anyone know where we can find his orphanage?'

'There's no one left to know.' Her voice is low. 'When the nuns retired, only my parents and David were left. After Mum and Dad died, the mission closed. David got involved with the orphanage instead.'

'The deputy manager at the hospital told Adam the same thing so he went to every orphanage in Molepolole. But no one knew Teko. I don't understand.'

'This is Africa, Em.'

'What does that mean?' A get-out clause? A reason bad things happen? A bad thing has happened, but that wasn't because of Africa; it was because of me.

'Things come to an end very quickly when the money runs out. David would have used his own finances to keep the orphanage going. Now he's dead, there'd be nothing to pay staff or to feed children with. It would have been disbanded in days, the children sent to state-run orphanages anywhere in the country.'

'What about his own children?'

'He didn't have any.'

'Your parents . . .'

'I told you, Em. Both dead.'

It's vanished, then, the world Megan grew up in, with parents who never had time to talk to her, the long queues they tended amid the dust and the flies, the songs from a tin-roofed church, weaving up into the burning air through the pine trees, the orphanage that grew out of that; a world of effort and children and tragedy. All gone.

'It's my fault. I know it is. If I hadn't contacted David in the first place this would never have happened . . . I feel completely responsible.' Her voice fades miserably.

'Teko could have come from any orphanage, nothing to do with you or David.' My suspicions about Megan were mad, I see that now. 'We presumed it was from his orphanage but there's no proof of that now. We were told people can simply turn up for a job here with no introduction . . .' As I repeat Kabo's words, I see Teko as a random stranger who came upon us by chance; if so, there is little hope of tracking her down. She could be anywhere in the country now, anywhere in the world.

'I could come out, if you like,' Megan offers. 'I could look after the girls and free you both up?'

There is no both, not since this morning: but the drift had already begun, though it's difficult to pinpoint when that was: when Sam was taken or when he was born? Maybe it was when I fell pregnant, or further back still, when Adam accepted the post, keeping it secret from the family.

'I'll look up flight times,' she continues. 'Just say when.'

I hold the phone tightly, wanting to accept, knowing I mustn't. She is needed at home; our family is not the one she used to know; I'm not the same either. 'I can't possibly let you come out, Megan, but thanks.'

Can she tell there are tears streaming down my

face? Tears of shame as well as loss. What have I ever given Megan that comes close to what she gives me? She wouldn't understand the question if I asked her: love isn't a balance to her, there's nothing to equalize.

'Tell me if you change your mind. I'm thinking about you all the time,' she says. 'Sam was on the front page of *The Times* today, Adam's picture was on the ten o'clock news. At work . . .'

There is a scream from outside. Alice's scream. Dropping my phone, I run down the steps and across the grass to where she is staring down into the leaves of a large cactus.

'What is it, Ally? Are you hurt?'

She points between the thick stalks as they crowd together. A dead snake lies twisted in the cobwebby depths of the plant. The jaws are open, the eyes swarming with ants. The long, sinuous body has been neatly skinned and is glistening with flies.

'It's dead. It can't hurt you.' I tighten my arm round her. 'It was a nasty kind of snake, darling. I asked Josiah to kill it.'

'Look,' she whispers, still pointing. Half hidden under the bloodstained body of the snake are the two little lizards, also crawling with flies. They've been decapitated and skinned.

'It's horrible, disgusting . . .'

'A rat must have got them. Or a mongoose.' I hope

she believes me. 'It would have been quick. A clean death.' Another euphemism.

'You let them go. It's your fault.'

She runs back to the house, disappearing through the door.

The bodies are stuck to the leaves with dried blood; they feel crusty in my hands. Could they be useful evidence of some kind? In Josiah's toolshed by the compost heap, I balance them on a rafter for now, further away from any ants. The harsh creosote smell in the shed brings back my father, painting a fence against the winter.

I'd gone home as a student, on the cusp of giving up; I couldn't remember why I'd wanted to do medicine.

*'It's too hard, Dad. It's not interesting.'*

*He doesn't look at me, just carries on painting. He is wearing glasses. Is he getting old? Can he hear me?*

*'I can't do it.' My voice gets louder.*

*Silence for a few minutes, maybe five; he paints very carefully, running the brush down each thin slip of wood, catching the drips before they fall.*

*'It's all right, Emmie. You keep going.'*

*'Why?'*

*'That's the wrong question.'*

*'Dad, I can't remember why I'm doing this.' I'm shouting now, starting to cry.*

*He moves his tin, and starts a new section. 'The question isn't why, the question is how.'*

*'What does that mean exactly?'*

*'It means you work out how you're going to do it first. The reason will come to you. Some things don't bear too much why.'*

*He smiles up at me and then I remember exactly why. His smile. So now I have to work out how.*

As I walk back to the house, the heat is fierce on my neck, the shadows short and black at my heels. I find the phone where I dropped it and text Megan to explain. Alice and Zoë are sitting at the kitchen table, watching while Elisabeth chops a pile of herbs. The air is fragrant with the woody lemon scent of wild thyme. Peo sweeps the floor, crooning a song.

'I'm sorry you were frightened, Ally,' I whisper as I rinse my hands. 'I've got rid of them now.'

For a moment she is quite still, staring at me as if I'm a stranger. She gets down and walks out. Zoë runs after her, asking questions; I hope Alice doesn't tell her what she saw.

I turn to Elisabeth. 'Alice showed me the snake Josiah killed. It had been skinned, and so had the lizards. Why would anyone do that?'

Her hands stop moving.

'Why, Elisabeth?'

'Spells,' she says quietly, and resumes chopping, but her knife misses, cutting into the board.

Someone from the village then, someone who has crept very close; even Elisabeth is frightened. We should take up Kabo's offer of guard dogs: I send him a rapid text.

Peo is murmuring to Elisabeth, who tries to smile as she translates, but her mouth quivers. 'Peo says all the people are looking from her village. Many men looking all the time.'

I stare out of the window at the arid landscape, as if expecting it to be crawling with men, spread out, searching with sticks through the undergrowth as they would in England. What do the villagers hope to find? If Sam had been left out there he wouldn't last a day. Why would they search the bush, unless they're looking for a body?

But the question isn't why.

I shower, change into clean clothes, brush my hair. There is a crunch of wheels on stone: the police are arriving later than usual.

Kopano walks round the back of the house. Goodwill comes into the sitting room to find me, his eyes darting over my thin sundress. Too exhausted to wash clothes, unwilling to burden Elisabeth further, I'm down to my flimsiest things. Adam has left a jacket on the chair. I shrug it on but it smells of his sweat and I discard it again. Goodwill watches, missing nothing.

The question is how.

'Where's Josiah?' I aim for a pleasant tone, conversational, even.

Goodwill moves to the window. His fingers tap on the sill as he looks outside, and he cranes his neck to see up into the sky, an expression of interest on his face, as if wondering whether it's going to rain. He is ignoring me. My heart thuds with anger or fear, I'm not sure which.

'Why did you arrest him, Goodwill, apart from the fingerprints on the cages?'

'Mma Babira from the clinic and Mrs Stukker in Gaborone were most co-operative,' he says, as though I haven't spoken. 'There was nothing suspicious to find in either case.'

It takes me a moment to realize he is talking about Esther and Claire. I feel a stab of guilt that they have been disturbed.

'The personnel in Mokolodi game park had heard of your situation. They were very sorry. All had been working at the time of the kidnapping. We made no arrests. We were quite wrong to suspect Mr Katse also,' Goodwill continues, shaking his head at me, as if I were the one who had thought Simon was guilty. He pulls out a handkerchief and coughs noisily into it, then folds it carefully, stowing it in his pocket. It's as though Josiah has ceased to exist.

'We have questioned Mr Katse at length. When he left your house, the day before your son disappeared, he went to pick up his wife and they drove overnight to Johannesburg to celebrate with relatives.'

'Celebrate?'

'His wife had already been elected. We have interviewed the relatives.' He nods now, his chin descending each time into stiff rolls of flesh.

'Why did you want to question Simon? What was it you suspected him of?'

I move a little closer and he steps sideways, repositioning his weight on widespread legs; it's as if we're partners in a dance, moving around something so terrible it can't be named. Today Goodwill is wearing a red striped tie; the colour glows in the dark room. He has the power; I must be careful.

'He was here just a few days before Sam was abducted.' For a large man his voice is unusually silky. 'We thought it possible that he might have encountered something relevant.'

'Relevant like his wife's political ambitions?'

Goodwill turns towards me, putting his hands on his hips, becoming bigger, more threatening even. If it is a threat, I ignore it.

'I know body parts can be used for power ... children's body parts,' I continue.

The obscene words are between us, as they have silently been all along.

'Such things do unfortunately happen from time to time, but not round here.' His eyes flick to the laptop on the table and back to me. 'You have doubtless read of an old case in Mochudi. Nothing was ever proved, of course.'

'I also know of a school child near here, who walked into the bush quite recently. He's never been found.' Does he know about Baruti? I watch his face closely for clues.

'Children who wander in the bush are always at risk.' He looks mildly exasperated. 'Snakes, other animals, the heat. Parents should keep them at home.'

Police complicity was suspected in Mochudi. Whose side is Goodwill on? In that moment, thick with conjecture, Kopano knocks and enters. He glances at Goodwill then faces me. 'Your daughter has just told me you found reptiles in the garden that had been skinned. I will need to see them. Can you show me?'

Weren't there rules here about questioning children on their own? Cheeks burning with anger, I lead the way. Kopano follows. Outside the house, I turn to him. He is younger than Goodwill, less guarded. He might be willing to let slip what he knows.

'What do you think Josiah has done, Kopano?'

No answer.

'Why are you interested in the reptiles?'

He glances back at the house as he walks beside me but doesn't reply.

'Why, Kopano?'

As we reach the shed, Goodwill's heavy tread comes down the veranda steps after us. I have to be quick. 'What do you know about medicine murders?'

But Goodwill is already beside me. Kopano silently holds open a plastic bag. As I tip in the bodies of the snake and lizards, his eyes slide sideways fearfully: so he believes in spells too.

They leave, Kopano carrying the bag at an angle from his body, as if it might be contaminated. Their car moves down the drive. I am no nearer knowing why they are keeping Josiah. Minutes later, Kabo drives in, Adam beside him in the car.

'I found your husband miles away.' Kabo gets out, shaking his head. 'He was starting back, but sunset comes quickly.'

Adam stands silently in the drive; he stares at his feet, his expression bleak.

'I got your message about the dogs.' Kabo's hand grips mine. 'I'll be near the kennels tomorrow for my niece's christening. I'll call in and bring them over in the afternoon.' He looks uncertainly at Adam, then back at me, pushing up his glasses.

'Stay for a cup of tea, Kabo.'

I make a pot and we sit on the veranda; Adam and I avoid each other's gaze.

'We should have christened Sam,' Adam says into the silence. His face is coated with dust, his eyes bloodshot. 'His name means "heard by God", remember? God would have heard him calling for us, if we'd christened him.'

Then I do look at him – stare at him. 'Surely you're not going to pretend you believe in God suddenly?'

Kabo shifts in his seat at my words, glancing from Adam to me. Adam looks up; swallows are flying in a V-formation across the reddening sky. For a moment I imagine they're migrating to England. I've lost track of the seasons. Is it spring there? Summer?

'Just because I need God now, doesn't make him less likely to be real,' Adam mutters.

It does, though; he's being irrational.

'Maybe I should start praying.' He laughs abruptly. 'If Sam is dead, shouldn't that mean he'll go to Heaven?'

'I don't think God makes bargains like that,' Kabo says gently. 'He'll look after Sam anyway.'

We are at the point of evening when a hush falls, a small hesitation before dark. Kabo's voice is quiet, as though he's in church, but Adam's is angry. 'God should have been on my side,' he says. 'I came to Africa to help.'

What had we imagined Africa would be like? The

very word had once been exciting but it's hard to remember exactly why. Adam had thought he could help and so had I. How arrogant that seems now, how naive. I doubt we have helped; our help wasn't needed. The kind of Africa we imagined doesn't exist. We found none of the things we thought we would. On the contrary, God or no God, it's been a place of loss.

# Chapter Thirty

*Botswana, April 2014*

The questions in my head distil. Is he alive or dead? Killed within moments of being taken? My mind hovers between possibilities as the hours and days tick by, not daring to settle. I hardly eat; my gums bleed. When I wake the taste of iron is in my mouth, as though I had sucked on knives in my sleep.

My milk supply has disappeared more quickly than I would have thought; from one moment to the next, my breasts stopped hurting. I can't rid myself of the thought that my body knows more than my mind, that my milk isn't needed now, because Sam is dead.

Adam goes back to the consulate three times a week, on his own. He doesn't mention God again; he is silent and eats little. Goodwill tells me the counter-trafficking department of the International Organization for Migration is involved now but surely it's too late. Sam could have been transported to another country at any time in the last two weeks. As Goodwill talks about grass-roots surveillance and witness protection, I can hardly take in the words.

My mind is full of images of Sam in some airless back room in a dirty cot, tear-stained and thin. At night I lie awake, wondering if he would remember me if we found him now.

Zoë follows me everywhere, asking to be held. Walking through the house is an effort; noises and light hurt. All day I search the Internet and scour every news channel. The children want stories, though I often lose my place and have to begin from the beginning.

The space between Adam and me widens. We hardly talk any more. We sleep in the same room but I go to bed later, when he is already asleep; he gets up earlier and has left to walk the bush or visit the consulate by the time the children and I have breakfast.

Yesterday a press plane flew low twice over the house; luckily the girls were inside. The gum trees bent and shook. The three guard dogs, housed in large crates near the garage, usually sleeping by day, woke and slunk in circles, whining.

Peo returns to her village early on a Wednesday. A knot of women wait for her in the road beyond the gate and she is quickly enfolded. Around us the journalists' vans are still closed. A man's cheek is pressed flat, a pale ham against the window. The women's ululations wake him and he stumbles out, aligning his camera. Others follow.

A tall girl detaches herself from the group around

Peo; she approaches me, unwrapping the sling around her. Mmapula. She holds out her baby to me. The group has become very quiet, though cameras click repeatedly. The baby feels light and warm; he mews in his sleep, like a kitten. For a moment I feel light-headed; Mmapula reaches to take him back. She gives me a small bunch of bush flowers.

'*Ka a leboga,*' she says, and smiles. Thank you.

Peo takes my hand. '*Ka a leboga.*' My accent is clumsy. The murmuring swells into chatter, which fades as the group moves down the road; I want to call her back.

Car doors open and slam, engines start: some of the journalists are leaving, having got what they wanted for the day. The gum trees tower above me as I walk back. Kabo told me trees have a powerful spirit and it consoles me to think that the ancient African tree gods might be watching over us. My hand against the silvery bark looks like a skeleton hand. Staring up into the canopy of leaves, I find myself praying for death. As a child I once persuaded my father into a medieval torture museum in Siena. Racks and spiked cages would be unnecessary to punish a mother; those twelfth-century Italians would only have had to take her child away from her and she would have agreed to anything for his safety, even death. But my torture won't end. I can't die.

Up at the house the girls' faces, like pale flowers, are pressed to the windows. The dried bunch I was given rustles as I place it at the foot of the tree, my offering to the tree gods.

Inside, the girls have slipped from the window and are watching a cartoon on television. What's happened to my resolve, to the normal structure of the day? I ought to turn off the television; read the girls a story or help Elisabeth, who is quieter without Josiah, thinner. She moves more slowly. I'm letting things go, letting the fabric of our lives unravel. I can't remember when the girls last did any work. We never heard from Simon's friend, and after the police questioned Simon, I couldn't pursue it.

Later that morning, both policemen turn up. Kopano disappears but Goodwill stands in the sitting room, rocking backwards and forwards on his feet, leather shoes creaking. Elisabeth takes the girls into Josiah's yard. Through the window I see her set down a bucket to milk the goat. Alice leans against the wall, near the dogs' cage. She taps the wire; one wakes and lumbers to his feet. She aims a little kick in his direction. The animal crouches swiftly, tail flat against his body. Alice never used to be cruel. Grief is changing us all. Meanwhile Zoë squats, looking up at Elisabeth, waiting to be told what to do.

Goodwill sits, but remains silent. Perhaps he is

finding the words for bad news; perhaps he is simply bored: this job has gone on too long with no end in sight. There must be others waiting for his attention. He is dressed as usual in spotless uniform, though his shirt strains at the buttons. School children along the road wear perfect uniform too, though their homes often lack electricity and running water. Goodwill might live in a hut like that, he might mind that we are wealthier than he is, though surely he knows we have lost everything; no one could possibly envy us now. Maybe the international attention bothers him; after all, there are missing children who are never mentioned. For a moment Baruti's face floats between us.

The kettle whistles in the kitchen. The task of spooning black leaves from the tin into the chipped yellow teapot and pouring the bubbling stream from the heavy kettle is calming. Back in the sitting room, Goodwill takes his cup, sips and sighs loudly, then looks down to his lap at the papers he has pulled from the case.

'Josiah,' he says finally, frowning deeply, as though the name itself is a statement of guilt.

'Yes?'

'We are concerned with this man. He is not telling us the truth.'

'Why do you say that?'

'Thirteen days ago, the day after your son

disappeared, Josiah went to his home in Mochudi. He told his brother he needed money, then he left. He didn't arrive back here until the following morning. He refuses to tell us where he went in the hours in between, but he seems frightened, which worries me.'

Goodwill would be frightening to a frail old man, pushing him into silence; even so, these words are a warning. What has Josiah done that he is keeping so secret?

Goodwill wipes his hand rapidly over his face. 'In my profession, fear means guilt. I am wondering where he might have gone that day, and how we might find out.'

'I'm afraid I can't tell you. I have no idea at all.'

What Josiah does when he isn't working and where his family lives are unknown to me. As with Teko, we didn't involve ourselves. A bleak wave of regret breaks over me, leaving a backwash of bitterness. Goodwill is still staring at me. He seems suspicious that I am protecting Josiah; he thinks I'm not telling the truth, but I am. Almost. They have forgotten about Elisabeth. They may not know she is his sister. She may be able tell us more, but if there is more to find out, I will do the finding.

I begin to think about Josiah as Goodwill must, like a detective: a man with no money who unexpectedly breaks his habits to disappear for a while shortly after our child has vanished and refuses to say where he's been. A man who had always singled Sam out for special attention.

Goodwill pulls himself to standing and drains his cup. 'Kopano is digging up the grave by Josiah's hut.' Casually imparted, but I feel his eyes follow me as I run from the room.

Kopano leans on a spade, soil scattered around his feet in crumbling heaps. The wooden cross is in pieces on the ground. There are scraps of yellow fur in the earth, a long shallow skull. I walk back to the sitting room on trembling legs. 'The dog,' I tell Goodwill. 'Just the dog.'

Goodwill leaves silently. He has sharp instincts: he thinks I'm keeping something from him. He must have known the grave was for Josiah's dog, but perhaps he meant to terrify me, believing I would talk more freely from pure relief.

In the kitchen, the girls are with Elisabeth, collecting empty jars from a cupboard to make butter from the goat's milk; she sends then to scrub their hands and begins to scour the jars at the sink. A pan of water containing clothes bubbles on the hob, filling the air with the steamy scent of hot cloth.

'About your brother, Josiah.'

The jam jars bob about in the soapy water as she washes them. She seems absorbed in her task: there is no indication she has even heard me.

'He is in trouble; the police may keep him. He

visited his brother, your brother too, of course, thirteen days ago, then disappeared for the afternoon. No one knows where he went before he came back here.'

Elisabeth looks out of the window above the sink. Her eyes rest on his small vegetable patch; the neat rows of leaves are dried and dying.

'*Ngaka ya setso*,' she murmurs.

That Setswana word, meaning traditional doctor. 'So he's ill?'

She looks at me and away, her glance is full of secrets.

So, it's more complicated than illness. The steamy air thickens, clotting into the shapes of a small heart, limbs and lips. I lean against the wall for a moment, 'Why did he go to see the doctor, Elisabeth?'

She shrugs and her mouth turns down: she has said too much already.

'I need to see this doctor. He may help us to help Josiah.' She turns at my words and this time her gaze lingers on my face. Can she guess what horrors are passing through my mind?

'Could you take me there?'

She inclines her head, so briefly it could be mistaken for an accidental movement.

'Shall we go this afternoon, when Adam is back?'

Another small nod.

'You will need money for the doctor,' she tells me. Zoë runs back into the kitchen followed, after a while, by Alice who, walking as though half asleep, stumbles against a chair and almost falls. I put my arms round her and she stands quite still, waiting for me to go. Elisabeth puts two jars on the table and pours goat's milk into them, screwing the tops on tightly. She shakes them and the milk slops up and down. Zoë laughs. No one notices me leave.

Josiah's room is stifling. The sun strikes through the metal roof, releasing a harsh clay smell from the plaster. The drawers have been pulled right out now; there are the marks of boots on the shirt and towel, which are lying on the floor. I fold both, lay the towel and the shirt back inside and close the chest. There is nothing behind the door; I even peer into the key-hole. My fingertips pick up a layer of gritty dust from the windowsill. The mattress is back on the bedstead, but has been slashed at one end with a knife, and some of the stained foam-rubber lining has been pulled out. Kopano must have done this on his return visit.

The room is so silent the air hums. The old man has gone and I am unable to grasp even the faintest echo of who he was. Questions begin to invade the barren space around me: could the emptiness itself be a clue, a screen behind which another Josiah is hiding? He seems to have so very little: is the real stuff of Josiah's life somewhere else? A stash of money or knives in a box? I begin to feel frightened.

# Chapter Thirty-one

*Botswana, April 2014*

My father once showed me grainy newsprint photos of ex-Nazis. 'Look what resolve can do,' he'd said of the hunters who'd tracked them down, but I'd stared at the pictures of the old men in the dock. It was hard to imagine the white-haired, stooped figures capable of such cruelty.

The sunlit patch of ground outside Josiah's hut is the same as it was back in December. The goat backs away, eyes wild and hoofs scrabbling, just as before. I still feel I'm trespassing. Apart from the grave this could be the day we arrived but underneath the surface everything is different. He was invisible to the journalists, but has the real Josiah been invisible to us as well? If he is a criminal, this house would be a good place to hide. He might have been here a long time or maybe his arrival coincided with ours, deliberately coincided. How would Elisabeth fit in? Innocent sister? Collaborator?

When Adam returns from the bush, he falls asleep on the bed for an hour. I find my purse in the wardrobe, slide out five hundred *pula* and stuff them into my pocket. I take the car keys from his jacket. The jeep I used is still being repaired. I am walking out of the door when he stirs. 'I'm taking Elisabeth to see a doctor. I'll need the car for a while. The children are in their room – they'll want supper later.'

He rolls on his back, eyebrows raised. His face is still streaked with sweat and dust. 'Can't we help Elisabeth ourselves?'

'She says it's private.'

He nods, accepting this.

Elisabeth is waiting by Adam's car. She is wearing her green woollen hat pulled low, a long mauve scarf covers half her face. Her eyes are watchful. As we get into the car, she murmurs, 'Mochudi.'

At the end of the drive the journalists gather around the jeep, knocking on the window and shouting questions. They have become more aggressive through boredom, or perhaps they think we're hiding something. Elisabeth shrinks back in her seat.

As we near Gaborone, the verges are cluttered with stalls: fruit is for sale under broken awnings. Children are everywhere, walking along the edge of the road, dawdling by the fences, trailing after adults, some barefoot. One or two toddlers trip and straggle behind on their own and my heart clenches in panic. By a junction, something white moves at the edge of my vision: a sheet or blanket spread out against a fence. I stop the car by the side of the road and run, panting, to inspect: close up, it's finely striped with red. Sam's blanket was white.

Driving through Gaborone, my hands grip the wheel as if I'm holding onto a boat in rough water. I haven't faced traffic for a while. At the crossroads a tall policeman in white gloves leaps and gesticulates with ferocious energy amid traffic that shoots and swirls around him. When Kabo drove us from the airport, we must have come a different way: the tall buildings with gleaming windows that I'd noticed then have vanished. The streets are crowded: people are walking or dawdling, pushing bikes and prams, talking, eating and dancing. At one intersection, two youths stagger and collide, throwing punches; there are bottles at their feet. The backdrop is a line of fences strewn with rubbish and, behind, concrete houses and huts made of tin. It seems like a different town from the one I saw when we first arrived.

After forty minutes, the first houses of Mochudi appear, dotted along the highway. Elisabeth indicates right: the roads twist and turn, the disjointed settlement thickening down a slope into a tight-knit jumble of streets lined with concrete huts.

She cranes through the windows, then holds up her hand. Pulling the scarf more closely round her face, she points to a wooden door in a white wall. The words 'Tuck Shop' are painted in thick red letters above a hatch; paint has dribbled from one arm of the T, bleeding a crimson trail down the wall. Elisabeth shrinks further into the seat. I park under a shady tree and she closes her eyes; perhaps she will sleep. I cross the narrow street, knock and wait by the door; the sun scorches off the whitewash. After a few moments, a child with a frilly pink collar and stiff plaits peers through the hatch; a bolt slides back and the door opens into a small earthen yard surrounded by sheds. She points to a bench and stands, stomach out, against a wall, watching me fixedly; a bone-thin dog with swollen teats walks slowly towards me, then half sits, half falls against a step to lie panting on her side. An old woman waits on the bench too, her twisted hands bunched on a stick; her corneas are white. Flies rise from dark puddles at our feet.

After a while, the door of a hut opens and an older girl, tightly wrapped in brilliant orange and blue, beckons me into the darkness. I indicate the old woman who was there before me, but the girl beckons again.

A small man sitting by a window is just visible in the gloom. The room smells musty and faintly of herbs. A woven rug stretches in front of him; to the side is a small patch of ash and burn marks scored on the concrete. The girl indicates a seat next to him; close up, his face is broad, the thin yellow skin finely

286

wrinkled. His slanted eyes flare with recognition. I'd forgotten that my image has been on television and in newspapers for weeks. I'd planned to start by asking if he knew Josiah, then pick up clues from there, but now he knows who I am, he might be evasive and, if guilty, vanish. I could inform the police but the door is shut now and the girl leans against it.

Playing for time, I pile *pula* on the floor in front of him; the girl gathers the notes carefully and slips them into an iron box next to his seat. He lifts his chin questioningly at me.

'Josiah . . .' I begin, then stop, at a loss.

He nods and, without turning his head, speaks in rapid Setswana to the girl by the door; as he talks I look around. There are plastic pots cramming wooden shelves that line the walls, little bottles, ceramic dishes and small cardboard boxes with faded labels in red and orange. A necklace of dried pods dangles from the top shelf, exactly like the one Alice made with Teko. The doctor is watching me; he nods, then points to a snakeskin pinned to the smoky wall. Though the edges are dried and curling inwards, the bars of bright coral shine as they did when I saw the living animal slither into the grass. There is a moment of utter silence.

The girl begins to speak to me. 'This doctor knows of you and your son. He says Josiah came with the pods and with the skin of that snake and other skins. He needed a charm, made with your things.' Then she adds quietly, almost as if it were self-evident, 'A special charm, so that your son would be found.'

If what she says is true, I've got it wrong. Very wrong. Josiah has been helping us all along. It must have been Josiah who skinned the snake, the frog and the lizards. Josiah who slipped the pods from the kudu horns. He would have borrowed money from his brother, then made his way here. After the doctor had made the charm, he would have journeyed home, waiting patiently for a bus, possibly all night.

Why didn't he tell the police? I know the answer to that, though: Esther told me months ago. Everyone is frightened of the power of these doctors. Josiah wouldn't dare say a word. If the police visited the doctor, what vengeance might he fear?

'How would it work then, this charm? Is it a medicine? Who would take it?' I am ready to believe. Despite a lifetime of evidence-based practice, I want to believe it's possible a charm might bring Sam back. I would trade everything I own and all my knowledge of medicine, if only it were possible.

The girl translates my question to the doctor, and he replies to her at length. She turns to me. 'No one takes this charm. It's not for the body. The doctor takes the pods and cuts the skin of the snake. He makes a powder together.' She demonstrates a grinding action, her fist in her palm. 'Then he made a fire with the powder. The smoke goes up.' She lifts her bunched hand high into the air and opens it suddenly, spreading her short fingers wide. Up and out, the movement implied, out into the room, the village, the miles and miles of bush around, molecules drifting across the spaces of Africa. I close my eyes, drifting with them in the warm air.

*The sun shines in my face.*

*I kick my legs hard, my arms pull though the water.*

*My father calls to me above the noise of splashing, he tells me I can do it.*

*My body moves forwards towards the boat.*

The doctor stands up. My eyes snap open. He holds a small bag made of leopard-skin; he demonstrates that I am to stretch out my hands. When I cup my palms he tips the contents of the bag into them, a heap of tiny bones.

They are cold in my hands: mouse vertebrae? Snake? There are yellow shards of horn and a domino buried in the mixture. The girl tells me I am to whisper my wish to them.

'Help me find Sam,' I murmur into my hands.

Then as he mimes opening his hands, I do the same, scattering the bones on the mat in front of him. Watching them closely, he moves them a little with a stick. Then, glancing back from time to time, as if their pattern spelt out a recipe, he gathers powder from different pots and mixes them in a stone dish. He pours liquid from a small bottle onto the powder. Purple flames leap and dance, and when they die down, he tips the powder into a small pot.

'Touch the powder to your face,' the girl says, handing me the pot, touching her eyelids.

'What will it do?'

'It is a powerful charm, from roots and leaves. It will to help you see your son,' she replies.

The doctor's hand is cool as he clasps mine; his eyes are remote, as if his thoughts have already turned to the next patient, the blind old woman on the bench outside.

'Josiah is in prison,' I tell him quickly. 'The police think he's hiding something from them.'

His eyes meet mine. They close and open once. Then he turns away.

On the journey home, Elisabeth unwinds her scarf. Her hands relax on her lap. We don't talk much as the miles go by but I tell her I've found out that Josiah has been very kind to us and her face softens. Once home, she disappears into the kitchen, pulling off her green hat. In the bedroom, I push the little pot of powder deep into the side pocket of my suitcase. I say nothing to Adam. He might be scathing if I told him what had happened; he might want to throw the powder away.

After supper he lets the dogs out; from the window I watch his torch bobbing up and down in the darkness as he follows them round the perimeter fence. There is, after all, nothing of importance to say. No clues sprang out today; despite what I'd like to believe no real steps have been taken that have brought Sam nearer. That night I lie next to Adam, wondering how I will convince Goodwill of Josiah's innocence without revealing the old man's secrets.

The next morning, I wake to the sound of the hoe falling on soil: Josiah is back in the garden, digging.

Later he comes to the door of his hut at my knock. He refuses money, though I tell him it's for the medicine. He takes my hand and smiles.

Behind him is the empty room. Now I know he isn't hiding anything; in any case he has nothing to hide – he owns almost nothing. I want to go in, ask his forgiveness, sit down with him, find out what he did when he was younger, and why he loved Sam. He made a journey, paid money and went to prison for our son. Did he remind him of a boy he knew? His own son?

*Ka a leboga*. It's all I can say, but he nods and smiles again, then releases my hand and turns back into his hut.

Goodwill doesn't come that day or the day after. After a while it feels we have gone backwards rather than forwards: Sam seems further away than ever.

# Chapter Thirty-two

*Botswana, May 2014*

'I'm worried about Alice,' Adam says at breakfast. The girls have left the table; in the sitting room, Alice has pushed Zoë aside and is sitting so near to the television screen that the blue light plays over her face.

I'm worried about her too. She is silent and seems fearful. She doesn't play or even read. The books on the table have hardly been touched since Simon was here.

'She needs to go home.' His eyes are wary: he's expecting an argument. 'So does Zoë. It's been two months – time for them to get back to some kind of normality.'

All the fragile leads we'd thought we had have snapped. Teko has disappeared without a trace. Simon and Josiah should never have been pursued. Our story is still in the news, a knot of journalists still camping outside the gates. Elisabeth tells me that Chief Momotsi continues to search. Adam walks out into the bush every day, but for the girls, time is hanging, motionless.

'She's unhappy enough to be careless,' he says. 'She sits in the heat without a hat. I've seen her walk in the grass over there with no shoes on.' He nods towards the side of the garden where it grows tall and spindly under the trees, and snakes could be hiding. 'It's as though she doesn't mind what happens to her, almost as though she's seeking harm.'

'She's grieving, Adam. Don't make it worse than it is. She forgets to take care.'

'I'll stay here, of course, and carry on searching,' he continues, as if I haven't spoken. 'The Met are sending a task force next week and the private detective arrives in a few days.'

'A task force?'

'I told you yesterday. Goodwill has agreed to work with them as there have been no positive leads.'

'How are we going to pay for a private detective?'

'I've re-mortgaged the house. Emma, we had this discussion two days ago.'

If we did, I can't remember it – or perhaps I didn't hear. When Adam talks, the words often jumble together; sometimes I watch his lips moving and hear the sounds as if at a distance.

Zoë jumps with a little cry of alarm when I pass her on my way to the quiet of our bedroom. She startles at everything now. In our room the bougainvillaea around the window frames the garden like a wreath. A blade of certainty slides between my ribs:

Sam is surely dead, or hidden so determinedly that he is irrecoverable. Why hope?

Adam follows me into the bedroom; I nod without turning my head.

'I'll get your tickets for a week's time,' he says. I can't tell if he is relieved or sad. 'Does that give you long enough?'

I email the girls' school, my work and Megan – she and I email once a week; whenever her name appears in the inbox my heart lifts just a little. Adam organizes our tickets. We don't speculate on how long it will be before he comes back to England.

I text Goodwill to let him know we're leaving. We debate if we should buy the police something, but in the end decide it might look like bribery.

The house takes on the look of a ghost house, the rooms emptying of most of our stuff. I move slowly, a victim sorting debris in the smoky remains of a bomb. My hair fades as grey thickens in the blonde and my face is thinner. I haven't put on makeup since Sam was taken. I wear whatever comes to hand.

As the last week draws to an end, Goodwill and Kopano come out to the house. Goodwill tells me they will continue working on the case. He stands at the window; as we talk, his eyes rest on Josiah, who is carrying logs to the house in a wheelbarrow.

'Did you ever find out where he was?' I am curious to see whether he knows the truth.

'A bus driver helped account for all his movements.'

'And the money?'

'Josiah told us he needed medicine. He is an old man. It is natural.' A little shrug.

'So you let him go?'

'We spoke at length to the owner of the house; he was prepared to vouch for Josiah's character, having known him for many years.' Goodwill nods emphatically as he watches me.

His expression remains carefully bland. There is something more that he's not telling me. Did the doctor use his power to make Goodwill let Josiah go or was it coincidence? If the doctor had power it was good power, an innocent man was freed.

'The skinned reptiles that Kopano took away, did they help?'

'The men who took your son might have seen the animals in the cages and returned later for their skins. They have a certain value. If we'd found the skins, they could have given us a lead.' He sighs. 'But we never did.'

One of the skins is on a wall in a dark hut in a back-street in Mochudi, I could tell him, and the others are atoms in the air. They haven't realized that Elisabeth is Josiah's sister. Though Josiah is innocent, it's worrying they missed all the clues.

'What's the latest news about Teko?'

He stretches his neck, as if the collar is too tight. 'We do not think she is responsible, as you know.' He looks down, his next words sound automatic. 'Nevertheless she remains our primary witness and we are looking for her everywhere.'

There is nothing more to say. I sense his anxiety to be gone; it is strange that I hardly know this man yet he holds my son's life in his hands.

'Do you have children, Goodwill?'

'Four boys.' He nods, pride deepening his voice.

'How old?'

'Twenty-five. Twenty. Eighteen.' He pauses. His smile is sudden and genuine. 'Two weeks.' His hands sketch a rounded shape, the size of a bag of sugar.

There is a small suitcase under our bed into which everything of Sam's has been packed. I tip folded babygros, towels embroidered with ducks and nappies into a bag, then hand it to Goodwill before I can change my mind. 'For your son.' So you remember mine, I add silently.

Goodwill has mauve marks beneath his eyes. The baby must be disturbing his nights. He nods quickly without smiling; I can't tell if the gift pleases him, or if he is reluctant to take cast-offs from a baby who has disappeared. He walks heavily out of the room without saying goodbye.

Kopano smiles and shakes my hand; his is dry and

light. An athlete's hand. For a moment I wish I'd found out more about these men, though I doubt we would have been friends. I was never sure how much I could trust them.

The next day Adam drives me to the clinic to say goodbye to Esther. As we sit in the crowded waiting room, Adam sleeps, his head swaying and nodding on his chest. The last time I was in this building, men were closing in around our house, creeping into the garden and watching through the windows. I am unable to sit still. Out on the porch a group of three girls sit on the steps, two perched above a third. The two girls are laughing, nudging their friend from behind. She gets up abruptly and walks away, her right foot dragging a little. My heart comes up into my throat.

I run down the steps, missing the bottom one and turning my ankle painfully. I begin to half run, half hobble after her. The girls on the stairs notice and call to her. She turns but it's not Teko: it's not a girl at all; I was fooled by her size. A thin-faced woman of fifty faces me, lips pursed, her hands on her hips. Perhaps she thinks I've joined in to torment her. I stammer out an apology and she turns away.

The silent gaze of the two girls follows me back inside. We are shown into Esther's room in an interval between patients. The nurse who was away on maternity leave has returned; she walks noisily round the little room that was mine for a while; her glasses flash through the gap where the door hinges to the wall. Esther is uneasy; there seems little to talk about although she tells me that Baruti has not yet been found. A gulf has opened up between us. I want to tell her that I'm the same person she knew two months back, although we both know I'm not.

We leave two days later, four a.m. on a Tuesday. The car is packed, the girls have been woken and dressed, and now are sleeping in the back seat.

Elisabeth stands by the door, Josiah is next to her. He pushes his shoulders back, standing as straight as he did when we arrived. How could I have known then how difficult it would be to leave them? I put my arms round Elisabeth and hold her close; she smiles and pats my shoulder. I shake Josiah's hand and he nods, looking away. We've given them presents already, money, my coat to Elisabeth. There is so much and nothing to say. The final moments pass so quickly they convey only a sense of emptiness.

As we walk down the steps, they go back into the house and the front door shuts behind them. Later Josiah will be in the garden; Elisabeth will strip the girls' beds and wash the floors. She'll cook Adam's supper. Later still Josiah will let the dogs into the garden; he's grown fond of them. I've seen him talking to them by the cages in the afternoon in a low sing-song voice.

The car slides out of the drive and the house disappears behind us. Soon I will be thousands of miles away; I am leaving, knowing nothing more than when Sam was first taken. I have failed him completely but, behind me, both girls are sleeping, trusting they will be carried from this place of tragedy back to their lives.

Kabo is waiting at the airport; in the place where we first met him, it's obvious that these last months have changed him. His jacket hangs on him now, and his hair is greying. He helps us unload our bags, and carries Zoë to the departure lounge. Alice follows slowly. Kabo and Adam talk quietly together, planning to run down the research as quickly as possible.

Three policemen in the lounge stand against the wall. They recognize us and nod politely. A group of journalists clusters by the bar, cameras around their necks: absorbed in their stories, they don't notice us.

Zoë pulls my hand: she needs the toilet. Inside there's a queue and she begins to whimper. We stand behind a wild-haired girl, who holds the hand of a sobbing boy. She releases his hand, and scoops her hair into a scrunchie, revealing a long, willowy neck.

Teko's neck. Teko in the act of stealing another child? The girl spins round at my touch. The acned face is unfamiliar. She stares at me questioningly, a pink bubble of gum protruding from her mouth, glances down at the crying boy, then back at me; she thinks I am drawing her attention to the child. She smiles and, bending, hoists him onto her hip, sucks in her gum and kisses him, bouncing him on her hip. The boy stops crying; not stolen then. I continue to wait in line with Zoë, who has watched this little drama silently.

As the call comes to board, Kabo hugs the children, then me; he pushes his glasses up and walks away quickly. I watch his back view recede and my throat constricts.

Adam kisses my cheek and bends to the children. Serious and silent, Zoe lays her head on his shoulder. Alice stays stiff in his arms; when he tells her how much he loves her, her eyes squeeze shut.

We board the plane, find our seats, and the girls sit down on either side of me, Zoë at the window. On take-off Gaborone grow smaller, then the great brown spaces of bush recede beneath. If he's alive, Sam is somewhere in that wilderness; I have to fight the urge to jump up and shout that I need to go back, my son has been left behind. Beside me, Alice groans. She is rigid, hands clasping the arms of the seat, sweat on her forehead. I put my hand over her clenched one. 'Ally, sweetheart. It's okay. We're up.'

She looks at me. Her eyes are expressionless.

'I know who took him,' she whispers. 'I helped.'

# Chapter Thirty-three

*London, January 2015*

Luckily the post comes late. There is a large white envelope on the mat when I return from dropping the girls off at school, the psychiatrist's report, by its weight: if Alice had seen and guessed, her first day back at school might have been wrecked.

Zoë's puppy has puddled the floor again. I wipe the tiny pool, throw the J-cloth into the bin, then wince at my mistake: in Botswana it would be washed and dried in the sun, used and reused.

The little black dog is warm on my lap. These days, I'm always cold. I walk around in two jerseys and sometimes my duvet. Weight loss. Loss.

Rain is lashing the windows. It will be midday in Kubung now, the heat reaching into the shadows. Josiah will be asleep in his hut, Elisabeth serving lunch. Someone else will be standing at the door, her hand shading her eyes, calling her children in.

Kodi chews the envelope while I read the report, my hands pulling at the satin triangles of his ears. Kodi: Setswana for kudu, Alice's idea.

*Report by Dr Harnham FRCPsych*
*Patient: Alice Jordan. DOB 10 August 2004*
*Diagnosis: Psychotic depression.*
*Generalized anxiety syndrome*

*Siblings:*
*Zoë Jordan. DOB: 19 June 2008. Alive and well.*
*Samuel Jordan. DOB: 17 November 2013. Missing, pre-*
*sumed deceased, March 2014.*

*Missing.* That word opening always into the vacant room: the empty cot, the black night beyond the shattered glass. *Presumed deceased.* I don't presume anything. Certainties have disintegrated. There are times I know Sam's alive, times when I hear him breathing in the silence of our room at night. Then, more often, and lately much more often, I know he's dead. I wish I hadn't opened the report. I wish it hadn't come. Though Adam and I have talked through everything that happened with the psychiatrist, it looks so much worse, typed out in black and white.

*10.8.2004 Full term, normal delivery of female infant. Weight: 3.175 kg. Apgar score: 10.*

Normal? It was cataclysmic, splitting me from the woman I had been; I'd become consumed, torn, embattled.

*Early childhood uneventful.*

(Uneventful? What about love? Breastfeeding, bedtime stories, walks in the park, the beach, the food? And what about the return to work, the tears, the promises, the late returns. The rushed talks. Events, good and bad, happened all the time.)

*School*
*Academic record: Consistent excellence across the board (see attached report)*
*Extra tennis, Mandarin lessons, violin . . .*
*Personal and Social Development*
*History of pilfering: . . . stolen items . . . self-validating . . .*

Alice calling for help, asking to be noticed. I flick back to Dr Harnham's report.

*Home Life and Early Psychiatric Morbidity (ages 4 to 8)*
*Father Consultant Oncologist (full time)*
*Mother Consultant Obstetrician and Gynaecologist (now retired)*
*Parents co-habit: high level of expressed emotion . . . eased in holidays but not sustained . . . Child care delivered by series of au pairs.*

They were safe, though. Efficient. I took up references . . .

*Reported symptomatology occurring at this time: poor sleep, obsessive tendencies . . .*

The footsteps I heard at night, months before we left for Africa, were Alice's, not Sofia's; Alice was listening to us even then.

The stolen things, the broken dolls, the rigid arrangement of hairclips: warning signs of a child who felt unsafe, attempting to order her world, the significance missed, then forgotten.

*Alice felt left out of important family issues, e.g., exclusion from the fact of her mother's pregnancy. Retrospective diagnosis at this stage: mild depressive disorder, with associated anxiety.*

I should have told her. I wish I had. She was tired but coping. That was what we thought. We didn't see anything . . . No: we didn't understand anything.

*Third sibling: born 37 weeks gestation normal delivery . . .*

*Alice experienced raised level of anxiety and depression around the welfare of the new baby and describes his birth in terms of a tipping point. She felt less visible to her parents from then on, and in addition to feeling more unsafe herself was concerned for the baby's wellbeing, and also her sister's. She has positive memories of time spent with a family friend, with whom bonding occurred, which mitigated these effects at this time.*

Megan saving us, as she still does, but even so, in spite of everything, sometimes I look at her peaceful face, and think, Could it possibly, still, be you?

*History of Presenting Incident*

*The family moved to Kubung, Botswana, in December 2013 in order for Dr Adam Jordan to take up a planned research sabbatical. Alice experienced further anxiety, due to interruption of normal routines; and the loss of relationships with the family au pair and the above friend. Alice had been informed by her mother she would be at home during their sabbatical so she experienced significant loss of trust when her mother unexpectedly returned to work at six weeks.*

She hardly seemed to notice when I went back to work. I thought she was fine, quiet but fine. The opposite was true.

*Two important relationships had developed concurrently. Alice became close to the nanny, Teko, hired to look after her brother. Teko provided a consistently supportive relationship.*

*Alice was positively attached to her tutor, Simon Katse, on whom she had projected idealized attributes. Delusional beliefs had clearly by then become part of her disturbed mental state and when the tutor left suddenly she developed further deterioration, which may have led to the auditory hallucinations (described in section 2.) below.*

1. *Delusional beliefs*

   *Alice believed her mother disliked her brother because of his facial birthmark. She'd heard her mother positively discuss African babies being given away; she claimed Teko was sympathetic, having overheard the same conversation.*

   *The latter delusion probably constitutes a psychological defence mechanism against self-blame; Alice was worried that the abduction was caused by wish-fulfilment; i.e., her desiring a safe home for her brother 'caused' the abduction; inventing Teko's sympathy would lessen her own responsibility for her feelings because someone else shared them, a mechanism known as psychological scapegoating.*

Alice must have overheard my stupid joke on the veranda; it would have fed into her deteriorating state with terrifying effect. She might have confided her worries to Teko in simple Setswana; if she believed Teko had understood a complex conversation in English, Alice must have been truly delusional.

2. *Auditory hallucinations*

   *Alice claimed she heard breathing noises, footsteps and voices in the days preceding the abduction. She attempted to tell her family but other explanations were found and her fears dismissed.*

We didn't listen when she mentioned footsteps. Not properly. Adam thought she had heard him getting up at night. She blamed him for the whispers she could hear. Even though she looked ill, it never once occurred to me she was hearing voices.

3. *Severe feeling of guilt and self-blame*
   *Despite 'inventing' Teko's sympathy (i.e., psychological scapegoating referred to above) Alice maintains she herself, not Teko, actively helped in the abduction.*

   *The night before the day her brother was abducted, Alice believes she was persuaded by a threatening shadow or ghost of some kind (possibly part of a nightmare) to assist in removing her brother from her own 'bad' family to a 'better' one where he would be loved. Alice becomes confused and highly distressed if encouraged to elaborate. Such hallucinatory episodes are known to have the subjective quality of nightmares; until Alice is comfortable with exploring this experience, there would be little benefit in encouraging her to relive it.*

   *The understanding at present is that Alice claims she was told in the nightmare/hallucinatory episode to take the household members away from the house on the afternoon of her brother's abduction. She did not inform the nanny, Teko, hoping the latter's presence in the house would protect her brother. When Alice realized her brother had been abducted despite Teko's presence, she assumed responsibility for his disappearance.*

*Making sense of catastrophic events through retrospective hallucinatory experiences by highly intelligent and sensitive children is not unknown though rare.*

*In the aftermath of Teko's disappearance Alice concluded that Teko had been subsequently kidnapped as well; she took on responsibility and grieved for both losses. As the search for Samuel continued she realized how distressed her parents were and became actively suicidal.*

*Since the family's return to England, in spite of, and subsequent to, her self-harming episode, Alice has worked closely with all members of the psychiatric team to uncover the sequence of beliefs and delusions related above.*

Alice and I talked on the plane journey to London from Gaborone or, at least, I tried to, but it was obvious something was very wrong. After her outburst she'd wept and insisted she was to blame. Between sobs she claimed Sam had been taken in order to save him. Nothing she said made sense. She was wild with grief. I held her, told her we loved her, that it wasn't her fault. Gradually she became silent, then slept. I knew we had a major problem, but I hadn't sensed she was psychotic.

Megan met us as planned and got us through the seething crowds of journalists at Heathrow, then helped us push past the reporters outside our house.

Once home, I phoned the psychiatric on-call team. I thought Megan was with Alice; she thought I was. Then Zoë told me she couldn't get into the bathroom; in the end, Megan unlocked it with a screwdriver. Alice was on the floor. She'd taken paracetamol from the cupboard and swallowed it, along with a handful of diazepam from my bedside drawer.

Adam caught the next plane back. By then Alice's stomach had been pumped and she was on the paediatric medical ward for liver-function monitoring. We spent the next few days beside her, holding her hand or lying with her on the bed as she slept. I watched her constantly, terror and love consuming me. We didn't sleep for two days. We could have lost her so easily. Alice as well as Sam. It doesn't take much paracetamol to poison a child. She recovered slowly from the overdose, and, as her psychosis unravelled, we knew we couldn't believe anything she said. The psychiatric team asked us to step back.

The puppy feels heavier – he has relaxed into sleep. When I lift him to my neck, he stirs and sleepily pushes his nose under my chin.

*After counselling and psychotherapeutic intervention, Alice is beginning to accept that she was not to blame. She admits that her understanding of events preceding and around the abduction were both delusional and hallucinatory, arising from psychotic depression and related anxiety at the time. As events recede she understands that she had and has no knowledge of why/how her brother went missing.*

*Despite grasping elements of the Setswana language, this would not have been sufficient to allow Alice to comprehend the conversations she claims she had with Teko; and it is currently unclear whether auditory hallucinations or delusional beliefs account for Alice's belief that they were able to communicate fully. Psychotherapeutic work is ongoing to try to distinguish this as it has prognostic implications.*

*Treatment*

*Supportive psychotherapy*
*Julie Edwards, child psychologist: two sessions a week*
*Paroxetine; 10mg o.d.; monthly review with Dr Harnham*

After a while I settle Kodi in his basket by the stove; he turns and falls in a soft heap, nose to tail; his back rises and falls under my hand, his skin twitching. I put the report on Adam's desk for him to read when he comes home. The polished surface is empty; his orderliness has become fierce.

The rest of the day passes. Washing the floor and making the beds is something to cling to: when I smooth the sheets with my hand, I feel calmed, as if I'm smoothing out my mind.

I check the street through the blinds; journalists often lie in wait outside the house. We've been on television three times, holding hands. Adam co-operates with the press but I avoid them.

There have been reports of sightings in Africa, in Kenya and Nigeria, all false and each one seeming to push Sam further away. I've had my own sightings too. Across the aisle in front of us in church at Christmas, Teko became a tall stranger when she stood up. Only three weeks ago I followed a girl with hair just like hers right up to the checkout in Sainsbury's until she turned to face me, her face full of fear. What Teko would have been doing in a north London supermarket was a question I didn't think to ask myself. I'm unsure why I'm compelled to do this because, unlike Adam, I know we have lost him.

We have lost each other too. We walk around at home silently, ghosts in a dead marriage, saying almost nothing. There is an unspoken pact about the girls. They mustn't suffer any more so we are polite. No one would know, though now I recognize other couples, like us, who don't talk or touch, who walk one behind the other in the street.

Megan phones halfway through the day. 'Hi, Emma.'

'Hi.'

'You okay?'

'Mmm. Clearing out a cupboard. You?'

'It's just . . . Hear me out. Mrs Ridley Scott talked to Adam this morning and he's asked me to call. Apparently she wants to know –'

'No. Not yet.'

I can't return to work. Not now, not ever. How could I deliver babies, watch them being held? It's not only that: before I finish a sentence I've forgotten the beginning. I could probably operate safely but I can't hold a conversation.

We exchange a few more words, then she has to go.

The girls return from school. Zoë plays with Kodi, and Alice hands me a brass pendant she's made in art. A step forward.

Adam comes home later. He reads the report and lays it aside. I see him thinking there's nothing really new in it. The facts don't hit him afresh each time as they do me. He wants to talk about the press conference in Gaborone in a couple of months' time: the one-year anniversary. 'Alice is better,' he says. 'She'll be fine without us.'

'Without us?' I stare at him. 'I'm not going, Adam. She's not ready. We can't possibly both leave.'

'The message will be stronger if we go together,' he says.

'Go without me.'

'I bumped into Dr Harnham in the car park today.' He carries on calmly. 'He thinks a short break from us could do Alice good. She's ready to be trusted with a little more independence. We'll only be gone a week.'

'Who would look after them?'

'Can't they board? I thought there was provision for day girls to board, if necessary. They'd be together. We can phone every day. Kodi can go to my registrar – his wife is nuts about dogs.'

He makes it sound so easy. Alice would be fine. Zoë would be fine. Even the dog would be fine. All we have to do is the journey, then the arrival at the airport, though the last time we did that I'd had Sam in my arms. We'd meet Goodwill and Kopano, other policemen. The Met have long gone, and so has Adam's private detective; after all, they were no more successful than the police already on the ground.

Then we'll go back to the house in Kubung, along with all the journalists. We'll be photographed in the garden. I walked past Highgate cemetery in the rain last week on my way to the library; the fresh scent of pine brought back the garden, the first night of searching and all the nights after that. I had to lean against the railings until the giddiness passed. Returning will be beyond me.

We go up to sit on the children's beds and talk. Alice tells us a little about her day. We don't talk about Sam: the psychiatrist told us to wait till she's ready. Zoë now says her prayers, kneeling by the bed and whispering into her fingers. She never used to pray. None of us did. I wonder who she is talking to and if she's asking for her brother. Sometimes when I watch her, the memory of my own whispered prayer and the cold bones in my hand floats for a moment in the pretty bedroom, unreal, like a dream or the memory of a dream. Adam watches her too; I think he's pleased. I think he secretly says his own prayers, too, but we don't talk about belief or anything else that might disturb the flat surface of our lives.

Sometimes I remember my father's voice as he called from the boat and the feel of his hands as he pulled me in, but there is a silence where his words used to be. I can't remember how he sounded – I can't feel his hands, I can't even bring his face to mind. He has vanished completely and I am on my own.

# Chapter Thirty-four

*London, February 2015*

Gulls lift and slide in the grey sky above the Post Office Tower. It must be rough at sea. The wood of the bench is dark; wet seeps through my jeans. There is a scrabble of dogs on the grassy slope below me: an Alsatian, spaniels, a thin greyhound. They bark and run and skirmish, same as a school playground, the leader, the sycophant, the small one on its own. Kodi is the class clown: he rolls on his back and jumps at the others, eager to please and mostly ignored.

Around the pack, women are chatting as they watch the animals. They have prams and pushchairs and children clinging to their legs. Standing well apart, two middle-aged men tuck their chins into their coats and shift their weight from foot to foot, glancing at me; they recognize me from somewhere but can't place where it was. One of the women follows their glance then nudges her friend. They stare and whisper. I call Kodi. It's time to fetch Alice anyway. He bounds over, a typical Labrador, sweet, obedient. Halfway down the hill, one of the pram-pushing women passes me. She is almost running, pulled along by the German Shepherd. As the pram moves ahead, all I can see are small white fingers curled on the cover. They must be icy. I want to tell the mother to put the little hand safely under that cover, but she's too far away now.

Later, in the kitchen, Alice wants a second doughnut. I try not to look too pleased; Dr Harnham says act normal but I can't remember how.

'So, Ally, how did it go today?' When I picked her up earlier, we'd talked about Kodi and the dogs he'd played with; giving her time.

Her head bends over her plate, her shoulders shake. I feel sick. Perhaps Dr Harnham upset her. When she lifts her head she is laughing, not crying. Zoë is staring with surprise so I laugh too, keeping Alice company. If it sounds real it is, a laugh of relief.

Zoë pokes her sister, smiling. 'What's so funny?'

'Nothing,' Alice says, her face growing still, eyes watchful.

But it was something, along with the second doughnut. Another sign of repair.

'What about you, Zoë? Did you have a good day?'

Zoë is colouring, leaning close to her paper on the table, her breathing loud. A slip of tongue protrudes between her teeth. Before she can answer, Alice says,

'Dr Harnham asked me how I was getting on at school.'

'Yes?'

'I told him it was okay.'

'That's great, Ally.'

She picks up her bag. 'Think I'll do homework in my room.' The bag swings as she walks to the door.

The kitchen is quiet. The February wind is spattering rain against the window. I love that sound. I used to long for rain in the heat.

As if on cue, Zoë says, 'We're doing Africa in assembly tomorrow.' Casually, like any piece of school news.

'Right.' My heart is instantly racing.

'They asked me to say something.'

'Fine.' But it isn't fine. How could it be? How could they ask?

'I can say anything I want.'

'Okay.'

What could she talk about? Not the animals. She lost the ones she'd collected. The scenery? Those desolate spaces would be too difficult for a child to describe. Maybe the people, but she only really got to know three or four. What if she talks about the day we lost Sam?

Zoë bends closer over her picture, pressing hard with a yellow wax crayon. 'I'm going to say it was hot. Look.' She holds up her picture of a yellow sun; it takes up the entire page.

319

'Brilliant, Zoë.'

The heat at Kubung hurt your skin. Grass withered; donkeys died of thirst by the road.


'We'll go to her assembly, of course.' The children are in bed and Adam is eating supper. I'm leaning against the stove, watching the rain still falling on the grass outside. They would be glad of this rain in Kubung. 'We have to support her.'

'Of course,' he replies. I wonder what the other parents will say when they see him again. He's always been thin but now he's skeletal. He moves more slowly.

'Talking of Africa . . .' He looks at me hopefully and I look away.

'Maybe.'

# Chapter Thirty-five

*Botswana, March 2015*

It's not just the smell of pine. The dusty scent of the bush reaching through Gaborone and into the hotel garden is instantly familiar. I needn't have worried about what it would be like, returning to the same place. It's as if we have come to another country; any country where it's hot and labour is cheap. The hotel is new since last year, a five-star monster. It has efficient air-conditioning, muted lighting and thick linen tablecloths. Beyond the plate-glass windows of the dining room the swimming pool glitters, surrounded by ranks of sun-loungers. We could be hundreds of miles distant from Kubung or maybe thousands of years. Compared to this opulence, the village had been medieval. Little running water, electricity or Internet. Not many goods in the shops or shoes on the children. It's only when I hear the warm tones of the Motswana chef and catch the smile of the young girl bringing our tea that I can begin to connect the two worlds.

We came straight to the hotel in a taxi. No one

knew we were arriving at the time we did, apart from the police. We want to use the journalists this time, not the other way around. We were caught in the media headlights before. Adam booked three days here for us to acclimatize and prepare for the press conference.

On the first day I'm restless. By breakfast on the second, I've Skyped the girls and swum in the pool. As I'm towelling myself dry, a chameleon on the branch of a jacaranda tree catches my eye. The same colours as the lichen markings on the wood, its eyes gleam as the lids close and open.

At the breakfast buffet the plates around us were piled high with layers of food, eggs and bacon on pancakes, haddock on top of that. Oiled bodies stretch out around the pool, iced drinks alongside. Children bicker in the background.

'I can't stay here, Adam. I'll go mad.'

He's been making notes since breakfast, anticipating the media questions and trying to craft replies that strike the right note between hope and being prepared. We mustn't look like victims, but we must be grateful to the police. Now the notebook lies on his face; we had both forgotten the heat.

'Can't you relax?' His voice is muffled. 'We need to rehearse soon.'

'I have to escape this place.'

The book slides off as he raises himself up on one elbow, studying me. 'You mean it, don't you?'

'I'll go to the main mall. I could buy something for the girls.'

'At least try to avoid notice. Wear a hat and dark glasses.'

'Not a false moustache?'

'I'm serious, Emma.' He scratches his neck. He's always serious.

'We have to control the media this time,' he continues. 'We want publicity on our own terms.'

I buy a large pair of sunglasses along with a wide-brimmed black cotton hat in the boutique in the hotel lobby. Then, up in our bedroom, rummaging in my suitcase, I find cotton trousers and a linen jacket, my smart sandals. My face is shaded by the brim of my new hat. I brought no makeup. Searching in my case for a tube of lipstick, my fingers close around a small plastic tub in the side pocket. I draw out the forgotten pot of ground herbs I'd stashed away a year ago. Unscrewing the lid, I inhale the acrid scent, which makes me sneeze. I dip a dampened finger into the powder and dab it on my eyelids, quickly, before I change my mind. Why not? What's the worst that can happen after all? A rash?

Down by the pool Adam is writing again. He glances up, then gives me a narrow-eyed stare. He nods. I've passed the test. As I climb into a hotel taxi, the blue of the jacaranda tree in the courtyard glows like wet plastic.

The mall is thick with people and stalls. I long to throw off the jacket, and wish I'd worn shorts and flip-flops. Stalls spill over the walkway, displaying pinwheel baskets, bags of sweets, piles of peanuts; lengths of blue cotton lie across a rack, the orange circles stand out sharply, the colours bright enough to sting. The stall owner begins an aggressive pitch. As I turn away, an iridescent line arcs across my left field of vision. A migraine, gathering strength.

A crowded little tea room fronts the mall; sitting at a tin table near the back, I rummage for paracetamol and swallow two with a sip of burning tea that the café owner brings. She rests a generous hip against the table edge. 'On holiday?'

I nod: easier to lie.

'You like our country, then?' She wipes her hands on her apron, waiting for my reply. Her rounded face is very kind; for a moment I want to tell her that we lost our son in her country and that everything she might be proud of, the wide sky, the warm people and the energy in the streets, has faded to dust for us. That I wish to God we had never set foot here. Instead I swallow the dark tea, hoping she will leave.

'You are happy here?' she persists.

I catch a brief memory of my outstretched hand rimmed by sun, the sensation of Sam's soft baby hair beneath my fingertips, then both vanish; I find I simply can't remember what happiness feels like. A man thumps on the counter, calling loudly for a cool drink; the café owner stares at me a moment longer, then hurries to the front of the shop.

I leave the tea unfinished and walk down the street but there is nowhere to go, no friend to visit. I can't risk another café or go back to the hotel and face a day by the pool, rehearsing for press interviews that I know will be pointless.

I take turning after turning, walking rapidly, looking intently at the houses and the yards full of washing and bikes and chairs; then the noise of children reaches me across the road. There is a large building on the opposite side of the street with at least thirty children playing in the yard. Two women stand inside the gate, leaning against the wooden frame, watching the children and gossiping together. A school or an orphanage, perhaps. Two small boys kick a punctured football about, and, as I watch, a thought arrives, welcome as a cool drink: I do have a friend after all. Claire. The address of her orphanage is still on my phone. I could get a taxi, sit in her kitchen, listen to her brisk but kindly talk. Adam will understand. Scrolling through my phone for her name and address, I cross the street, reach through the gate and show the screen to the women. They nod in recognition; they know Mma Stukker well. She runs a smaller orphanage than theirs but, still, a good one. Talking loudly, contradicting each other and starting afresh, they indicate I can easily walk there: it's about five blocks distant. Right. Two lefts. Second right, then turn down by the large garage. The orphanage is halfway along on the left. I'll know it by the big tree over the gate.

Tidy stacks of tyres line the pavement outside the garage; the smell of hot rubber follows me down the street. Halfway along there is a large mopane tree hanging over a white metal gate; inside, a wooden bench has been placed under its branches. I collapse in the shade, catching my breath; it was further than I'd thought. Ahead, a flight of wooden steps leads to a red door. Children's voices are coming from inside, with the clash of crockery. Lunchtime; I should wait a little. The door opens and two young girls emerge. One is talking loudly as she takes off her apron, the other is wearing a hat; both are smiling. Assistants coming off duty, happy to be outside and on their way home. The talkative girl is short and well built, her black dress stretched so tightly that the fabric shimmers in the sun. Her friend is small too, but slim and, unusually, blonde. The neat bob glints under her hat, too perfect to be real, a wig perhaps. She wears a pretty red and green African print dress and carries a large package. Her dark glasses, like mine, are huge, hiding her face. As she descends the steps, her right leg seems to drag behind just a little. The limp is so slight I could be imagining it. Perhaps I am.

The girls pass without a second glance, slap hands and part at the gate; the short girl runs across the road, waving and calling goodbye. The blonde sets off to the right and, unable to help myself, I start to follow. She walks rapidly, despite the tiny limp, turning quickly at street corners. Out of sight, I run to catch up; she seems a little taller than Teko was, or perhaps she's fatter.

Adam will be dismayed that I'm still following strangers, but he needn't know. I won't tell him. This is the last time, I promise myself, as I hurry. The very last time.

# Chapter Thirty-six

*March 2015*

The girl turns right again at the fifth junction, but when I follow, she has disappeared. I lean against the wall of a building, blinking sweat out of my eyes, scanning the crowds. Then I catch sight of the red and green dress on the opposite side of the road, she's in a queue by a yellow coach just beyond the taxi rank.

I cross over and stay out of sight, hidden in the crowds milling around the taxis; the blonde girl is intent on the phone in her hands, her package by her feet. Under the hat, her hair swings forward in an unfamiliar movement. I should stop this, go back to the hotel, join Adam, prepare for the press – any of these taxis will take me – but at the exact moment I turn, the girl's free hand flutters up to touch her neck and, though she isn't wearing a necklace, my heart begins to race.

Backing against the door of a stationary red car with a 'Taxi' sign in the window, I find the handle by fumbling behind me; opening the door I turn and sit down in the back seat. The taxi driver looks round, startled, a man in his early twenties, mouth working on gum, tight yellow T-shirt, dark glasses pushed up into oiled curls. There is an unsmiling moment as we stare at each other, he in surprise, while I assess him: too good-looking, too young. An older man, a father, would be better, tougher, if necessary. I nod an apology and am about to slip out when I catch movement, a blur of green and red, up ahead. The girl is boarding the yellow coach.

At that moment the young man gives me a smile of such luminous sweetness that I feel warmed through. 'I am glad to carry you today, ma'am. Where to?'

'There is a woman on that yellow coach. I need to follow her.'

He smiles at the cliché and, without asking further questions, starts the engine, then pulls out behind the coach.

I'd forgotten the way Teko's hand would reach towards her neck. Even if I'd thought to tell Goodwill, it would have been hard for anyone else to spot that fragmentary movement. I should call the police, but if the girl is Teko, the sight and sound of police cars would warn her. She could slip from the coach when it slows and melt into the suburbs, disappearing for ever.

'Do you know where the coach is going?'

'Tshabong, non-stop.'

Tshabong: the name is familiar. A town in the south. Adam went there last year to pick up medical supplies trucked in from South Africa. 'How long will it take?'

The smooth shoulders rise in an elaborate shrug. 'Seven hours, maybe.'

Seven hours. Can I really let myself travel miles across country after a girl in a coach just because of the way she touched her neck? What shall I tell Adam? If he knows I've started following strangers again, he'll talk about abnormal grieving and anti-depressants; on the other hand he might send the police after Teko and we'll lose her. There will never be another chance like this. I have to take it.

I quickly punch a message to Adam: *Encountered old colleague. Possibly helpful. Back later.*

It's not a complete lie, after all. I turn off my phone. 'Are you all right to take me all the way there and back again?'

'As long as you pay me.' There is anxiety under the smile: he is taking a risk.

'I will pay you whatever you ask.' In my bag I have the cash we took out at the airport for car hire to Kubung, and for presents to give Elisabeth, Josiah, Peo and her husband. Adam has more at the hotel. I don't care what it costs.

The driver turns, flashing another smile. 'My name is Bogosi, and you know what? This is my lucky day.'

We have reached the suburbs of Gaborone. The road has widened, the houses are larger and more spaced out; trees show above garden walls. The coach has picked up speed and is lurching along rapidly, swaying slightly from side to side. Ten minutes later we are in open country, flat and sandy, with thorn trees; this is how it will be for hundreds of miles.

I feel a sense of calm, of being carried forwards irrevocably into the next few hours. It could be Teko just ahead of me, jammed up against the window, eyes closed, unaware that soon she will be tipped back into the past. In a few hours, we might have answers that will help, even if they close down hope.

The car speeds silently on. Sedated by heat and the steady motion, I feel myself drifting into darkness.

# Chapter Thirty-seven

*Botswana, March 2015*

I am woken by the car slowing down. My head thumps, my throat feels dust-caked. Wet lines of sweat have accumulated in bent elbows and knees. Bogosi is pulling up behind the yellow coach in a roadside garage forecourt. The driver, a short man with thick grey hair, is stretching and yawning by the petrol pump, his large belly filling his blue shirt like a beach ball. A young boy refuels the coach for him. Bogosi gets out and puts petrol in the taxi himself, waving away another boy waiting hopefully to help: no one touches his car. He disappears into the shop, emerging after a while with bottles of water, packets of chewing gum and nuts. He exchanges words with the coach driver, clapping him on the back and laughing. The driver laughs too, nodding and spreading his hands wide to illustrate a point.

Bogosi gets into the car, handing me a bottle of water and some peanuts. 'My aunt's first husband,' he says, still smiling. 'He does this journey twice a week. People come to town to see relatives, meet up with friends and so on.' He settles in the seat, stripping the cellophane from the packet of chewing gum with his teeth.

'You didn't tell him we were following someone on the bus?'

His eyes meet mine in the rear-view mirror as he shakes his head. In that moment I understand two things: he knows who I am, and he is on my side.

'Do you want to get out?' he asks. 'I'll go between you and the bus to the toilets.'

I'd been wrong to think an older man would be better. Bogosi is lending himself to this with the joyous enthusiasm of a boy. I pull the hat lower over my face and we walk together as far as the shop. He waits outside while I use the pit latrine at the back of the building. I look dishevelled in the fragment of mirror that's wedged between the basin and the wall – strands of hair stick to my skin with damp – but there is a difference in the set of my mouth. I look as I did in the scrub-room mirror before a difficult operation, summoning determination. It's working. I feel stronger. The headache has receded.

When I emerge, Bogosi is leaning against the wall, talking on his mobile – cancelling customers, maybe, or appeasing a girlfriend. This journey must have disrupted his routine but he smiles when he sees me, putting the phone away. He's bought a newspaper, and as we walk back side by side, he spreads the printed sheets wide to screen me from the coach windows.

'Put your feet up, ma'am. It will be better for you,' he tells me, as we get in. He starts the car, following the coach as it swings out onto the road again. I settle, spreading his newspaper on the seat. He is right. when I lift up my feet, resting them on the paper, I feel more comfortable immediately.

'*Ka a leboga.*' I smile at him in the rear-view mirror, pulling off my hat. 'It's the only thing I know. I wish I could speak your language as well as you speak mine.'

'My auntie taught me.' He smiles back modestly. 'She worked in England. I watch American films on television also.'

'So what kind of place is Tshabong?'

'It's a border town, small, very boring.' He looks out of the window at a group of teenage girls walking along the verge towards the garage, smiles and waves. Most ignore him, but one girl giggles and glances away. Bogosi looks gratified.

'So what do they do, the people who live there?'

'Some work in Kgalagadi game park to the west. There's a couple of car-repair centres. And there's crime, of course. Plenty of criminals.' He lowers the window, spits his gum into the road. 'You can escape to South Africa just by stepping across the street. Stuff gets smuggled There are border controls, but in time they get used to you . . .' He leaves the sentence hanging. His fingers tap the wheel. 'It's quiet. Not many people. No one goes there much. Camels wander through sometimes.' Bogosi turns on the radio and the car fills with the strong beat of drums. If the girl on the bus is Teko and she's part of some gang, they may have guns to guard what they have stolen. I wipe my hands on my trousers, leaving a sweaty smudge on the linen and wrench my mind to Alice and Zoë. They looked happy on Skype today. Dr Harnham may have been right and they needed this break from me. Who knows what depth of sorrow I've infected them with? My mobile shows ten missed calls and four messages from Adam.

I text: *I'm fine. I'm safe.* My watch reads five p.m. *I'll explain all in two hours.*

Despite the fear that seems to pulse in time to the music, my eyes start to close.

I wake to a quieter light: the car is slowing and pulling in behind the coach as it draws into a bus stop. Around us there are small concrete houses with yards and little dirt tracks running between them; a powdery haze of orange sand hangs in the air.

The clock on the dashboard reads seven p.m. exactly; the first passengers disembark, mostly women with baskets and carrier-bags, stepping stiffly down. Handclasps and goodbyes are exchanged with the driver; the blonde girl is almost the last to step out.

She ignores the bus driver's cheerful nod and sets off, carrying her package, walking quickly up the road.

I am about to open the back door of the car to follow her when Bogosi turns. 'The blonde lady with the hat, right?'

'Yes, but –'

'Wait here. She will notice you, but not me,' Bogosi says, with authority.

'I'll come back when I've seen where she lives.' He gets out and slams the door, puts his head back through the open window, says, 'I am enjoying this,' and is gone before I can object, pacing fast up the street with an easy stride. I watch until the girl turns right by a group of trees, Bogosi following after a few seconds.

The minutes lengthen. Putting on the hat and dark glasses, I climb out of the car. My back aches as I stretch. The hot smell of desert has a dark undertone of meaty decay, as though an animal has died and been left to rot in the heat. The quiet is immense but gradually the screech of cicadas and frogs seeps into the silence, bringing back the evening garden at Kubung, and then my mind is flooded with the kind of memories I've learnt to keep at bay: Sam lying on our bed, kicking his fat legs in the sunlight, crowing with delight at Zoë; Sam in the cot, his face soft with sleep; Adam holding him as he walked around the garden playing hide and seek with the girls. The empty road blurs. I shouldn't have come here. I shouldn't have come back to Botswana at all. There are memories everywhere I look. I want to go back: this has been a useless escapade. The girl isn't Teko. I ought to go home.

No one is about. Where have all the people gone who got off the coach a few minutes ago? Two hours have passed since I texted Adam. In the car, I punch in another quick message: *All fine, nearly done. Bear with me. Will explain v. soon.*

Five more minutes pass, ten. In the silence, whispers start in my head, telling me I should have called the police, that I don't know Bogosi at all. He might have caught up with the girl by now, warned her that I'm round the corner. If it's Teko, she would be easy to blackmail: he knows the story from the press. She will be called to account for negligence, he might say, unless she gives him money. Buying time, she'll start counting notes into his hand –

'I've seen where she lives,' Bogosi gasps. He is by the car, bent over, holding the doorframe and dripping sweat on to his shoes. 'We can get closer.'

The imaginary scene disappears. Bogosi registers my congratulations with a smile. After a moment he gets back in, starts the engine and drives slowly down the road, turning right up a little track.

'It's not far,' he says, still out of breath. 'But she stopped once or twice to rest – I had to step out of sight.' He smiles but his fingers tighten on the wheel: he's warming to the chase.

'We'll get near enough to describe the house, then tell the police. They can check it from then on. Let's leave that part to them.' It could go wrong if he becomes too involved: he might scare them off.

The track ends. He turns the car round to face the road, nodding as he does to a wooden gate in a high wall behind some trees.

'She went in that way,' he says. 'I saw her unlock it with a key from her bag, but she was carrying something so maybe she forgot to lock it up again.' He smiles. 'It might be worth taking a look.'

'A look? Are you mad, Bogosi? Even if the gate is unlocked, there could be people in the garden or dogs. I'll be seen straight away.'

'The front door is further round,' he continues, as though I haven't spoken. 'I'll go and knock, then whoever comes, I'll keep them talking while you check out the garden.' He is playing a part culled from a film: I'm to case the joint while he provides the distraction.

'What will you talk about that could possibly be convincing?'

'My new door-to-door taxi service.' He waves a hand nonchalantly. 'Cheap rates for special customers. I've done doorstep advertising before. People like it.'

'In Gaborone, perhaps, not in a tiny settlement in the countryside, miles from anywhere,' I hiss. 'We ought to phone the police. They'll deal with it.'

'Trust me,' he says, with a grin, getting out of the car quickly. Before I can stop him, he's walked towards the corner of the wall, swaggering a little. Just before he disappears he turns and points exaggeratedly at the gate. Quick, the gesture says, I'm buying you time.

A distant bell rings, answered by the deep bark of dogs. I was right. In an isolated place like this, people have dogs. Fifteen months ago, I thought I'd known better than to follow Kabo's advice. Regret washes over me, receding slowly.

Voices drift towards me in the still air: Bogosi is talking to a woman; another voice joins in, lower-pitched. Bogosi doesn't reappear. Perhaps he's charmed his way in after all. A minute ticks by. Another. My scalp crawls with tension. The dogs went to the bell: it might be safe to chance the gate. I could take photos for the police. Slipping on my sandals again, phone in hand, I run to the gate before I can change my mind. The handle turns smoothly. Bogosi guessed right, the gate is unlocked.

Another world opens up. A striped square lawn, shockingly green after the dull browns of the bush; red flowers in a stone urn, a couple of teak sun-loungers, angled parasols. The still water of an oval pool shines in the sun but the house is forbidding: all the windows are closed and barred. There are large empty kennels at either side of the back door.

Inside the gate, and keeping close to the wall, I photograph everything I can see. The house, the windows, the lawn. A door slams somewhere inside the house. Turning to go, I catch sight of four cots with their sides up, pushed into the shade near a little path running along the side of the house. Is this, after all, simply an orphanage? If so, where are all the children? Orphanages should be noisy places full of children and toys. Unease prickles. There are only moments left.

In the first cot there is a sleeping baby of a very few months, lying on his side, the dark skin of his cheeks flawless against the white sheet. The baby in the second is awake, the brown eyes watching the pattern of light and shade above him, his open palm pink as a shell. The child in the third cot is a little girl, older than the boys. There are pink ribbons in her hair and her lashes curl against her cheeks as she sleeps, a tiny thumb in her mouth. I photograph them all. Fighting the urge to leave, I risk a glimpse into the fourth cot.

My heart jolts. The boy in this cot is white, sleeping face down. For a second I can't breathe, but in another I see it can't be Sam: this child is too old, too big, so tall his legs are bent, feet jammed against the end of the cot. Does this orphanage take white children, then? I take a photo but the click disturbs him: he is turning his head, rolling on to his back.

The world stops turning. Colours fade. A dull beating sets up in the pit of my stomach, rising to my chest, thumping so strongly it could knock me to the ground. My vison narrows and the only thing I see is the birthmark: it covers most of his right cheek; the edges are crenellated like the edges of a map.

Even as I'm reaching in and carefully, quickly, lifting him out, I can tell he is perfect, both exactly the same and different. I settle him against me and instantly I am complete. I press my cheek lightly against his hair, gold still but darker, thicker. The shape of his head is exactly the same. My arms are full of him. He has grown more than I would have thought possible. He's a boy of fifteen months, not a four-month-old baby. I knew that, of course, but I hadn't felt it. He'd stayed unchanged in my heart.

He's heavy too. Hot and heavy with sleep. I've dreamt this often but he was tiny in my dreams, a pale, cold baby, lifeless in my arms, as I called for help, running up and down empty corridors. Never this beautiful child, this breathing boy, flushed with sleep, a dried line of mucus on his chin. My heart is banging strangely. I mustn't die, not now. People don't die of joy, of thankfulness.

I hold him closer, the soft pad of a nappy crinkling under my hand. Halfway to the gate, a door opens behind me. The girl from the bus steps out of the house. She is still wearing the red and green print dress but the dark glasses, the hat and the wig have gone. Her face is a little fatter, but her eyes are the same, the same nose, the same mouth. Dark hair neatly braided around her head. Teko. Though I tracked her down, I'm frozen with surprise.

Sam makes a sleepy protest as my arms tighten. Teko sees me and stops dead. We stare at each other, waiting. Will she scream for help? Summon the dogs? There is a whimper: one of the babies in the cot wakes. The noise widens into a cry. Teko gives an almost imperceptible nod; her left hand moves a fraction. She is telling me to leave. Now.

I take a step backwards, turn, and run the last yards of garden and through the gate, kicking off my sandals as I go.

The taxi isn't there. My hands clench around Sam as I search the track. Has Bogosi lost his nerve and absconded?

Then red metal glints from overhanging shade further along: the car has been moved and is tucked close to the wall. Bogosi is inside, hunched over the wheel. I stumble towards him, gasping for breath. He is out and round to the side, opening the door.

'I moved the car . . . Less obvious . . . Cooler . . . Sorry,' he says breathlessly.

He pushes me inside; Sam is jogged against my

shoulder and makes a small noise. Bogosi, back in the driver's seat, turns the key in the ignition.

As the wheels spin on the rutted track, two great dogs bound from the gate, barking and springing at the car, their muzzles hitting the window; saliva dribbles down the glass in a thick bubbling trail. As the car jerks forwards they fall back, and a burly figure emerges from the front of the house: a Motswana man in a cowboy hat. He catches one of the dogs by the collar. He has something in this hand – a stick, a gun?

A woman comes to join him. Her arms flash white as she grabs the other dog in a practised movement. She is talking and looks half amused, half irritated, blonde hair tumbling around her broad face.

Recognition hits, like a smashing punch to my mouth.

Claire.

How can it be Claire? Her orphanage is in Gaborone. The impossibility clashes against the reality: the blonde hair, the thick arms, the wide face. She hasn't noticed me, so focused on the dogs she's scarcely looked at the car, let alone who is inside. She has no idea I've taken back my son.

We are moving faster all the time. Disbelief coalesces into white hot anger, scalding my face and arms. Claire is the criminal we have all been hunting. The truth flashes like fire along every nerve and into my brain. I want to stop. I need to get out, take her by the shoulders, scream my questions into her face.

Why? Why choose Sam? Why choose us? Why drag us all to the brink of hell for a year?

Even as I am leaning forward to ask Bogosi to brake, we are already round the corner and Claire has vanished from sight.

# Chapter Thirty-eight

*Botswana, March 2015*

The car settles on the road, gathering speed.

'You have your son,' Bogosi announces, his voice breaking a little.

Yes, I have my son. He is saved, I am, we all are. Anger must be trodden down, every second savoured. I lower Sam carefully to the seat, where I can look at him and he can sleep stretched out comfortably.

His eyelashes are longer – they sweep in a curve to his cheek, silky as a girl's. His skin is translucent. The birthmark, I touch it with my lips, feels the same.

'. . . worried for a second there . . .' Bogosi is saying. 'I thought something might have happened to you.'

Something has happened to me. Life has started again: I feel as though I'm drawing breath for the first time in a year. I cup my hand over Sam's foot; in sleep, he pushes strongly against my palm. He could be walking now. I hadn't thought of that.

'The dogs got out through the gate at the back but those guys came from the front. They had no idea he'd been taken. Did you see the gun?' There is awe in his voice. 'They would have shot us, if they'd known.'

Sam's fingernails have been neatly cut. I close my hand carefully round his satiny fist. The image of severed hands in the dust fades, then disappears.

He'll be frightened when he wakes – he'll have no idea who I am. He won't know Adam or Alice or Zoë. Two bereavements in one short life, though he's older now: it will be worse. We'll have to be very careful, very patient. I lay my hand lightly on his chest, letting it move up and down with his breathing. That's fine: we have all the time in the world.

We are passing the last houses of Tshabong when three police cars speed by us, heading in the direction we have just come from. In the mirror, Bogosi's eyes are shining. 'I phoned them from the garage,' he says happily. 'To put them on the alert. I gave them the exact address once I saw the house. I didn't know you would find your son, but I thought they'd be interested in the woman we followed.' He glances at his watch. 'It's been five minutes. Once they see your son has gone, those guys will know the game's up. They'll be packing their car very fast. At the speed the police are going, they'll catch them before they reach the end of the drive.'

Five minutes. Is that all? But it doesn't take long for lives to change. It took a moment to conceive him, another to lose him. I put my face next to his, the small rubbery ear is cool against my cheek.

Bogosi, humming, glances back. He wants to carry on talking. 'So, that woman who opened the door, she wasn't smiling . . .'

'I know her.'

'You do?' His voice lifts in surprise.

'We met by chance. She's called Claire. We'd just arrived from England and stayed overnight at a hotel.'

But we needn't have broken our journey at all: we could have carried right on to Kubung. Claire would have taken her group of children home again after their swim and Teko would never have come to our door.

'She was with a group of orphans by the pool. She was friendly.' The memory is bitter, like vomit in my mouth. 'She seemed interested in my husband's research.'

Though, of course, it was Sam she was after.

'We didn't talk long. She left before we did.'

That would have been so she could instruct Teko and begin to lay her plans. She might even have driven Teko to Kubung herself early the next day, leaving her to walk the last mile to wait for us, removing her shoes as she went, fooling us all.

The tiny hairs on Sam's temples glint, gold dust. His mouth opens and his thumb slides out, puckered with damp. The frilled edges of new teeth gleam.

'. . . didn't say much. She asked who I was so I told her about my taxi services,' Bogosi is continuing. 'She was holding the dogs back. Then the man appeared, wanting to know why I picked on them. I said I was visiting all the houses in the area, but he didn't like it. He started shouting for someone to check the back garden. He thought it was a trick. He was quite right there.' Bogosi chuckles. 'When he saw me looking over his shoulder, he shut the door in my face.' He turns to grin at me. 'I could hear him swearing inside.'

'Claire's South African, I think. Was he?' They might have friends just over the border. They might still get away.

'Hard to tell. He didn't have an accent.' Rummaging in his shirt pocket, he pulls out a packet of gum, bites a piece off and starts chewing. 'His English was perfect.'

'English?' Surely he would have called out to Teko in Setswana: she doesn't understand English.'

'Even better than mine.' He winks in the mirror.

'Did you hear a reply?'

'A girl called back, said she was on her way.'

'And that was in . . .?'

'English. Does it matter?' He sounds puzzled.

Yes, it matters. It means Alice was telling the truth. Teko spoke English as Alice had told us, though we didn't believe her. Teko, hovering at the edge of things, head inclined, must have been listening all the time.

The car is moving steadily on through the landscape. It all looks the same but everything has changed. An earthquake has broken open the familiar shapes of the past. What was hidden has been exposed.

Alice didn't lie. If we'd listened, we could have worked it out. My mind jumps back a year: Teko, understanding English, must have known in advance about Adam's conference, passed it to Claire and the abduction was planned accordingly.

Sam curls towards the back seat and I slip my hand between his face and the leather. Teko would have let the kidnappers in through the front door but, blocked from escaping by Adam's return, must have shattered the glass doors, aping a break-in. It would have only taken minutes.

Alice didn't lie.

Sam's breath is hot on my fingers. He is sleeping as deeply as if he's been drugged – perhaps he has been. Sedated babies are less trouble. I check his heartbeat and breathing, both normal. He'll sleep this off. I put my lips against the soft curve of his cheek.

She wasn't psychotic. The whispers and footsteps that frightened her must have been real: Claire's men, closing in, leaving fingerprints on the wall. We ignored all Alice's warnings. When she snapped, we thought she was psychotic; instead she was anxious, alone and afraid. Tears start. Will she ever forgive us? Bogosi's face in the mirror softens but I am crying for more than he knows: joy that I have my son safely back, and joy that Alice was never psychotic, tears of shame that we thought she was.

Sam's hair is shining in the sun; it glints in the same way as Zoë's. His skin is immaculate. They looked after him well but what kind of return were they expecting?

'There were other babies, Bogosi. African, younger than Sam. What should we do about them?'

He shakes his head. For a moment he looks unhappy. 'The police are there now. They will know what to do.' He leans forwards and turns the radio louder.

He doesn't want to discuss it. His head bobs up and down in time to the music. The unfairness may trouble him: the white baby of rich parents got the world's attention, but no one spoke for the other babies, or if they did, no one listened. Where was the media when their parents needed a voice? Other explanations hover, dark wings of the monsters we've escaped; baby trafficking, witchcraft, possibilities that Bogosi wouldn't dare name. I cup my hand over Sam's sleeping head. He is safe.

It's time to tell Adam. Past time. He picks up immediately and his voice is so loud it hurts my ear.

'Jesus Christ, Emma. Where the fuck have you been? I'm waiting in a queue in the police station to report you missing.'

'The police know exactly where I am. They passed us not long ago.' I start laughing and for a while I can't seem to stop.

'What the hell are you talking about? Have you gone fucking nuts? It's been hours and hours of hell. I've been out of my mind with worry –'

'I've got him, Adam. I've got Sam.'

Adam says nothing. I can't even hear him breathing.

'He's fine. He's beautiful. He's the most beautiful thing you've ever seen.'

There is silence for so long that I think he must have decided I've really gone mad and is wondering what to do. Then a soft gasping sound breaks into the quiet: he has started to cry. I stay on the phone because it feels like I'm holding his hand and I want him there with me when Sam opens his eyes.

# Chapter Thirty-nine

*London, January 2016*

We're building a den in the loft for the girls. I went up last week to clear it out before the builders start. I'd expected a mess but I'd forgotten the boxes, shoved in and stacked high. After my father died we emptied his study into tea chests, put them in the loft, closed the hatch and left it all for years.

I walked around them; the air was sour with dust, dead flies crunched under my feet. This was Dad's stuff: difficult to touch, worse to throw out. I drank tea, turned on the radio then began: the papers at the top were crackling with age. Tidy piles became toppling heaps: old research documents and published papers, committee reports, academic prizes. No letters; the ones from my mother were already in a box in his desk. In the last tea chest there were hundreds of bank statements and insurance documents. Files. The receipt from the sale of his boat. At the bottom my fingers, scraping plywood and tea leaves, closed on his passport. He'd renewed it the year before he died.

He looked unfamiliar. Not sad, not smiling, just different. The light from the casement was too bright but, tilting the page in the half-shadow, I got what it was. I'd seen it before: it was the look Josiah had, the look of an old man who was content. I sat on the edge of a chest. He'd got there, then, without my help; he'd found it on his own. It occurred to me that he might have felt like that for years. When I went downstairs to put the passport in his desk my body felt fluid, as though I was floating, as though a hand had let me go.

I stuffed everything else into bags, haphazard armfuls packed in and trodden down, though, when it came to it, I kept the receipt from the boat sale. It took three trips to the dump – the bags tumbling over the edge of the containers landed with a soft crash. When I drove away, the empty car seemed to swing round the corners more quickly.

# Epilogue

We both work part time: we're balanced, though balance may not be the right word. The Relate counsellor asked us to think of our lives like circles that overlap, rather than weights on a machine. My circles are family, marriage, work and swimming. Sam is learning to swim; Adam comes along. Sam clings to us. We're taking it slowly. There are more good nights now; less waking, less clinging and crying. He said his first word two weeks ago: dog. I hope that's Kodi, not the slavering animals who guarded him. The psychiatrist said he could have problems later, but he's been wrong before.

Adam and I are taking it slowly too. We swim together on Tuesdays when Megan has Sam. Adam beats me at butterfly; I'm faster at crawl. It gives me a kick to touch the side first; some things are too ingrained to change.

Zoë's growing up determined. She says she wants to be a vet. She's quieter now: we're watching her, too, just in case.

It's different with Alice. She talks all the time. Going back, going forward, going through it all again and again. The psychiatrist was right about the anxiety, feeling unsafe, the worsening fear when Sam was born; what no one could have spotted was how this played straight into Claire's hands.

After we arrived in Kubung, Alice heard Teko whispering on the house phone in English. Teko begged her to keep the secret, in case she was sacked for lying, she said. Alice agreed: she needed a friend and Teko seemed to be a good one. They both overheard me talking about giving babies away and Teko sympathized with Alice's fears about Sam, while skilfully deepening them. When Teko disappeared, Alice had no idea she'd been involved in her brother's kidnap.

The night before Sam was taken, Alice surprised a man hiding in the kitchen, as she'd told us. He claimed he was there to rescue Sam from being given away. He said she had to help or there'd be trouble. Terrified but wanting the best for Sam, she agreed to keep the family out of the way the next afternoon. She realized her mistake when she saw our anguish. Later, regretful and despairing, she threw Sam's elephant in the pond: she'd thrown her brother away, what point was there in keeping his toys?

Mostly I listen. She knows it's not her fault; she knows we're sorry; even the psychiatrist apologized.

We can't blame Teko, not completely. Was it poverty or did she really think Sam needed saving? We'll never know. She walked out minutes after we left, taking nothing with her, vanishing into the bush.

When the police arrived, Daniel and Claire were back in their house, unaware that Sam was missing or that Teko had gone. By the time the case came to trial, months later, they were blaming each other and the truth came spilling out.

Megan went to listen on our behalf. 'I want to,' she'd said. Sam was on her lap; she moved her coffee out of his reach, then leant towards me over his head. 'I persuaded you to go to Botswana. Then I didn't follow up when David failed to get back. It's the least I can do.'

If she felt guilty, so did I. She must never know that, in spite of everything, she had been a strand in the mesh of possibilities until Sam's discovery.

The courtroom had been packed. Claire and Daniel ran a legitimate orphanage in Gaborone. As their defence barrister pointed out, the business had been inspected by government agencies and had passed with flying colours. Even Goodwill had been wrong-footed. The house in Tshabong was the base for a secret trade in babies conceived or stolen to order for illegal adoption; white babies were hard to find for white South African couples. Sam had been special. It must have helped that I'd told Claire his birthmark would disappear quickly.

Teko had been told to co-ordinate the abduction from inside, but she'd become fond of Alice and things got delayed. Daniel began visiting Teko at night, bullying her into submission. When Alice came across him in the kitchen, he threatened her too. He damaged my car to delay my return; spying out in advance where Sam slept, he'd left his finger-marks on the wall.

Claire must have hoped that by revealing so much about Daniel, she would get off lightly, but they both got prison sentences of indefinite length. Their accomplices, the men who snatched Sam for them, were never found.

To date, no one has claimed any of the other babies. All have gone to government-run homes. I sent the photos I took to Goodwill and Chief Momotsi in case they hear of parents who are searching. No one has come forward. They might be too afraid. There might have been contracts that Claire didn't mention, unwritten ones worth thousands, with businessmen, politicians or the *boloi* themselves, men whose beliefs run counter to common sense, to humanity. A mother, fearful for her other children, wouldn't dare involve the police. Baruti's mother didn't.

Today at breakfast, we start talking about summer holidays. It's the kind of cold, rainy morning that makes everyone want sunshine, though at the same time it feels good to be inside. The kitchen smells of toast and coffee. It's my day off, and I'm in pyjamas, about to feed the dog.

Adam wants to go to Iceland. Alice says Provence. Zoë, stroking Kodi, looks up and smiles. 'Africa,' she says brightly.

Dog biscuits clatter into the bowl. Adam, on his way to fetch his shoes, stops in his tracks. 'Really, Zoë?' he asks.

Sam is eating a banana. He squeezes it tightly in his fist, watching as it bulges out between his fingers.

'We've been there already, Zo-Zo,' I tell her. Sam is sucking his hand now; banana is in his hair.

'Rosie saw elephants when she went.'

We saw other things. The sun on the trees. Birdsong. Kindness. Poverty, what it can do.

I wipe Sam's hands and he wriggles down from his chair, squatting next to Zoë. They watch Kodi crunching his biscuits. When he has finished, Zoë stands up. She tugs my hand. 'I want to go to Africa again.'

I kiss the top of her head. Her face darkens, but then her gaze falls on Kodi's empty water bowl. 'Sorry,' she says, bending to stroke his head. She picks up the bowl and stretches on tiptoe to fill it from the tap. Sam stands next to her, copying, stretching up as high as he can. The bowl slips, water splashes on him and on her uniform. There is a little fuss. By the time they are both dried off, she's forgotten what she'd been asking.

The girls leave with Adam. I check anoraks are done up, scarves in place and kiss everyone goodbye.

I haven't forgotten anything.

Sam settles for his nap. The pot of powdered herbs is still in the side pocket of my case where I left it ten months ago. The contents look like ordinary dust: grey, soft, settled. I stand on a chair in the study and put it high on a shelf, beyond anyone's reach, next to the medical encyclopedias at the very top.

Read on for the first chapter
of Jane Shemilt's stunning
debut novel

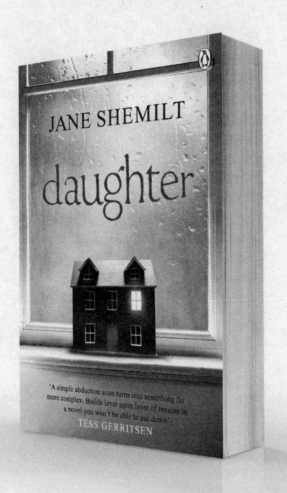

JANE SHEMILT

daughter

'A simple abduction soon turns into something far
more complex. Builds layer upon layer of tension in
a novel you won't be able to put down'
TESS GERRITSEN

'Taut and thought-provoking'
*Woman & Home*

# I

*Dorset 2010*

*One year later*

The days grow short. Apples litter the grass, their flesh pockmarked by crows. As I carry logs from the stack under the overhang today, I tread on a soft globe; it collapses into slime under my feet.

November.

I am cold all the time but she could be colder. Why should I be comfortable? How could I be?

By evening the dog is shivering. The room darkens; I light the fire and the flames pull me near as the regrets begin to flare, burning and hissing in my head.

If only. If only I'd been listening. If only I'd been watching. If only I could start again, exactly one year ago.

The leather-bound sketchbook Michael gave me is on the table and in the pocket of the dressing gown there is a bitten red stub of pencil; he told me it would help to draw the past. The pictures are in my head already: a scalpel balanced in trembling fingers, a plastic ballerina twirling round and round, a pile of notes neatly stacked on a bedside table in the dark.

I write my daughter's name on the first unmarked

page and underneath I sketch the outline of two black high-heeled shoes lying on their sides, long straps tangled together.

Naomi.

## Bristol 2009

### One day before

She was swaying to music on her iPod so she didn't notice me at first. Her orange scarf was looped round her throat, schoolbooks scattered everywhere. I closed the back door quietly behind me and slid my bag to the floor; it was heavy with notes, my stethoscope, syringes, vials and boxes. It had been a long day: two surgeries, home visits and paperwork. Leaning against the kitchen door, I watched my daughter, but another girl was in my mind's eye. Jade, lying in a bed with bruises on her arms.

That was the chilli in my eye. They squirt chilli juice into an elephant's eye to distract him while they mend his wounded leg. Theo told me that once. At the time I didn't believe it could work, but I should have taken it as a warning. It's easier than you think to lose sight of what matters.

As I watched Naomi, I imagined painting the curve of her cheeks as she smiled to herself. I would outline them with a paler shade for the light trapped against her skin. With every step her blonde fringe jumped softly against her forehead. When it lifted, beads of sweat along the hairline glistened. She had pushed up the sleeves of her school jersey; the charm bracelet moved up and down, up and down the smooth skin of her arm, almost slipping off. I was glad to see her wearing it; I thought she had lost it years ago.

'Mum! I didn't see you there. What do you think?' She pulled out her earphones and looked at me.

'Wish I could dance like that . . .'

I stepped forward and quickly kissed the velvety bloom along her cheek, breathing her in. Lemon soap and sweat.

She jerked her head away, and bent to pick up her books in a swerving movement that had her quick, glancing grace. Her voice was impatient: 'No, I mean my shoes – look at them.'

They must have been new. Black, very high heels, with straps of leather binding her feet and wrapping tightly round her slim legs; they looked wrong on her. She usually wore pumps in coloured leather or Converses.

'The heels are incredibly high.' Even I could hear the criticism in my voice, so I tried to laugh. 'Not like your usual –'

'They're not, are they?' Her voice was triumphant. 'Totally different.'

'They must have cost the earth. I thought you'd spent your allowance?'

'They're so comfortable. Exactly the right size.' As if she couldn't believe her luck.

'You can't wear them to go out, darling. They look far too tight on you.'

'Admit you're jealous. You want them.' She smiled a little half-smile that I hadn't seen before.

'Naomi –'

'Well, you can't have them. I'm in love with them. I love

them almost as much as I love Bertie.' While she was speaking she stretched down to stroke the dog's head. She turned then and, yawning widely, went slowly upstairs, her shoes hitting each step with a harsh metallic noise, like little hammers.

She'd escaped. My question hung, unanswered, in the warm air of the kitchen.

I poured myself a glass of Ted's wine. Naomi didn't usually answer back or walk out while I was talking. I stashed the doctor's bag and notes in the corner of the cloakroom, then, sipping my drink, started walking around the kitchen, straightening towels. She used to tell me everything. As I hung up her coat, the sharpness of the alcohol began to clear my mind; it was part of the bargain and I'd weighed it all up long ago. It was simple. I did the job I loved and earned good money, but it meant I was home less than some mothers. The bonus was that it gave the children space. They were growing up independently, which was what we'd always wanted.

I pulled the potatoes out of the cupboard. They were covered in little lumps of soil so I rinsed them quickly under the tap. Thinking about it, though, she hadn't wanted to talk properly for months now. Ted would tell me not to worry. She's a teenager, he would say, growing up. The cold water chilled my hands and I turned off the tap. Growing up or growing away? Preoccupied or withdrawn? The questions hummed in my mind as I hunted in the drawer for the potato peeler. Last summer in my surgery I had seen an anxious adolescent; she had carefully sliced the delicate skin of her wrists into multiple red lines. I shook my head to drive the image away. Naomi wasn't depressed. There was that new smile to set against the impatience. Her involvement in the play against the silences at home. If she seemed preoccupied it was because she was older now, more thoughtful. Acting had given her maturity. Last summer she'd worked with Ted in his lab and she'd become interested in medicine. As I began peeling potatoes it occurred to me that her new-found confidence could be key to success in interviews. Perhaps I should celebrate. The starring role in the school play would also increase her chances of getting a place at medical school. Interviewers liked students with outside interests; it was known to offset the stress of becoming a doctor. Painting worked like that for me, dissolving the stress of general practice. With the tap back on, the brown mud swirled around and around in the sink and then disappeared. I'd almost finished Naomi's portrait and I could feel the pull of it now. Whenever I painted I was in a different world; worries melted away. My easel was just upstairs in the attic and I wished I could escape more often. I dumped the potato peelings in the bin and took the sausages out of the fridge. Theo's favourite had been bangers and mash since he was a toddler. I could talk to Naomi tomorrow.

Later Ted phoned to say he was held up at the hospital. The twins came back home ravenously hungry. Ed lifted his hand in silent greeting as he took a heaped plate of toast upstairs. I could hear the bedroom door close behind him and pictured him turning on music, falling onto his bed, toast in hand, eyes closed. I remembered that about being seventeen: hoping no one would bang on your door or, worse, walk in and talk to you. Theo, freckles blazing in his pale face, shouted out the day's triumphs as he crunched biscuits, one after another, emptying the tin. Naomi came back through the kitchen, her wet hair lying in thick points on her neck. I hurriedly pushed sandwiches into her rucksack as she was on her way out, then stood at the open door for a few minutes, listening to her footsteps going slowly down the road, gradually becoming fainter. The school theatre was a street away but she was always late. She'd stopped running everywhere now; the play was sapping her energy.

'Though just fifteen Naomi Malcolm's Maria is mature beyond her years.' 'Naomi mixes innocence and sexuality in a bewitching performance as Maria; a star is born.' Being tired and wound up was worth it for those reviews on the school website. Two more performances after this: Thursday, then Friday. Soon we would all get back to normal.

## Dorset 2010

### One year later

I know it's Friday today because the fish lady comes to the cottage. I crouch down under the stairs as her van draws up outside, the white shape smudged by the old glass of the door. The woman rings the bell and waits, a squat, hopeful figure, head bobbing as she searches the windows. If she sees me I will have to open the door, compose words, smile. None of these are possible today. A small spider scrabbles over my hand. Bending my head further,

I breathe dust from the carpet and after a while the van rumbles away down the lane. It's a day for being on my own. I lie low and wait for the hours to pass. Fridays still hurt.

After a while, I get up and find the book I left on the hearth last night. I turn over the page with the picture of her shoes and, on the next one, draw the little overlapping circles of a silver ring.

## Bristol 2009

### The night of the disappearance

I knelt on the kitchen floor, opening up my medical bag to check the drugs against a list to see what I needed. This job was easier away from the surgery; there were fewer interruptions if I picked my time. I was groping into the depths of the leather pockets so I didn't notice her come silently into the kitchen. She walked past me and the bag she was carrying knocked against my shoulder. I looked up, keeping a finger on my list; I was running low on paracetamol and pethidine. Naomi glanced down at me, her blue eyes clouded with thought. Even through the thick make-up she'd already put on for the play there were dark lines under her eyes. She looked exhausted. This wasn't the moment to ask the questions I'd wanted to.

'You're almost done, sweetie. This is the second-last performance,' I said brightly.

Clothes were spilling from her carrier bag; the heels of her shoes had made little holes in the plastic.

'Dad and I will be there tomorrow.' I sat back on my heels and looked up, studying her face. The black eyeliner made her look much older than fifteen. 'I'm longing to see if it's changed since the first night.'

She looked at me blankly and then gave me the new smile; only one side of her mouth lifted, so it looked as if she was smiling to herself.

'What time will you be back?' I gave up and got to my feet reluctantly; I never managed to finish anything. 'It's Thursday. Dad usually picks you up on Thursdays.'

'I told him not to bother ages ago. Walking with friends is easier.' She sounded bored. 'The meal will finish around midnight. Shan will give me a lift.'

'Midnight?' But she was tired already. Despite myself, my voice was rising. 'You've got the play again tomorrow, the party straight after. It's only a meal. Ten thirty.'

'That's not nearly long enough. Why do I always have to be different from everyone else?' Her fingers started tapping the table; the little ring that some boy at school had given her was glinting in the light.

'Eleven, then.'

She stared at me. 'I'm not a baby.' The anger in her tone was surprising.

We couldn't argue all night. She would be onstage soon and needed to calm down; I had to finish sorting the medicines before cooking supper.

'Half past eleven. Not a second later.'

She shrugged and turned, bending over Bertie where he lay at full stretch, sleeping against the stove. She kissed him, pulling his soft ears gently; though he hardly stirred, his tail thumped the floor.

I touched her arm. 'He's old, sweetheart. He needs his sleep.'

She jerked her arm from my hand, her face tense.

'Relax, it's okay. You're a triumph, remember?' I gave her a quick hug but she turned her face away. 'Only one more day to go.'

Her mobile went off and she stepped back, her hand resting on the draining board as she answered. Her fingers were long. She had freckles, tiny ones that went as far as the second knuckle, light gold, like grains of demerara sugar. The nails were bitten like a child's, at odds with the pretty ring. I folded her hand in both of mine and kissed it quickly. She was talking to Nikita; I don't think she even noticed. She was still young enough for the knuckles to feel like little pits under my lips. The phone call finished and she turned to go, a little wave at the door, her way of making up for being irritable.

'Bye, Mum,' she said.

Later I fell asleep by mistake. I put the kettle on for her hot-water bottle at about eleven, and lay down on the sofa to wait; I must have drifted off almost immediately. When I woke up my neck ached and my mouth tasted stale. I got up and, pulling my jersey down, went to put the kettle on again.

The kettle was cold under my hand. I looked at the clock. Two in the morning. I hadn't heard her come in. I felt sick. She'd never been as late as this. What had happened? The blood thumped painfully in my ears for a second until common sense took over. Of course, she had let herself in by the front door and gone straight up to bed. Asleep in the basement kitchen a flight below, I wouldn't have heard the door shutting behind her. She must have dropped her shoes soundlessly in the front porch and then tiptoed upstairs, quietly, guiltily, past our room and up to hers, on the second floor. I stretched as I waited for the kettle to boil; she could still have her hot-water bottle. I would wrap it up and tuck it in beside her; she might sleepily register the warmth.

I went upstairs slowly past the boys' rooms. Ed snored suddenly as I passed, making me jump. Up another flight to Naomi's room. The door was open a crack and I went in quietly. It was pitch dark and stuffy, smelling of strawberry shampoo and something else, bitter with citrus at the back of it. I felt my way to her chest of drawers and, pulling out a shirt, slipped the hot-water bottle inside. I stepped carefully over to the bed, half tripping on strewn clothes. My hands moved to turn the cover back around her, but it was smooth and flat.

The bed was empty.

I snapped on the light. Tights spilt from open drawers, there were towels and shoes on the floor. A thong lay on top of a red lacy bra on her bedside table, a black half-cup bra on the chair. I didn't recognize any of these things; had her friends changed here too? Naomi was usually so tidy. A bottle of foundation had tipped over on the dressing table; a stick of lipstick lay in the small beige puddle. Her grey school jersey had been left on the floor, with the white shirt still inside it.

The cover of the bed was slightly dented where she had sat on it but the pillow was quite smooth.

Fear curled in the pit of my stomach. I put my hand on the wall and its coldness seemed to travel up my arm to the inside of my chest. And then I heard the front door shut two floors down.

Thank God. Thank you, God.

I put the hot-water bottle under the duvet, far enough down to make a warm place for her feet. They would be cold by now in those thin shoes. Then I ran downstairs, careless of the noise. I wouldn't be cross, not tonight. I would kiss her, take her coat and send her up. I could be cross tomorrow. My footsteps slowed as I rounded the corner of the stairs and Ted came into view. Ted, not Naomi. He stood looking up at me. He was wearing his coat and his briefcase was by his feet.

'She's not back.' I was out of breath; the words were difficult to push out. 'I thought you were her coming in.'

'What?' He looked exhausted. His shoulders were hunched; there were deep circles under his eyes.

'Naomi hasn't come home yet.' I went close to him. A faint smell of burning clung about him; it must have been from the diathermy spluttering heat, sealing cut blood vessels. He'd come straight from the operating theatre.

His eyes, the same sea-blue as Naomi's, looked puzzled. 'Her play ended at nine thirty, didn't it?' An expression of panic crossed his face. 'Jesus, it's Thursday.'

He'd forgotten that she had cancelled Thursday pick-ups, but he never knew what was happening in the children's lives anyway. He never asked. I felt the slow swell of anger.

'She walks back with friends now. She told you.'

'Of course she did. I'd forgotten. Oh well.' He looked relieved.

'But tonight was different.' How could he be so relaxed

when my heart was pounding with anxiety? 'She went out for a meal with the cast.'

'I can't keep up.' He shrugged. 'So, she's out with her mates. Perhaps they're having such a good time they stayed on.'

'Ted, it's after two . . .' My face flushed hot with panic and fury. Surely he realized this was different, that it felt wrong.

'That late? Gosh, I'm sorry. The operation went on and on and on. I hoped you'd be asleep by now.' He spread his hands in apology.

'Where the hell is she?' I stared at him, my voice rising. 'She never does this, she lets me know even if she's five minutes late.' As I said it, it occurred to me that she hadn't for a long time now, but then she had never been as late as this. 'There's a rapist in Bristol, it said on the news –'

'Calm down, Jen. Who is she with, exactly?' He looked down at me and I could sense reluctance. He didn't want this to be happening; he wanted to go to bed.

'Her friends from the play. Nikita, everyone. It was just a meal, not a party.'

'Perhaps they went to a club after.'

'She'd never get in.' Her cheeks were still rounded; she had a fifteen-year-old face, younger sometimes, especially when she was tired. 'She's not old enough.'

'It's what they all do.' Ted's voice was slow with tiredness. He leant his tall frame against the wall in the hall. 'They have false IDs. Remember when Theo –'

'Not Naomi.' Then I remembered the shoes, the smile. Was it possible? A club?

'Let's give it a bit longer.' Ted's voice was calm. 'I mean, it's kind of normal, still early if you're having fun. Let's wait until two thirty.'

'Then what?'

'She'll probably be back.' He pushed himself away from the wall and, rubbing his face with his hands, he began to walk towards the steps at the end of the hall that led down to the kitchen. 'If not, we'll phone Shan. You've phoned Naomi, obviously?'

I hadn't. God knows why. I hadn't even checked for a text. I felt for my mobile phone but it wasn't in my pocket. 'Where the bloody hell's my bloody phone?'

I pushed past Ted and ran downstairs. It must have fallen out and was half hidden under a squashed cushion on the sofa. I snatched it up. No text. I punched her number.

'Hiya, this is Naomi. Sorry, I'm busy doing something incredibly important right now. But – um – leave me a number and I'll get back to you. That's a promise. Byee.'

I shook my head, unable to speak.

'I need a drink.' Ted went slowly to the drinks cupboard. He poured two whiskies and held one out to me. I felt the alcohol burn my throat then travel down the length of my gullet.

Two fifteen. Fifteen minutes to go before we would ring Shan.

I didn't want to wait. I wanted to leave the house. I wanted to go down the road to the school theatre, wrench open the doors and shout her name into the dusty air. If she wasn't there, then I would run down the main street, past the university, storm into all the clubs, pushing past the bouncers, and yell into the crowds of dancers . . .

'Is there any food?'

'What?'

'Jenny, I've been operating all night. I missed supper in the canteen. Is there any food?'

I opened the fridge and looked in. I couldn't recognize anything. Squares and oblongs. My hands found cheese and butter. The cold lumps of butter tore the bread. Ted silently took it from me. He made a perfect sandwich and cut off the crusts.

While he was eating, I found Nikita's number on a pink Post-it note stuck to the cork board on the cupboard. She didn't pick up either. The phone was in her bag. She had pushed it under the table, so she could dance in the club they'd managed to get into. Everyone else wanted to go home, all their friends were leaning against the wall, yawning, but Naomi and Nikita were dancing together, having fun. No one would be able hear Nikita's phone ringing in the bag under the table. Shan must be awake too, waiting. It was only a year since her divorce from Neil; this would feel worse on her own.

Half past two.

I phoned Shan and, as I waited, I remembered her telling me a week ago how Nikita still shared everything with her and the stabbing moment of jealousy that I'd felt. Naomi didn't do that any more. Now I was glad Nikita still confided in her mother. Shan would know exactly where we could pick them up.

A sleepy voice mumbled an answer. She must have fallen asleep, like me.

'Hello, Shan.' I tried to make my voice sound normal. 'I'm so sorry to wake you. Do you have any idea where they are? We'll pick them up, but the trouble is . . .' I paused, and attempted to laugh. 'Naomi forgot to tell me where they would be.'

'Wait a moment.' I could see her sitting up, running her hand through her hair, blinking at the alarm clock on her bedside table. 'Say all that again?'

I took a breath and tried to speak slowly.

'Naomi's not back yet. They must have gone on somewhere after the meal. Did Nikita say where?'

'The meal's tomorrow, Jen.'

'No, that's the party.'

'Both tomorrow. Nikita's here. She's exhausted; she's been asleep since I picked her up hours ago.'

I repeated stupidly, 'Hours ago?'

'I collected her straight after the play.' There was a little pause and then she said quietly, 'There was no meal.'

'But Naomi said.' My mouth was dry. 'She took her new shoes. She said . . .'

I sounded like children do when they want something they can't have. She had taken the shoes and the bag of clothes. How could there not have been a meal? Shan must be mistaken; perhaps Nikita hadn't been invited. There was a longer pause.

'I'll check with Nikita,' she said. 'Phone you back in a moment.'

I was outside a gate that had just shut with a little click. Behind it was a place where children slept safely, their limbs trustingly spread across the sheets; a place where you didn't phone a friend at two thirty in the morning.

The kitchen chairs were cold and hard. Ted's face was

white. He kept bending his knuckles till they cracked. I wanted to stop him but I couldn't open my mouth in case I started screaming. I picked the phone up quickly when it rang and at first I didn't say anything.

'There was no meal, Jenny.' Shan's voice was slightly breathless. 'Everyone went home. I'm sorry.'

A faint buzzing noise started in my head, filling in the silence that stretched after her words. I felt giddy, as if I was tipping forwards, or the world was tipping back. I held tightly to the edge of the table.

'Can I speak to Nikita?'

By the tiny space that followed my question, I could measure how far away I had travelled from the gate that had clicked behind me. Shan sounded hesitant.

'She's gone back to sleep.'

Asleep? How could that matter? Nikita was there, safe. We had no idea where our daughter was. A wave of anger was breaking on top of my fear.

'If Nikita knows anything, anything at all that we don't, and Naomi might be in danger –' My throat constricted. Ted took the phone from me.

'Hi there, Shania.' There was a pause. 'I appreciate how difficult this will be for Nikita . . .' His voice was calm but with an edge of authority. It was exactly how he talked to the junior doctors on his team if they rang him for advice about a neurosurgical problem. 'If Naomi doesn't come home soon, we may need to call the police. The more information you give us . . .' Another pause. 'Thanks. Yes. See you in a few minutes, then.'

The boys were sleeping in their rooms. I leant into the warm, breathing space around their heads. Theo had burrowed under the duvet; his hair, sticking up in a ruff above its edge, was stiff under my lips. Ed's black fringe was damp; even in sleep his eyebrows swooped down like the wings of a blackbird. As I straightened, I caught my reflection in his mirror. My face, lit by the street lamp shining through the window, looked as if it belonged to someone much older. My hair was dark and shapeless. I dragged Ed's brush through it.

As we drove past the school theatre, Ted stopped the car and we got out.

*I don't know why. I still don't know why we had to check. Did we really think you would be there, curled up and sleeping on the stage? That we could wake you and that you would smile and stretch, sleepy and stiff, with some explanation about taking too long to change? That we would put our arms round you, and take you home?*

The glass doors were locked. They rocked slightly as I pulled at the handles. There was a night-light in the foyer and the bottles in the bar were shining in neat rows. A torn red and yellow programme lay on the floor just inside the door; I could make out red letters spelling 'West' and 'Story' on different lines and part of a picture of a girl with a blue swirling skirt.

Ted drove carefully though I knew he was tired. He had pressed the button on the dashboard that made the back of my seat warm up. It made me sweat and nausea seemed to rise from the deep leather upholstery. I glanced at him. He was good at this. Good at looking serious not desperate. When Naomi was in difficulty during her birth, his calmness had stopped me panicking. He had organized the epidural for the Caesarean section and he was there when they lifted out her small, bloodied body. I wouldn't think about that now. I looked out of the window quickly. The streets were shining and empty. A fine rain had started to mist the windows. What had she been wearing? I couldn't remember. Her mac? What about her scarf? I looked up into the roadside trees as if the orange cloth might be there, tangled in the wet black branches.

At Shania's house Ted knocked firmly. The night was silent and still around us, but if anyone had been passing in a car, they would have seen a couple like any other. We were wearing warm coats and clean shoes as we waited quietly, heads bowed in the rain. We probably looked normal.

Shania's face was prepared. She looked calm and serious as she hugged us. It was hot in her house, the gas fire flaming in her tidy sitting room. Nikita was hunched on the sofa, a cushion held tightly to her, her long legs in rabbit-patterned pyjamas tucked beneath her. I smiled at her, but my mouth felt stiff and trembled at the corners. Shan sat close to her on the sofa, we sat opposite and Ted took my hand.

'Ted and Jenny want to ask you about Naomi now, babe.' Shania put her arm round Nikita, who looked down as she twisted a thick lock of her dark hair in her fingers.

I moved to sit by her on the other side, but she shifted slightly away from me. I tried to make my voice gentle.

'Where is she, Nik?'

'I don't know.' She bent and pushed her head into the cushion; her voice was muffled. 'I don't know, I don't know, I don't know.'

Shania's eyes met mine over her head.

'I'll start, then,' Shan said. 'I'll tell Jenny what you told me.' Nikita nodded. Her mother continued: 'Naomi told Nikita that she was going to meet someone, a bloke, after the play.'

'A bloke?' Ted's voice cut across my intake of breath. 'What bloke?' The word in his mouth sounded dangerous. Not a boy. Older. My heart started banging so loudly I was afraid Nikita would hear and refuse to tell us anything.

'She said . . .' Nikita hesitatingly began. 'She said she had met someone. He was hot.'

I uncrossed my legs and turned round to face her properly. 'Hot? Naomi said that?'

'That's all right, isn't it? You asked me.' Nikita's forehead puckered, her eyes filled with tears.

'Of course,' I told her.

But it wasn't all right. I'd never heard her use that word. We had talked about sex, but as I desperately scanned my memory for clues, I couldn't remember when. Relationships, sex and contraception – Naomi didn't seem interested. Had she been? What had I missed?

'Was he . . . did she . . .' I groped in a forest of possibilities. 'Was he from school?'

Nikita shook her head. Ted spoke then. Lightly, casually, as though it wasn't important.

'This guy. She must have met him before?'

Nikita's shoulders dropped fractionally, she stopped twisting her hair. Ted's calmness was working, but I felt a stab of anger that he could manage it so easily. I could hardly keep my voice from trembling.

'Yeah. I think he was around in the theatre sometimes.' She glanced down. 'You know, at the back.'

'At the back?' Again, barely inquisitive.

'Yeah. Where people waited. Maybe.' She looked up and there was reluctance in her dark eyes. 'I didn't really see.'

'What did he look like?' I asked quickly.

'Don't know.' Nikita didn't look at me. There was a pause. 'Maybe dark hair?'

She moved nearer Shan on the sofa and closed her eyes. I didn't think she would tell us anything else, but Ted was asking another question.

'And tonight? What did she say to you about tonight?'

There was silence. Nikita was completely still. Then Shan stood up. 'She's tired now.' Her voice was firm. 'She needs to go back to bed.'

'Tell us, Nikita, please.' I touched her on the arm lightly, carefully. 'Please, please tell us what she said.'

She looked back at me then, her brown eyes wide with surprise. Her best friend's mother was a busy figure in the distance: cheerful, running in and running out. In charge of her life and her family. She didn't plead.

'She said' – Nikita paused for a fraction – 'she said, "Wish me luck."'

# Acknowledgements

I would like to thank Eve White, Jack Ramm and Kitty Walker at Eve White Literary Agency.

Many thanks to the team at Penguin: my editor Maxine Hitchcock, also Hazel Orme, Beatrix McIntyre and Eve Hall. Lee Motley designed the beautiful jacket.

Warm thanks to Jessica Jackson, my publicist.

I am grateful to the many friends who showed me the magnificent country of Botswana; special thanks are due to Tebogo Basupang and Boston Naledi Basupang for their friendship and patience. Thanks also to Evelyn Lorato Botshabelo, then the acting headteacher at Kubung Primary School, to teachers Edith Nthaba, Motswaki Mothokatse and Polite Mmopi and to all the children we met there. Thank you to Agnes Motlhabedi and Matilda Ranko, nurses at Kubung clinic.

Many thanks for his wisdom are due to the chief at Kubung, Boitshwarelo Mabutlwane and to his wife, Oefile Mabutlwane.

Modiri and Keletso Ramahobo, Thongbotho Nkaelang, Kabo Garebakwena and Frank and Moses Peter in Tonota were very helpful, as were the staff at

World Spine Care near Mahalapye in the Central District of Botswana.

The Kubung village in *The Drowning Lesson* drew only its name from the real Kubung village in Botswana; all the people mentioned in the book are also entirely imaginary.

Thanks are due to Alexander McCall Smith, met by chance at Gabarone airport and most generous with his time and thoughts.

My daughter Mary came with me, fellow traveller and lovely companion. Thank you.

Many thanks for her wise counsel are due to Tricia Wastvedt.

My writing group continues to meet; for friendship and inspiration thanks to: Tanya Attapattu, Victoria Finlay, Emma Geen, Susan Jordan, Sophie McGovern, Peter Reason and Mimi Thebo and now further away, to Hadiza El-Rufai and Vanessa Vaughan.

Thanks for their continuing support to Kathryn Atkins and her family of Durdham Down Bookshop in Northview in Bristol.

My enduring gratitude and love go to my family: Steve, my bedrock, and our beloved children Martha, Mary, Henry, Tommy and Johny.

# Reading Group Discussion Questions

1. 'Our relationship was evenly weighted with work and success, but the balance could tip at any moment.' Discuss what it means to be equal in a relationship. To what extent do you think Emma and Adam's competitive marriage contributes to what happens in the novel? What kind of secrets are allowed in a marriage?

2. Emma is amazed that Megan put her career aside to look after her husband. Does Emma rely too heavily on her job to give her a solid identity?

3. When Sam is born with the birthmark on his face Emma is upset that he is not 'perfect'. Perfection is something she strives for, but does she really know what this is? What does Emma really want from life?

4. At first Emma is uncomfortable with having staff in her Botswanan home, though she is perfectly happy employing staff in London. Discuss the reasons for this.

5. Did Emma have a responsibility to be a better mother to Alice, Zoë and Sam? Do you believe she was suffering from post-natal depression? How far is she responsible for what happened?

6. What did Emma learn from the drowning lesson in the quarry as a child?

7. How much does our relationship with our parents influence our choices as adults? Is it inevitable we will repeat the same patterns of behaviour?

8. Sam is not the only missing child in *The Drowning Lesson*. Compare and contrast his abduction with Baruti's disappearance. How might the investigation have differed if the disappearance had taken place in the UK?

9. Discuss the different representations of female relationships throughout the novel. Do women really need female friends?

10. Alice is in trouble but no one sees. Mental health issues in children can slip below the radar. How many of Alice's problems could have been avoided?

11. Things are not always what they seem, yet judgements are often made on appearance. How important is it that Emma learns to look below the surface?

# He just wanted a decent book to read ...

Not too much to ask, is it? It was in 1935 when Allen Lane, Managing Director of Bodley Head Publishers, stood on a platform at Exeter railway station looking for something good to read on his journey back to London. His choice was limited to popular magazines and poor-quality paperbacks – the same choice faced every day by the vast majority of readers, few of whom could afford hardbacks. Lane's disappointment and subsequent anger at the range of books generally available led him to found a company – and change the world.

*'We believed in the existence in this country of a vast reading public for intelligent books at a low price, and staked everything on it'*
**Sir Allen Lane, 1902–1970, founder of Penguin Books**

The quality paperback had arrived – and not just in bookshops. Lane was adamant that his Penguins should appear in chain stores and tobacconists, and should cost no more than a packet of cigarettes.

Reading habits (and cigarette prices) have changed since 1935, but Penguin still believes in publishing the best books for everybody to enjoy. We still believe that good design costs no more than bad design, and we still believe that quality books published passionately and responsibly make the world a better place.

So wherever you see the little bird – whether it's on a piece of prize-winning literary fiction or a celebrity autobiography, political tour de force or historical masterpiece, a serial-killer thriller, reference book, world classic or a piece of pure escapism – you can bet that it represents the very best that the genre has to offer.

**Whatever you like to read – trust Penguin.**